CAPTIVES OF CHEYN...

'The truth is all this excites you, isn't that it?' he said.

She was breathing faster now. 'Y – yes, Master.'

'Are you a masochist?'

Gail took a deep breath, chewing her lip again in an innocently childish display of uncertainty. 'I ... I don't know, Master. I never thought so before now. I was terribly afraid at first. But I can't help getting excited and – coming, even when I'm being hurt. As long as it's sexy as well.'

'Is that what this is for you? A sex game?'

'No – a bit, maybe ... but I am really sorry for what I did, Master. I deserve to be punished.'

He slipped a finger into the mouth of her sex. 'You mean you want to be punished?'

'Yes, Master!' she gasped.

'Then say it.'

'Please punish me, Master! Do anything you like to me!'

By the same author:

**THE OBEDIENT ALICE
ALICE IN CHAINS
ABANDONED ALICE**

CAPTIVES OF CHEYNER CLOSE

Adriana Arden

This book is a work of fiction.
In real life, make sure you practise safe, sane and
consensual sex.

First published in 2006 by
Nexus
Thames Wharf Studios
Rainville Road
London W6 9HA

www.nexus-books.co.uk

Typeset by TW Typesetting, Plymouth, Devon

Printed and bound in Great Britain by Clays Ltd, St Ives PLC

ISBN 0 352 34028 2
ISBN 9 780352 340283

You'll notice that we have introduced a set of symbols onto our book jackets, so that you can tell at a glance what fetishes each of our brand new novels contains. Here's the key – enjoy!

cp (traditional)

cp (modern)

spanking

restraint/bondage

rope bondage/hojojutsu

latex/rubber/leather/enclosure

fem dom

willing captivity

medical

period setting

uniforms

sex rituals

One

Tara was the first to be caned.

They bent her over the sign, mounted on two short concrete posts, which rose from the grassy traffic island at the top of Cheyner Close. The edge of the plank which backed the metal strip bearing the raised lettering dug into Tara's belly, but Roberta Pemberton, who had a hank of Tara's hair coiled round her fist, would not let her shift to ease the pain. Tara could only stare at the grass in front of her face while her full bare breasts, their nipples painfully stiff, hung pendant and trembling in the cool night air.

Tara pinched her lips tight. She was determined not to make a sound whatever they did to her. Even naked with her wrists bound behind her back, she would not give way to fear and shame before the people she loathed.

Kneeling on either side of the sign, Jim Curry and Stan Jessop caught hold of her ankles and pulled her legs wide apart. The orange streetlight illuminated the twin moons of her buttocks and the softly furred mound that nestled at the base of their cleft. The full extent of her exposure made Tara's stomach churn. Though there was little traffic on the Styenfold road at half past one in the morning, anybody who did pass could look up the Close and witness her humiliation.

There were a few appreciative murmurs from her hateful audience at the helpless display of her private parts. They had probably never seen anyone so beautiful naked and live before them, Tara thought, her emotions swinging dizzily to perverse narcissism. They should feel privileged to have her like this.

As Major Warwick took up position behind her and raised the length of garden bamboo, the cameras held by the other residents started flashing again.

Swish . . . crack!

Tara bit her lip to prevent herself yelling out loud. It was as though a red-hot wire had been laid across her buttocks. She had never been physically punished in any way, let alone caned. Blinking back tears she clamped her jaws together, making only a throaty squeak as the second blow fell a little lower than the first, lifting her buttocks even as the shockwave rippled through her flesh. It hurt even more than the first but she would not show it. As the remaining four blows fell she cherished their stinging pain and exulted in her self-control.

They dragged her to her feet. Despite her burning bottom she held her head up proudly. These people would not break her.

The rest of the girls, bound and naked as she was, watched her return to their line with mingled looks of horror and disbelief.

'You said they wouldn't really hurt us!' Hazel wailed. 'They can't do this . . .'

'You all agreed, remember?' Jessop said, taking hold of Cassie and marching her over to the sign.

Cassie looked daggers at both their captors and Tara before she was bent over, but at least she maintained her self-control, tossing back her blonde straight hair indolently and letting out only a few yips of pain as she was caned. Tara found herself unable to look away as the bamboo lashed across Cassie's tight, firmly moulded buttocks, leaving stark red weals where it had landed. In the still night air the crack of bamboo on flesh reverberated round the Close. Despite everything she was fascinated. It seemed so intense and real. Exciting, even? Yes, in a twisted sense. Because this was their welcome to the unknown; their deliverance into the hands of others to do with as they wished.

Walking awkwardly, lips firm but tears glistening in her eyes, Cassie was led back to the group and Sian put in her place. Her slight body trembled and her slender bottom looked too small to take such a beating, but she got one all the same. They could expect no mercy from their captors. Sian gave a little yelp as each stroke of the cane scored her flesh, the impact making her whole body jerk. She came back sniffling quietly with her head hung low.

Gail went to the sign mumbling: 'Sorry . . .' over and over again, her melon-like breasts visibly wobbling as the tremors shook her. She cried quietly from first to last, punctuated by incredulous gasps as the cane marked her.

Hazel disgraced herself by peeing in fear even before the first landed. Even though she was the youngest of the Elite, Tara had hoped she would have more control. As the stream of urine splashed over the sign and dripped to the grass, the onlookers laughed at her shameful display. Warwick held back until the last drops had fallen then brought down the bamboo across her pale bottom, still lightly padded by puppy fat.

Daniela, sniffing and woebegone, went unresisting to her appointment with the cane and suffered her six strokes with feeble grunts and moans, as though already accepting this was her lot and the punishment justified.

3

And then they were done and they all stood once more in a line; sore and chastened, uncertain of what would come next. Unexpectedly the residents led them down the Close to Number 2, with its tiny unkempt front garden and boarded ground floor windows. Roberta Pemberton produced the key and opened the door. They were herded into the living room, which was bare except for a worn fitted carpet. Evidently it had once been separate dining and sitting rooms, but these had been knocked together and the room now extended from front to back of the house.

The girls were sat down in a row with their backs to the wall and their ankles were bound with more repair tape. The carpet felt like sandpaper to their sore bottoms and they squirmed unhappily. Warwick smiled down at them.

'You shouldn't be disturbed,' he said. 'Roberta promised the agent she'd keep an eye on it as there was so little interest in the property – thanks mainly to your activities. I hope you have a nice uncomfortable night. It might give you some idea what we've had to suffer in the past. But you'd better make the most of it, because this'll be the only one you'll spend alone for the next week.'

Hazel whimpered and Gail bit her lip.

Warwick and the other residents went out, switching off the light and closing the sitting room door. They heard the key turn in the lock. Then the front door shut and they were alone in the empty house. A faint orange glow from the streetlight filtered round the window boards, but otherwise the room was completely dark.

'Oh . . . shit, shit, shit . . . that hurt!' Cassie spat. 'How the fuck did you get us into this, Tara?'

'It was better than the alternative,' Tara said, trying to keep her voice level. 'You all agreed.'

'You said they wouldn't have the nerve to do anything very bad to us,' Sian moaned. 'My bum feels like it's on fire.'

'Just keep calm,' Tara said. 'We'll get through this.'

'I . . . don't think I can take a week of this sort of thing,' Hazel said in a small voice. 'You said they . . . they'd rather use us for sex. That we could wear them out like that . . .' Sian groaned at the idea. Hazel continued: 'But they're going to do just what they want with us. They're so angry about the things we did to them –'

'Shut up, Hazel!' Tara snapped. 'Get some sleep.'

They lay quiet, trying to get as comfortable as possible. Thoughts tumbled though Tara's mind.

How could this have happened to her? It wasn't fair. Yesterday she had been beautiful, rich and confidently in charge of her life. Today, and for the next week, only her beauty would count for anything. Was that a blessing or a curse?

Fear and anger fought against mental and physical exhaustion and lost. Tara slipped into a restless half-sleep, troubled by transient dreams and fragments of memory . . .

Cassie brushed the blade of her knife lightly across Daniela's bare nipples, making the girl squirm helplessly at the touch of cold steel. Grinning, she let the knife rest against the smooth swell of Daniela's left breast and glanced expectantly at Tara.

'Are you ready to be initiated into our society?' Tara asked.

The tip of the knife pressed deeper into the side of Daniela's naked breast, threatening to break the skin. The girl stifled a yelp of pain and said quickly: 'Yes I am . . .'

'Tell us what you hate.'

Daniela recited the litany: 'Slappers, style freaks, crumblies, nerds and losers . . .'

Tara smiled in approval. At least Daniela had memorised the responses properly.

'. . . the grey, the dull, the ordinary, the common,' Daniela concluded.

'And who are the Elite?' Tara demanded.

Daniela took a deep breath. 'The young, the stylish, the elect, the quintessence, the crème de la crème, the nonpareil, the ne plus ultra, the winners.'

Tara had plundered a thesaurus to compile the list, but she felt the effort had been worthwhile to hear them trip off the lips of a pretty young supplicant.

'And how do the Elite treat common people?'

'We keep them in their place by look, by word and by deed.'

'Are you ready to prove your fitness?'

'I am . . .'

Tara jerked awake. The others lay still about her. The glow from the streetlight had gone, leaving only an outline of pale grey light in its place. Tara eased herself into a slightly less uncomfortable position.

She had been dreaming about Daniela Hammond's initiation into the Elite Society not three weeks ago. She could not have known then, but that had been the trigger of her downfall. But at first everything had gone so well . . .

Tara's laptop displayed a montage of snatched pictures taken over some months and in different weathers. They showed a dozen different people, their names and personal details added as captions, together with a double row of houses and gardens seen from various angles. The houses were basically boxes with a bay stuck on the front to try to make them seem more interesting. Some were rendered with pebble dash. In the middle of the last century they had been desirable middle-class dwellings. Now Tara hated them. They were situated less than fifteen minutes' walk from her own home in Fernleigh Rise, but as far as Tara was concerned it was another world.

The girls crowded round the screen, despite the fact that they had all seen the pictures many times before. Tonight the images took on a special significance.

'These are the occupants of Cheyner Close,' Tara told Daniela solemnly. 'They're everything we're not. They get annoyed when you try to have innocent fun anywhere near them. They think they're as good as we are. They need to be reminded that they're not.'

Tara froze the last image. It was a map of Cheyner Close showing a keyhole-shaped array of nine houses opening off the Styenfold road, with back gardens radiating out into fields crossed by a few hedgerows. Tara enlarged the map to show more detail. Beside each house, except for Number 2, was listed the names of its occupants. Another click and an image of Number 3 filled the screen. Inset was a slightly blurred picture showing the profile of a thin-faced man in his late twenties wearing glasses.

'His name is Tom Fanning and he moved into the Close about a month ago. He bought privately from the Elliots . . .' she grinned '. . . apparently it was the only way they could get a sale. Anyway, I heard that Fanning works in electronics. I don't mean he owns a company or anything, he just makes electronic devices of some sort. He lives alone but I don't think he's gay because . . .' she called up a full length shot of Tom Fanning '. . . he actually wears patched corduroy trousers in public.'

The girls sniggered at the damning image.

'So he's a nerd and a loser and he hasn't received a visit from us yet. That means he doesn't know his place.' Tara looked at Daniela. 'Tonight you're going to put that right.'

Daniela gulped and then nodded ...

And Daniela had proved herself. Under cover of darkness she had made her way across the fields to the Close, scaled the back garden fence of Number 3 and put Fanning in his place. She recorded details of her raid for the rest of the Elite on a camera set up for flashless nighttime photography. There were views of number 3's back door with FANNING IS A SAD WANKER spray-painted across it; a large x on the lawn formed out of cut flower heads; Daniela scattering the bag of slugs and snails that Tara had provided her with over the vegetable patch and, finally, close-ups of her squatting down and peeing over a row of lettuces.

The raid was acclaimed a great success and Daniela was accepted as a full member of the Elite Society. It inspired Tara to conceive of a daring plan that would elevate her campaign against the Close to new heights. It would take a lot of organising but it would be such a thrill to carry out.

And so, on Friday morning, Tara had waved goodbye to her parents as she steered a hired MPV, loaded with tents, backpacks and the rest of the Elite Society, away from Fernleigh Rise.

Tara's proposal that she should take the others to visit Katy Mitchell, an old school friend who had moved to the West Country a couple of years ago, had been welcomed by all their families. Of course all the girls would be going on holidays variously to Tuscany, Venice, California, Monaco, Fiji and the Seychelles later in the summer, but it was still reassuring to know they were not above spending ten days on a simple camping holiday exploring the modest delights of Cornwall.

They had travelled less than two miles down the road, however, before Tara made a right turn into a small lane which led nowhere near Cornwall. A second turning off this became a meandering unpaved track into Manor Woods. They passed through a gate set in a tall hedge, beyond which was a small but neat cottage. Tara drove round the back, where its semi-wild garden merged with the woods, and parked under the trees.

As the girls piled out of the vehicle a young man in his late twenties emerged from the back door of the cottage.

He was Simon Pye, big, strong and rather simple, with shaggy dark hair that tended to fall over his eyes. He gardened and did odd jobs around Fernleigh Rise, and reminded Tara of a shy, not too bright, but obedient dog.

'Is everything ready?' Tara asked.

'Yes, Miss Tara,' Simon said. 'A letter came for you this morning, Miss . . .'

She took the envelope from him. It bore Simon's name and address but a small circled T had been written in one corner in red ink. 'Get the tent up,' Tara told him as she ripped it open.

'Yes, Miss Tara,' Simon said, hurrying off to obey.

'It's from Katy,' Tara told the others as she read the letter. 'She's got the phones and credit cards we sent and promises not to spend more than we agreed or lose the pin numbers. She'll send them all back in time for our "return", with plenty of photos of beautiful Cornwall. She'll send the texts you wrote spaced out over the next few days to seem natural. Any live calls we can make from here and they'll go

9

through her landline set back into our cells. Any problems contacting us we can blame on signal blackspots around her area. And she says remember that we promised to send her full pics and details of raiding the Close when we're done.'

Tara beamed at them. 'So as from tonight we're all in Cornwall, and we'll have the phone records and card receipts to prove it. If the residents try to blame us for anything that happens over the next few days, they're going to look very stupid indeed.'

By evening the big tent had been set up under the trees, with smaller tents housing a portable shower and chemical toilet close by. An extension cable run out from the cottage powered lights, a portable television and CD radio. The girls lounged about, resting or talking idly.

Gail, who had been walking through the woods as dusk fell, now appeared out of the gathering gloom and sat down on a folding chair. 'I like it here,' she announced. 'We should have come before now. It's so peaceful.'

'Only because my father had the woods properly fenced when he bought it from the old Manor estate,' Tara said. 'Plenty of barbed wire to keep out trespassers, so we won't be disturbed. That's what makes it such a good place for our base.'

'Does that mean we have to go all the way round by the lanes to get to the Close?' Sian asked.

'No. I had Simon make a concealed opening in the fence so it opens onto the fields. We can cut across them by keeping to the hedges. You'll see it all later.'

Cassie had been looking thoughtful. Now she said: 'Is Simon . . . you know . . . all right?'

Tara was surprised. 'You've seen him round the Rise often enough. He's harmless.'

'But we're staying in his garden. Can we ... trust him?'

'Well, he's not suddenly going to jump on you, if that's what you mean.'

The other girls sniggered derisively at the idea. Sian grinned. 'I dunno. He's got a great butt on him.'

'Don't forget the six-pack abs,' Hazel added with a giggle.

'What matters is that he won't tell anyone we're here and does what I tell him,' Tara said. 'He built those special bits of equipment to my designs and never asked what they were for.'

'Seems like you've got him well trained,' Cassie smirked.

'It's because this cottage came with the woods,' Tara explained. 'It was easier to leave it standing and let Simon stay here as a sort of unpaid keeper. That makes him cooperative. Of course, when my father decides to develop the land it all goes.'

'And Simple Simon gets the boot?' Cassie said with a knowing chuckle.

'Probably,' Tara agreed.

'That's a bit ... unfair,' Gail said.

'If anything goes wrong with the plan,' Daniela pointed out, 'he might get blamed as well –'

'Nothing will go wrong,' Tara declared firmly.

'Don't worry about Stupid Simon,' Sian said. 'He's no better than the people living in the Close.'

'At least he knows his place,' Tara corrected her. 'The residents in the Close don't. That's what this week's for: to remind them exactly where they belong.'

They had set off just after midnight.

Tara looked round the nervous but excited group as they stood ready to depart. All were gloved,

11

booted and masked and their clothing was dark and loose. Each carried torches with shaded lenses, as the night was darker than when Daniela had made her raid on Fanning's house.

'Right,' she said crisply. 'You've studied the map and you know your targets. We enter exactly at one o'clock. Get in, do your stuff and get out fast. We meet back at the big oak where the three hedges join. Any questions? OK: let's go.'

She led the way along a path that wound through the trees away from the cottage. In a few minutes they reached the edge of the wood where it was separated from the open fields by a high mesh fence topped by three strands of barbed wire. They made their way along this until they came to the section Simon had modified. The mesh appeared continuous but it was held in place by hooks and could be folded back. They squeezed through the gap and headed out over the fields, hugging the shadow of hedgerows towards the lonely fuzz of yellow streetlight that illuminated Cheyner Close . . .

By ten to one Tara was kneeling in the cover of tall oilseed stalks looking across the narrow strip of rough grass that edged the field at the back fence of Number 8. It was Major Warwick's house and her target for the night. She felt an almost sexual excitement coursing through her. The challenge of successfully overcoming so many obstacles and then seeing the effects of her actions on the residents was more rewarding than any sport.

When she'd first started raiding anybody could slip through a couple of loose boards in the fence and come out in the gap between and the shed. However Warwick had soon nailed them back in place and capped his fence with spiked strips of hard plastic.

Other residents had taken similar measures, but they had all been bypassed with the devices Simon had made for her. Alarm wires strung along the fence tops had been negated with lengths of fishing line used to set off numerous false alarms from a safe distance. Security lights linked to motion sensors had been put out with a borrowed high-power air rifle. It was too expensive for the residents to keep replacing them so eventually they were removed. For that Tara had allowed them a few weeks' rest from raids, serving as both a reward and a reminder that they were not to try too hard to spoil her fun.

At one o'clock exactly the raid began.

Tara broke cover and crossed to the fence, extending a lightweight sliding ladder as she went; thrilling at the knowledge that at that moment the others were using similar devices to effect their entries.

Bracing legs unfolded from the end of the ladder, bridging over the fence and resting on the roof of the shed. Tara climbed the ladder, dropped onto the roof of the shed, then lowered herself down into the gap between it and the fence.

Hardly daring to breath Tara crouched against the side of the shed, straining her ears and eyes. But all was silent and dark. She edged out of its shelter and started forward. She heard the footsteps behind her just too late . . .

A sack was jammed over her head and pulled down to envelop her upper body, trapping her arms. Before she could cry out she was shoved forwards so that she sprawled face down onto the ground. Somebody knelt across her back, driving the wind from her lungs and pulling a drawstring round the neck of the sack tight, binding her arms to her sides. As she gasped for breath, the coarse material of the sack was forced

13

into her mouth by a rope being tied about her head, forming a crude gag.

As she lay on the damp grass, wheezing and confused, Major Warwick's voice spoke softly but triumphantly in her ear: 'This is the end for you, Tara Ashwell!'

Tara jerked out of her restless sleep again. She ached all over. The heat of the day had drained out of the house and a pre-dawn chill had entered the room. Still desperately tired, she huddled down against the warm flesh on either side of her . . .

It had been the worst shock of her life.

Warwick hauled Tara to her feet and marched her forward. Hooded by her sack, numb with shock and half-choked by her gag, she was in no condition to resist.

Grass became flagstones under her feet, then a gate was unlatched and swung open and she was shoved through. The cloying orange glow of a streetlight filtered through the coarse weave of her sack. She was dragged forward again through another gate, stumbling over a curbstone, across asphalt and back onto grass once more, where she was forced down onto her knees. In her confusion Tara swayed unsteadily and would have toppled over but for Warwick's steadying hand on her shoulder.

Dimly she was aware of hurrying footsteps. A crowd seemed to be growing, conversing in urgent whispers. Muffled whimpers and grunts beside her suggested she was not the only captive.

Then somebody proclaimed loudly: 'This is the last one. We've got them all!'

As a tremendous cheer went up, Tara's stomach knotted. How could all the Elite have been captured? It wasn't possible. It was a nightmare . . .

'No need to keep them quiet now,' Major Warwick said, as the echoes died away. 'We want everybody to see their faces for the record.'

The gag rope was released and a second drawstring about the top of Tara's sack was loosened far enough for it to be pulled down over her shoulders, leaving her arms still confined. Spitting out hemp fibres, Tara looked fearfully about her.

She was kneeling on the small grass traffic island around which the Close road looped. Huddled about her were the rest of the Elite Society, all confined as she was by identical drawstring sacks. The implication penetrated Tara's dazed senses. The residents had been ready and waiting for them. They'd walked into a trap.

Brilliant white starbursts began exploding silently round the huddled captives. Tara flinched and turned her head aside, but there was no escape. Every resident of the Close seemed to be wielding cameras and eagerly making a record of their disgrace; Fanning, Stan and Louisa Jessop, Jim Curry, the Indian couple Raj and Narinda Khan, Roberta Pemberton and the lesbian pair Hilary Beck and Rachel Villiers. Even old Gerald Spooner in his wheelchair.

Sobs and groans rose from the others as they realised the totality of their downfall. Gail was shaking her head in disbelief while Hazel and Daniela were openly crying.

'Simple fuckin' Simon told them we were coming,' Cassie rasped, fear threatening to overwhelm the anger in her voice.

'You said we could trust him,' wailed Sian. 'Now look at us. Why did I ever listen to you?'

The lightning storm of flashes died away, leaving only Fanning walking round operating a digital camera on video mode, recording them from every angle.

'Simon Pye did not betray you,' Major Warwick said with a smile. 'We have Mr Fanning to thank for the intelligence that brought about this little coup.'

Tara could only gape in confusion at Fanning, who grinned back. 'Didn't you know?' he said. 'I build security and surveillance systems. After your first visit the other residents told me how you'd been persecuting them, so I put cameras and directional mikes in the trees round your house. When we learned about your fake holiday plan I gave Simon Pye's place the same treatment. We recorded every scheming detail. So, still think I'm a sad wanker?'

The residents laughed uproariously, but not at Fanning. Daniela turned her head aside in shame.

Tara licked her lips, which seemed to have gone very dry. 'What – what are you going to do now?'

'Call the police, naturally,' said Warwick. 'We have all the evidence we need. This is the end for your precious little gang. What your families will say when they learn the truth I can only guess, but I suspect when what you've been doing becomes public knowledge none of you will be able to show your faces anywhere in this county.'

The full implications penetrated Tara's numbed mind as Major Warwick took a phone from his pocket and prepared to punch in a number. This couldn't be happening . . .

'B – but you can't,' she choked out.

The Major's finger hovered over the keypad. 'What possible reason have we not to?' he demanded, and there was a murmur of agreement from the other residents.

'We – we can pay you,' Tara said desperately.

This offer was greeted by such a growl of derision

that Tara shrank back from the ring of angry faces. The Major scowled at her in undisguised contempt.

'You stupid girl! Don't you understand you can't buy yourself out of this? We'll get compensation for damages from you or your parents in due course. That will be for the courts to decide and hopefully it will make up for the material loss we've suffered. But that's nothing compared to seeing you and your friends receive proper punishment for the misery you've put us through.'

'Narinda could not sleep at nights,' Khan said angrily, pointing to his wife.

'Do you know how much it hurts to be called those disgusting things?' Roberta Pemberton hissed.

'I had to go on tranquillisers,' Curry admitted, looking ashamed but defiant.

'Justice, that's what we want,' the Major concluded. 'And we'll settle for nothing less.'

A fresh cheer went up from the other residents.

'Please don't do this,' Gail begged, finding her voice at last. 'I – I can see now what we did was wrong. It was just a game. We didn't think it would really hurt anybody . . . We'll try to make it up to you somehow. But please don't tell the police. I've never been in trouble before. It would kill my mother . . .'

Her tone was so pitiful that Warwick hesitated, but only for a moment. 'I'm sorry for any distress it may cause, but your mother will not die of shame or embarrassment. Perhaps this will teach you to choose your friends more carefully in future . . .' He punched in the first digit.

'I'll make you a better offer!' Tara shrieked desperately.

The Major paused. 'What are you talking about?'

'Put the phone away, turn that bloody camera off, and you'll find out. Just give me two minutes, then you can do what you like. What've you got to lose?'

17

The Major and Fanning exchanged shrugs. Fanning turned the camera off while the Major closed his phone. 'You have two minutes,' he said, checking his watch, 'and you had better not be wasting our time.'

'Maybe we can't buy you off,' Tara said, choosing her words with care. 'But money still buys good lawyers, and whatever our families think privately about what we've done, they'll get the best for us. You say you've got evidence using hidden cameras. Isn't spying on somebody's private land illegal? It might not be allowed in court.' Tara had no idea where the law really stood on that point, but she hoped the residents were equally ignorant.

A slight uncertain murmur from the crowd told her she was right.

Fanning tapped his camera. 'This is evidence recorded on our property. You being here now is proof enough.'

'Actually, isn't this road public property?' Tara said. 'And you brought us here and tied us up. We haven't done any damage to your property tonight, but we could accuse you of assault.'

'And false imprisonment,' Cassie added desperately.

'So it might not work out quite the way you hope. OK, so we'll probably get fined and it will be embarrassing for us and our families. But will that satisfy you?'

Tara's tone was measured but secretly she was terrified. Despite her assured words she had no faith in lawyers. In her mind's eye she had an image of Hazel or Gail or Daniela crumbling in the witness box and telling everybody how she had incited them to persecute the residents of the Close. Tara wasn't even sure she could trust Sian or Cassie in those circumstances. All the blame would be heaped on her. She might even go to prison. And even if she escaped that there would be the public ridicule and contempt, her picture in the gutter press being pawed over by the masses. Anything was better than that.

'So what is it you're offering instead?' the Major asked.

Tara took a deep breath. 'Why don't you punish us? Yourselves. Personally.'

An incredulous murmur rose up from the residents, while the rest of the Elite stared at her in disbelief.

'What do you mean?' Fanning asked.

'Just what I said. You do ...' she gulped '... whatever you want to us. Any punishment you like, as long as it doesn't do any lasting harm. But in secret. That's the deal. Our parents and the police never know. Call it ... natural justice.'

'Tara!' Sian spluttered. 'What are you saying?'

'It's better than the alternative,' Tara hissed.

'I couldn't ...' Hazel moaned.

'You'd let them get their hands on us?' Cassie said in horror.

'Would – would our parents really never need to know?' Gail wondered.

'I wish I'd never heard of your stupid society!' Daniela sobbed.

Curry sneered. 'She thinks they can get away with having their bottoms spanked and being told to be good in future.'

'You could spank us if you wanted,' Tara said, trying not to let her voice quiver.

'I think we should turn them over to the proper authorities as we planned,' said Khan. 'It's not right to take the law into our own hands.'

'Isn't that what we've just been doing?' said Louisa Jessop.

'Yes, but we had no choice,' pointed out Rachel Villiers. 'We had to get indisputable proof.'

'But will it be enough?' Spooner wondered, frowning at Tara. 'I don't trust that girl an inch, but she has a point. It might be the proper thing to hand them over, as Raj says. But once we do it's out of our hands. At least this way we'd be sure the punishment was suitable.'

Khan hesitated, looking thoughtful.

'Well, I wouldn't mind a bit of DIY justice,' said Roberta Pemberton. 'But we've had to live with their persecution for over a year. How hard and how long would their punishment have to be to make up for that?'

'What about as long as they planned to carry on this latest stunt?' Jessop said. 'We have them all to ourselves to do with as we like for the week they're meant to be staying in Cornwall.'

'You can't be serious,' Fanning exclaimed.

'Why not?' said Jessop.

'Might teach them some discipline,' the Major agreed.

'Does she mean we could really do anything we wanted to them?' Hilary Beck asked slowly. 'Not just punishing them, I mean, but anything that gives us pleasure to . . .'

The strange tableau on the island of grass was silent for a moment as the full implication sank in. Somewhere out across the fields an owl hooted.

'You could do what you want with us,' Tara said quietly.

The rest of the Elite were staring at her in utter disbelief. She said quickly, forcing the first words out: 'Please . . . give us time to talk. In private . . .'

The residents also seemed to need a recess for confidential discussion. In a body they moved a little way up the road and began debating urgently, leaving the Elite kneeling on the traffic island still confined in their sacks.

'You can't seriously mean letting them have – have sex with us,' Cassie spat. 'These are the people you hate. Look at them. It's disgusting!'

'It doesn't change anything,' Tara insisted. 'We're still the Elite. We can still prove we're better than them.'

'By being their – their sex slaves for a week?' Sian said.

' "Sex slaves"!' Hazel groaned.

'What do they know about keeping slaves?' Tara said with contempt. 'They haven't got the imagination. And half of them are nearly past it. A few pokes and it'll be over.'

'Oh God! Do you have to put it like that?' Cassie said.

'Beck and Villiers are lesbians, aren't they?' Daniela said hesitantly. 'You mean we'd have to do it with them too?'

'Haven't you ever tried it with other girls just for fun?' Tara said impatiently.

Daniela looked surprised. 'No.'

'Well, the bottom line is that sex is better than punishment,' Tara persisted. 'And the more sex we give them the less time there'll be for punishment. We're young and healthy. We can wear them out. I bet they won't be able to think up anything very original. At the end of it we'll still be the Elite and they'll still be nobodies. They can kid themselves that they've had their revenge, but what'll they have to show for it? They'll realise they should have handed us over to the police after all, only by then it'll be too late.'

'I . . . don't think I can pretend to like them,' Hazel said. 'That sounds like being a prostitute.'

'If we act like slaves we don't have to pretend,' Tara said. 'Just do what we're told for a week –' she lowered her voice '– and flatter those stupid people into believing they've beaten us.'

There was a thoughtful silence. Then Gail said, 'At least this way our parents will never know. It'll be our secret. That's something.'

'Isn't there any other way?' Cassie groaned.

'Letting Warwick call the police right now,' Tara said bluntly. 'Do you want that?'

Slowly Cassie shook her head. 'No ... I suppose not. But the thought of it makes me sick. It's all your fault, Tara. When this is finished I don't want to speak to you ever again, understand?'

At that moment Tara could not have cared less. 'Just let's get through it first. Are we all agreed?' One by one they nodded. 'Right. They're coming back. Remember, we're the Elite. Whatever they do can't change that ...'

The girls watched anxiously as Curry hurried off to his own house while the rest of the residents came back up the road. To their surprise they freed them from their sacks and then stood back. Fanning turned on his camera, panning it to show there was nothing between them and the main road, then focusing on the girls once more.

'Go on, get out of here,' Major Warwick said briskly.

Tara was confused. 'What do you mean? Don't you – don't you want to punish us?'

'You'd never make that sort of offer unless it was a trick,' Jessop said with contempt. 'Well, we're not falling for it.'

'Tara Ashwell volunteering her gang to serve our pleasure,' Roberta Pemberton said mockingly. 'Is that likely?'

'But it isn't a trick!' Tara protested. 'We want to be your slaves ...' she faltered, realising what she was saying. 'I mean, you do what you want with us in exchange for not going to the police. That's the deal.'

'We don't accept. We're letting you all go,' the Major said.

'Just like that?' Tara asked.

The Major grinned wickedly. 'Of course not. Maybe we'll go to the police tomorrow with our evidence, maybe we won't. Maybe it'll be the next day. We thought you should learn what waiting for the axe to fall feels like; the way you've kept us waiting for you to perpetrate your next nasty little prank.'

'No,' Gail wailed. 'Please don't. I couldn't stand waiting ... not knowing ... that's cruel!'

The residents smiled grimly at her anguish while the other girls looked bewildered. Tara knew Gail had spoken the simple truth. The uncertainty would be unbearable.

Curry returned to the group. He was carrying a couple of thick reels of repair tape, a bamboo garden cane and a roll of black plastic sacks. He handed the cane to the Major and the sacks to Roberta Pemberton.

Warwick held out his phone to Tara. 'Then get it over with. Call your families and have them pick you up if you don't want to go back to your camp. Of course, it might be awkward explaining why you're just down the road instead of in Cornwall, but I'm sure you'll think of something. Or call the police, if you want to make charges against us for false imprisonment. We're ready to chance what happens next. Are you?'

'We'll do anything you want if you promise not to turn us over to the police!' Tara said, hating the desperation that tinged her words even as her eyes followed the wagging of the bamboo he held in his other hand.

'Do you really mean that?' Warwick asked, his voice grave, as he ran his eye over the huddle of miserable girls. 'Will you all say it here and now? Publicly beg to accept whatever punishment or restraints we inflict and any use we make of you for the next week?'

There was a shameful chorus of mumbled assents.

'We want each of you say it loud and clear for the record,' Warwick snapped, in tones that would not have been out of place on a parade ground. 'I warn you, if anyone doesn't sound convincing you all go back to your camp and wait for the police to call. Well?'

Fanning moved closer with his camera, focusing on their distraught faces. Gail said suddenly: 'I do!'

'Do what?' Warwick demanded. 'Speak up, girl.'

'I – I beg to accept any punishment or restraints or – or use you make of me for the next week,' Gail said, her eyes glistening with tears.

'Who's next?' Warwick asked. 'We haven't got all night.'

Daniela and Hazel spoke together, their trembling voices tumbling over each other: 'I beg to accept . . . any punishment or restraint . . . or use you make of me . . . for the next week.'

Through gritted teeth, Sian and then Cassie made the same pledge. Then there was only Tara left. As the hateful unreal words flowed from her lips she realised they had been manoeuvred into this declaration on camera. Resentment at being so comprehensively trapped burned hotly within Tara, together with, surprisingly, an echo of the arousal she felt every time she had perpetrated a raid on the Close. But how could something so degrading get her excited?

They stood there fearful and uncertain.

'Strip,' the Major commanded. 'Take everything off: watches and jewellery included.'

There was a moan of dismay from the others but Tara understood. Of course they would do this. The first obvious humiliation to which they could be subjected. It was what she would have had done in their place.

As trembling fingers began to undo buttons and zips, the camera's began to flash again.

'You'll get your clothes and other possessions back when we release you at midnight next Friday,' Warwick continued. 'Until then you'll be nothing but naked slaves.'

Tops and jeans and trainers were cast down onto the grass, with many a miserable sniff and choked-back whimper of shame, which became louder as flimsy pieces of underwear joined the pile. When they were totally naked, Roberta Pemberton gathered up their discarded clothes and put them in the bin bags. The other girls clenched their thighs together and tried to hide their breasts and pubes from the gaze of their captors, but Tara fought the shameful impulse and stood proud and defiant with her arms by her sides. She was beautiful and she knew it. There was nothing they could do to change that, or what she was inside.

'Hands behind backs, wrists crossed,' the Major ordered, and reluctantly they obeyed. Curry and Jessop went around behind them with the reels of tape and began binding their wrists together.

'You don't have to tie us up,' Tara protested. 'We've promised to do what you want.'

'Think of it as insurance,' Warwick said. 'We can't risk any of you losing your nerve and running off. You're all going to see this through to the end, so get used to it.'

Tara's heart was thudding as her own wrists were bound. To her horror she felt her nipples begin to rise.

'We don't have time for anything elaborate right now,' Warwick explained with a smile. 'But you should have a taste of what's to come.' He pointed at Tara and swished the bamboo meaningfully though the air. 'You first . . .'

Two

The unlocking of the sitting room door roused the girls from their uneasy slumber. They peered about blearily as the lights came on.

Warwick, Khan, Roberta Pemberton and Hilary Beck entered. They were each carrying bulging plastic bags together with short lengths of cane. As they blinked the sleep from their eyes, the girls saw the canes had sprigs of holly taped to their tips. Khan put down his bags, took out a knife and cut the tape binding the girls' ankles. Assisted by the others he hauled them upright, ignoring their groans as their stiff limbs were forced to bear them.

'Stand straight,' Warwick barked, and clumsily they obeyed. He flicked his spine-tipped cane across their bare bodies, bringing forth gasps and yelps of pain. 'Form a proper line ... that's better ... eyes front, chests out ... don't be coy, girl, you've nothing to hide from us.'

Tara wanted to scream at the wretched man that nobody talked to her like that. But either her mind was still too cold and sluggish to assemble the suitable invective or else the force of his personality was temporarily too overwhelming. She could only stand mute with the others in a naked trembling line, feeling unkempt and miserable.

'We've let you sleep late this morning because we had preparations to make,' Warwick said. 'But that is the last concession you will receive for the next week. From this moment on you these are the rules you will live by.

'You will address us respectfully at all times, either as "Sir", "Ma'am", "Master" or "Mistress", depending on how you are instructed. You will remain naked at all times unless directed otherwise. You will perform any sexual act required of you by whoever you are serving at that moment . . .' He paused while the plaintive whimpers died away. 'That is what you agreed to, remember. You are here to pay for your crimes in whatever manner we see fit and suffer whatever punishments we choose to inflict upon you. Do you understand?'

'Yes, Sir,' they said miserably.

Warwick reached out and caught Tara's left nipple between his thumb and forefinger, digging his nail in until her eyes watered. With her arms bound she could not pull away, only grit her teeth and try not to cry aloud.

'Do you understand, Tara Ashwell?' he asked, looking her full in the face.

He read her defiance and she saw his determination. For one fleeting moment, in a twisted way, they understood each other perfectly. The corner of his mouth twitched in a faint smile.

'Yes . . . Sir,' she said.

He released her. 'Good. Now before we proceed further, Miss Pemberton has a job for you.'

Roberta had taken a phone and a small notepad from her pocket. 'You've got a couple of calls to make,' she told Tara. 'We've written down what you're to say. Be convincing or else you'll get another six of the best with the bamboo.'

Five minutes later Tara had spoken to Simon, telling him there had been a change of plan and he was to mind the camp until further notice, and also to Katy in Cornwall, giving her a new number to ring if she had any calls from their parents that had to be relayed.

'Now to get you freshened up,' Roberta said.

Leaving the Major in the sitting room unpacking bags, the girls were prodded upstairs, Khan coming last.

'What a pretty sight such a fine row of rumps makes,' he observed heartily, watching their bottoms proceed him. 'I'm glad to see the Major left room for more stripes. A good caning will make them more ready to please.'

Tara pinched her lips while Hazel and Gail whimpered.

'Don't worry, girls,' Khan continued. 'I've already told the others I do not care to soil myself with you. My wife is the only woman I wish to know intimately. But I will still enjoy seeing you humiliated in every way possible. Perhaps it will teach you to be better people in future.'

They lined the girls up in a row on the landing, with their backs to the wall. Hilary and Roberta drew Tara into the small bathroom, lifted the lid of the toilet and sat her down on the bowl.

'Please . . . Ma'am,' Tara asked, hating herself for sounding so servile. 'Aren't you going to undo my hands?'

'No, girl. And I think I'd like you to address me as: "Mistress.".'

'But . . . Mistress, how do I clean myself?'

'You don't, we use one of these.' Roberta was uncoiling a short length of garden hose from her bag. One end was fitted with a tap adaptor while the other held an adjustable spray nozzle. She fitted the adaptor to the bath tap. 'By tonight everybody in the Close will have something like this in their bathrooms, if they haven't got bidets. We'll make sure you're clean and fresh as required. In between you won't be needing your hands free because there's to be no playing with yourselves for any reason, unless you're ordered to for our amusement, of course.' Groans of despair could be heard from the landing at these words.

Tara gulped, then looked through the open bathroom door to where Khan stood on the landing grinning at her. 'Please, Mistress, will you close the door?'

'No privacy for the next week,' Roberta grinned. 'That's part of the punishment. You're going to spend the rest of your life knowing we've seen you perform all your most intimate functions. Now get on with it, girl; you're holding everybody up. No, keep your legs wide. You've nothing to hide from us . . .'

'Bloody-well do it, Tara,' Sian called out from the landing, 'we're bursting out here!'

Blushing furiously, Tara closed her eyes and managed to release her sphincters, emptying her wastes into the toilet bowl.

Hardly had she finished before Roberta made her squeal by directing a jet of cold water from the hose up into her pudenda and the pit of her anus. Her pubes bulged as the stream flushed it out, bubbling like a fountain as Tara squirmed and gasped in surprise.

'Get used to it,' Roberta told her. 'There's plenty more of the same to come.'

Hilary had taken soap, flannel, a comb and towels from her bag. After leading Tara over to the washbasin, she gave her a quick wash and brush up while

Cassie took her place on the toilet. After the combing, Hilary snapped elastic bands round their hair to make ponytails, ensuring it was held clear of their faces.

Fifteen minutes later the girls were led back down to the sitting room. Warwick had spread a plastic tablecloth on the floor and laid it with six brand new pet bowls. Their names had been written on the side of each one in bold black felt-tip. They were made to kneel before their respective bowls.

'Luckily Pet Village over in Felgate opens early,' Roberta said. 'We picked up several useful bits and pieces from there.'

The bowls were filled with muesli, fresh banana and a little milk, mashed together so that it formed a thick paste.

'Eat,' Roberta commanded, 'like the animals you are . . .'

Miserably they spread their knees wide and bent forward, pushing out their bottoms to maintain their balance as they dipped their mouths into their respective bowls and ate as best they could. The posture stretched their buttock clefts wide, exposing their anuses and mounds of Venus even more blatantly than during their canings the night before. While they ate, their captors walked round behind them, encouraging to them to lick their bowls clean with flicks of the holly switches across their unwillingly offered hindquarters.

Tara silently cursed the residents. They were proving to be far more inventive than she had imagined.

Eating had left their cheeks smeared with cereal, so they were paired and ordered to lick each other's faces clean. Tara and Cassie could hardly look each other in the eye as they grimly obeyed. Gail gave Sian a helpless smile as they went about the task, while

31

Hazel and Daniela broke into nervous giggles as they lapped each other's cheeks and lips.

When they were done, Warwick looked at his watch. 'We have a little time in hand. Perhaps, as I won't have any of them to myself this morning, I could give them a little drill practice in the back garden until Jim arrives. Some ideas for suitably slavish postures and responses occurred to me last night. They might help break them in and make them easier to control.'

The others nodded in approval. Khan said: 'Don't break them all at once, Major. We want to do our bit as well.'

Warwick smiled grimly. 'Oh, I think there'll be plenty left for you to do, Raj. I won't be able to whip this sorry bunch into order that easily, but it might make them a little more malleable.' He turned back to the girls with a stern eye, swishing his holly cane. 'While other preparations are being finalised, I'm going to give you some exercises appropriate to your new circumstances. You will learn to obey orders promptly and without question, respond in the proper manner and to present yourselves respectfully. I wish I had a month to teach you some real discipline, but we must do the best in what time we have. Now stand straight.'

The command was so perfectly pitched and their natural resistance so weakened that they obeyed without thinking.

'I think you can free their wrists now, Raj,' Warwick said. 'The back garden is secure enough.'

The tape binding their wrists was cut away, but their arms were so stiff they could hardly lift them. Warwick gave them no time to rub the life back into their limbs.

'Form up in a line, Ashwell at the front!' he bellowed. 'Hands folded neatly in the small of your backs! To the back door ... march! Left, right, left right ...'

Roberta ran ahead and opened the back door and they marched out in single file into the back garden, where a crumbling crazy paving patio opened onto a strip of rough lawn with overgrown flowerbeds on either side. Suddenly emerging naked into the open air in daylight rekindled their sense of shameful exposure. But the back gardens of the Close were only overlooked by their immediate neighbours. The only people who might see them were more of their captors.

'Halt. About face!' Warwick called. 'Look to your right ... form a line from Tara ... straighter than that! Feet spread so they are further apart than your shoulders, toes touching your companions' on either side. Keep your hands behind your back, bow your heads meekly and look at the ground. We shall call that position: "Standing at Submission". Remember how you got there. Now, bring your right foot to your left smartly and stand straight, heads up, eyes front, shoulders back, clasp your hands to the back of your necks with your fingers interlocked, and chests out.'

They obeyed, acutely aware of Hilary, Roberta and Khan watching with interest from the patio. Warwick strode down the line of girls with their clenched thighs and trembling breasts, looking them critically up and down as though inspecting soldiers on parade.

'I want to see those nipples properly displayed,' he said, tweaking and pinching each pair as he came to it. 'Think what's waiting for you and get some blood pumping.' he continued over their moans and yips of surprise. 'For the next week your skin is your uniform. And, like well polished brass buttons, I expect your teats to stand out.' He continued to flick and twiddle their breasts until all their little crowns of pink and brown had been teased into unwilling erection. Striving not to show her humiliation at the way Warwick had pawed her, Tara tried to derive a perverse sense of pride in the fact that at least her nipples had stood up quicker than the rest.

'That's better,' he said, turning on his heel to survey the line of tumescent papilla. 'This is "Standing at Attention". Whenever you are on parade I want to see you like this with your nipples hard and ready . . .' he swished his holly cane through the air, '. . . or else!' A renewed shiver of fear ran down the line. 'Do you all understand?'

'Yes, Sir!' they chorused.

'Now I will teach you the basics of conducting yourself as a slave before an audience. You will move smartly at all times, you will obey orders immediately and without question, you will show discipline. Understood?'

'Yes, Sir!' they replied.

'Good. Now you will learn some more basic postures. Time permitting I will drill you in them every morning until you perform them without thinking. Next is: "Kneeling while on Display". At the command, still keeping those hands behind your neck, you will go down onto both knees, thighs spread at ninety degrees, rears resting on your heels, your backs straight, eyes forward, chins up. Ready . . . Kneel!'

Hurriedly they obeyed, opening their groins to the morning air. Warwick walked along the line of spread knees inspecting them. 'The purpose of this posture is to demonstrate that you no longer have any "private parts". You are so open to inspection that, if anybody wished, they could count every one of your pubic hairs.' Daniela stifled a whimper but Warwick

34

ignored her, looking down at Hazel. 'Wider, girl,' he told her, flicking his cane back and forth between her fleshy inner thighs so that she gasped and shuffled her knees further apart. 'That's better.' He stopped in front of Cassie. 'Don't you know what ninety degrees means, you stupid girl? A right angle, like the corner of a box. Could you get a box between your thighs?' Gritting her teeth, Cassie opened herself wider, showing off the dark golden pelt that furred her delta. Warwick paused again before Tara. She had her thighs spread until the big inner tendons stood out and was staring rigidly ahead, daring him to find fault.

'That's very good, Tara,' he said unexpectedly. He addressed them all once more. 'Now you will "Kneel at the Ready". On the command you will bring your thighs together, rise onto your knees keeping your back straight, and bring your left foot to the ground beside your right knee. Do so – now!'

They shifted position into the half-crouch. Warwick nodded in approval. 'Good. This position enables you to rise easily to obey a further command. For instance . . .' He moved to the opposite side of the lawn. 'When I call your name, you will run to me, go down on your knees, kiss both my feet, look up and say clearly: "Your slave, Master", then return to your place in line. Do you understand?'

'Yes, Sir,' they said, a strained edge to their response.

Could they actually say such shameful words aloud, Tara thought dizzily? Could they really behave like obedient dogs, coming when their owner called? She'd never imagined it would be like this. Were the others waiting for her to protest? If one of them spoke up she'd do so as well. But none of them did . . .

'Gail,' the Major called.

Gail scrambled to her feet and ran quickly over to him, her heavy breasts bouncing. She knelt and kissed his toecaps, then lifted her head up and said tremulously: 'Your slave, Master.'

He patted her on the head as one might a dog and said: 'Good girl.' As she returned to her place Tara saw she was actually smiling with relief.

Sian was called next. She responded less readily than Gail and mumbled her words. That earned her a warning flick across the bottom with Warwick's holly cane and the order to repeat herself clearly. Hazel, who followed her, practically sang out her words and was rewarded with a reassuring pat.

Tara began to understand. The Major's pats and encouraging words counterbalanced the flicks of his holly cane. Contrasting threat and reward made obedience easier, though nonetheless degrading. But knowing this did not stop it being disconcertingly effective and left Tara in a state of confusion. Should she now deliberately misbehave and risk additional pain just to show she could still think for herself, or should she continue not to give Warwick the excuse of punishing her? It was only words and a symbolic show of deference, however humiliating it might feel. It didn't mean anything . . .

Tara was called last. She ran quickly over to Warwick, knelt and obediently kissed his boots, lifted her eyes to him and said clearly: 'Your slave, Master.' She returned to her place unable to deny the small glow of relief his 'Good girl' and pat had given her even as she silently cursed him for both looking and sounding so sincere as he had done it. Did he have to play so fair even when he had them all at his mercy?

'Now you will practise "Following to Heel",' he told them.

He walked up from behind their line, passing close by a girl at random, calling her name and saying: 'Follow!' And they did so just like dogs on invisible leads, staying two steps behind and to his left, their eyes locked onto him to match any change in pace or direction. When he stopped they went down into the ready position. It was the same way Tara had seen well trained dogs sit at the curb by their masters, waiting for the road to clear. All that was missing was their tongues lolling from the sides of their mouths. Another step further on the road to utter degradation; and shamefully exciting to watch. Hazel and Gail trotted after Warwick like little angels. How rapidly he was breaking them in. Why hadn't she ever thought to play this sort of game with them? Tara wondered.

But surely she could not do it herself. There must be a limit to what she would submit to, even if there seemed none yet in sight to the residents' inventiveness. The trouble was she was experiencing a disturbing sense of anticipation at the humiliating spectacle she would make. Perhaps she could turn the feeling on its head. It was an illicit sensation, in a perverse way similar to the thrill she had felt making the raids on the Close. She could enjoy it if she chose, and tell the other girls later it was just an act.

And so when her turn came she followed dutifully at his heel, stopping when he did and matching his every move. By the time he was done, her nipples were hard and there was a slickness between her labia.

Next came jogging round the perimeter of the lawn in what amounted to a high-stepping pony trot, while Warwick stood in the middle. 'Lift those knees high,' he instructed. 'I want to see those breasts bouncing in time with your step. Yes, even small ones like yours can jiggle if you make them, Sian.'

And round and round they went, like ponies in some dressage event. Tara felt her attention wandering as she lost herself to the simple pleasures of physical exertion and fresh air flowing over her bare skin. Her breasts bobbed heavily to the rhythm of her steps. Daniela's golden tan backside rolled and wiggled hypnotically ahead of her. Was that how her rear was moving? God that was sexy!

'Halt!' Warwick commanded, checking his watch. 'Form a line and stand at submission!'

They obeyed almost without thinking, forming up to the right of Tara, flushed and sweaty, chests rising and falling steadily.

'We have time for one last drill position,' Warwick said. 'This is called: "Presenting your Privates for Inspection".. At the command you will bend forward until your head is level with your knees, displaying your pudenda and rear orifices to the maximum. Present!'

And they bent over as instructed, Tara feeling her buttocks open, realising she was even more exposed than when eating from her bowl. He could see right up into their pussy slits and anuses. Looking back between her spread legs she had an upside-down view of Warwick surveying the row of female genitalia before him.

'I want to see those sex pouches pouting and wet,' he told them. 'Any girl who has not become even slightly aroused, however unwillingly, by what I've put you through this last hour must have something wrong with her. It's a perfectly natural reaction, you know. A dry vagina will receive three strokes of my cane, a properly wet one, just a single. However many strokes I deliver, you will each thank me properly for them. Do you understand?'

'Yes, Sir,' came the strained reply.

'You should be grateful. Your pubes will be getting a lot more use this morning, so they might as well be lubricated beforehand.'

Tara felt dizzy, but not from bending over. Where did Warwick learn how to handle women so well? The army had never taught him that – had it? She had seriously underestimated him. And what about the other residents?

Warwick was standing behind Hazel. 'Mmm ... that's a fine rear you have there, girl.'

'Th – Thank you, Sir,' came Hazel's tremulous reply.

'And properly wet labia. That's a good response. Just one stroke ...'

There was the sound of a swish followed by a little squeak from Hazel, then: 'Thank you very much, Sir.'

Warwick moved on down the line. Sian received two strokes with a warning to try harder for her own good. The others were all better aroused. Finally it was Tara's turn.

He stood right behind her, cupping her pubic mound in his hand while his thumb twirled about the tight pucker of her anus. This can't be happening to me, she thought. But he had his fingers inside her now, rubbing them between her sex lips, assessing her arousal. Despite her shame she held still. All that was left to her was to endure what came without flinching. Warwick slid two fingers into the mouth of her vaginal sheath, sampling her hot tight slick depths. Tara bit her lip.

Then the hand was removed. 'That is a prime cut of flesh you have there, girl, and very well oiled.'

She felt a stinging swipe of holly across her taut buttocks, the spines scraping her pouting pubes.

'Thank you, Sir,' she said, dizzy with relief.

'Attention!' Warwick snapped, and they straightened up; confused, blushing, humiliated.

Jim Curry was standing with the others by the back door. 'I see you've been putting them through their paces, Major,' he said, grinning approvingly at the line of flushed and sweaty girls. 'Well, I've been busy as well.' He held up a carrier bag. 'Got the stuff ready.'

'Right face!' Warwick commanded. 'Into the house, quick march!'

Bottoms swaying, they marched back into the front room, forming up into a neat line against one wall. What was coming next, Tara wondered.

Curry pulled a handful of leather dog collars from a bag and showed them to the others. 'Their names are stamped on the tags like Narinda suggested.'

'Excellent,' said Khan. 'They will look even more like little animals once they've got them on.'

Curry worked his way along the line of girls, buckling the collars about their necks and then fitting small padlocks through eyeholes in the protruding ends of the straps. While the padlocks were in place they could not be pulled back through the buckles. Tara felt a helpless shiver as her collar was locked about her. She couldn't wear this for a week as though she was an animal. But then that was exactly the idea.

Next Curry produced lengths of chain with leather loops at one end and spring clips at the other: leashes. The residents practised clipping them onto the girls' collars. Tara felt her leash drag her down far more than its mere weight could account for. Whoever was on the other end could lead her round like a pet dog. Her stomach churned at the thought even as her nipples tingled.

Curry took out a clinking bundle of short chains and metal rings that he separated out into half a dozen toy handcuffs.

'I've put on heavier chains,' he explained. 'The cuff rings themselves are solid enough and they all use the same key. It's a simple pattern but it should be good enough to keep this lot secure.'

They snapped the handcuffs onto the girls' wrists, confining them behind their backs once again. At least it gave them a little more freedom to wiggle their arms, though the metal felt hard and uncompromising.

The final items to emerge from the bag were small rubber balls that had been pierced through with loops of elastic cord, forming simple ball-gags. These were forced between their teeth and the loops stretched over their heads to hold them in place. Tara looked at the rest of the Elite and they gaped back at her mutely, their white teeth champing on the balls that stretched their mouths wide, as though frozen in permanent 'Os' of surprise or alarm. Even the power of speech had been taken from them by their captors. Nor could she eat or drink unless they permitted it. They were turning her into a helpless chattel, dependent on them for her most basic needs.

'You've been busy, Jim,' Roberta remarked as she looked the gagged girls over with satisfaction.

Curry grinned. 'Oddest morning I've ever spent in my workshop. But it gave me some ideas for a few devices we can try out on them. I think I can build a –'

'Shh,' said Hilary. 'Don't spoil the surprise.'

Warwick addressed the girls. 'While you're here we thought we'd put you to some practical use. Up to now I imagine your lives have been pretty pampered. Apparently the only things you have ever expended much energy on are enjoying yourselves, tormenting us and concocting elaborate alibis to deceive the police. You probably haven't had either the need or inclination to do much serious domestic work in your own homes. Well, now you're going to learn what it's like.' He smiled. 'Though we have added a few wrinkles to ensure you won't find it boring. I don't have to tell you what will happen if you don't do your jobs properly.'

Miserably they shook their heads.

There came the sound of a wheelie bin being trundled down the side alley. The back door opened and Tom Fanning came in from the kitchen.

'Are they ready?' he asked, blinking at the line of naked, cuffed and gagged girls. 'Which one do I get?'

Warwick unfolded a piece of paper from his pocket and then pointed at Hazel. 'Remember to have her back at Number 9 by one o'clock.'

Looking eager, if rather self-conscious, Fanning took Hazel by the arm and led her out the back of the house. A minute later the bin could be heard rumbling back up the side alley.

Shortly afterwards Stan Jessop appeared. 'I've got my wheelbarrow and a blanket. Will that do?'

'Just a precaution during the daytime,' the Major said. 'In case somebody comes up the road while we're moving them between houses.'

Jessop was allocated Cassie. As he led her away she flashed Tara a mute look of fear and anger.

'If you don't need me here anymore I'll take mine now,' Curry said.

'You'll be entertaining Sian this morning, Jim,' Warwick said.

Curry grinned at Sian who seemed to shrivel under his gaze. 'Well, I don't need wheels to carry that slip of a thing,' he said, unpacking a large sack from his bag. He bundled Sian into it and with a grunt and a heave, slung her over his broad shoulders and walked out.

She might as well have been a sack of potatoes, Tara thought with a shudder. That was what they had been reduced to: commodities on a list.

Roberta Pemberton came with a bin and took away Daniela. Rachel Villiers arrived with a wheelbarrow and she and Hilary departed with Gail, leaving Tara alone. She looked uncertainly between the Major and Khan.

'I absented myself from this list to simplify the allocation process,' Warwick explained, then added with a smile: 'but I'll have you all to myself tonight, Tara.'

More wheels sounded outside. Warwick motioned to Tara and Khan led her out the back door, where his wife was waiting with another wheelie bin laid on its side with its lid open. Khan forced Tara onto her knees and she crawled inside. The lid was closed, the bin was was lifted upright, rolling Tara ignominiously about, and then she felt it trundle off back the way it had come.

Three

Tom Fanning examined Hazel closely as she knelt on the rug in the middle of his cluttered study.

She was the youngest of the gang and there was a certain elfin sharpness to the line of her chin, heightened by her eyes which were slightly uptilted at the ends, counterpointing the broadness of her cheeks. Her nose and mouth were neat enough, her shoulder-length hair was a very dark blonde and her skin was clear. From the set of her face Tom suspected she often contrived a look of petulant self-assurance, perhaps to make herself seem older. If that was the case then the facade had certainly slipped, as her present woebegone expression showed.

Hazel had not quite shed her puppy fat, which gave a little extra weight to the curve of her stomach, an appealing swell to her soft white buttocks and fullness to her breasts. These stood out in plump rotund cones, capped by large pale areolae, from the centre of which rose the domes of small pink nipples. A dark triangle of hair sprouted from the junction of her nervously spread thighs.

Every few seconds her eyes flicked up to meet his own, then shied away again, as though she was fearful of giving offence yet desperate to know what he planned for her.

The unreality of the whole thing suddenly assailed Tom. He was contemplating the intimate humiliation of a young woman he had never even seen up close before last night! True, she had submitted herself to his will. But was that under duress? No, he reminded himself, it was to escape what she felt was a worse punishment. It had been her choice. But he had already seen this girl humiliatingly wet herself in public and receive six strokes of the cane, apart from whatever trials the Major had been putting them through in the back garden of Number 2 earlier. Wasn't that punishment enough?

He recalled the expressions on the other residents' faces, the day after his house had been vandalised, when they explained the war of terror the girls of Fernleigh Rise had been waging on the Close for so long. It was only then that he had learned how miserable Tara's gang had made their lives. And if nothing was done their suffering would continue. The law could not help so he had enabled them to gain the upper hand, never dreaming it would lead to a bound and naked girl kneeling on his carpet at his mercy. It was the stuff of fantasy and, he couldn't deny it, very arousing. But was it right?

Something Jim Curry had said last night, as they debated Tara's startling offer in a huddled group, came back to him.

' "There's no rule that says we shouldn't enjoy punishing them. Unless the rest of you think we should put ourselves through another week of misery finding ways to punish them that we don't enjoy either? Now that would be crazy." '

The so-called 'Elite' had made the process of punishment uniquely personal by rejecting conventional justice. Now they should be left in no doubt that they were unwillingly giving pleasure to their former victims through their degradation and suffering. This was no time for misplaced guilt.

'Stand up,' he told Hazel.

She struggled awkwardly to her feet, her eyes wide and pleading about her gag-stretched mouth.

He held up a short-handled duster with a flexible section of shaft, topped by a spray of thick floppy yellow bristles. 'This is an anti-static brush,' he told her. 'I use it to keep all my equipment clean.' he indicated the worktops that ringed three sides of the room, on which were arrayed two computers, a scanner, three screens, a couple of printers, several keyboards and a few other devices with more obscure functions. 'Today I want you to give them a really good dusting.'

Immediately she twisted round, trying to take the brush with her cuffed hands.

'No, I don't want you to hold it like that,' he told her. 'Come closer. Spread your legs . . .'

He saw her eyes widen as she understood. Trembling, she shuffled forward to where he sat in his swivel chair. He reached out and cupped the pouch at the apex of her thighs, running his fingers through her tight, dark curls. She shuddered at his touch and closed her eyes, but did not pull away. He toyed with her cleft, his fingertips brushing the crinkled tongue of her inner labia which protruded shyly from its depths. It was already coated with a moist sheen which emanated an intimate aroma. With growing confidence he probed deeper, finding the mouth of her vagina and twirling his fingers around it encouragingly. After a few seconds he felt a fresh warm slickness begin to ooze forth from the hidden passage. Was Hazel becoming aroused so easily? He saw a scarlet blush colouring her cheeks while her areolae were darkening and spreading into pink helmets that swelled before his eyes. Wonderingly he stroked the taut, blood-suffused domes, aware that he himself was now erect as the bulge in his trousers testified. Hazel shuddered, her eyes rolling, and she made an indistinct throaty sound.

The intensity of her response to his touch so surprised Tom that he asked: 'You're not a virgin, are you?'

She shook her head.

'But you're getting very wet. Does being tied up, being naked and helpless like this, excite you?'

She looked at him in mute despair, her blush deepening. Then her head dropped and she gave a tiny shameful nod.

He felt a pang of sympathy for Hazel. Added to her understandable fear and apprehension she was now in a state of sexual confusion as well. On the other hand, perhaps it would make what followed easier for her.

'You know you've got to be punished for what you did?' he said, stroking her cheek.

Hazel nodded, a look of tragic resignation in her eyes.

'But if you're a very good girl and do everything I tell you, then I'll only give you a light spanking, say three little slaps on your bottom just for show. But only if you've very good, mind. Will you do that?'

Looking slightly more hopeful she nodded, trying to smile round her gag.

'Then let's get this inside you . . .'

Holding the duster by its bristles he rubbed its chunky black foam handle up and down her furrow until it glistened with her secretions, and then slid it up inside her. Hazel gave a little squeak, lifting herself momentarily up onto tiptoe, then sank slowly back down as the handle impaled her to its fullest extent, leaving only a short length of shaft and the spray of bristles dangling between her thighs. Tom laughed at the sight and bent the flexible section of handle until its end thrust outwards.

'That's better. Now, use that chair to stand on when you need it, and I want to see everything spotless ...'

Tom watched Hazel as she worked her way diligently round the room, nudging the chair along with her feet and climbing up it so that her duster was level with screens and keyboards. Picking up his camera he took a few pictures. Some caught her head half-turned to the lens, blushing shyly. He grew transfixed by the motion of her bottom, with its slight excess of fleshy padding, as she oscillated her hips to work the duster into every nook and cranny. When she had to bend forward and spread her legs he could see her swollen pudendal pouch plugged by the duster shaft. There was a notable glisten on her inner thighs. He had never seen anything so vulnerable.

When Hazel was done she stood trembling nervously as Tom inspected her work.

'Very good', he pronounced at last, sitting back on his chair. 'Just three small spanks for you.'

Hazel's face lit up and she came almost eagerly over as he patted his knee and bent her plaint body across his lap. The brush was still inside her and it pressed against the side of his thigh. Tom felt a moment's heady rush of blood as he realised she hadn't tried to get him to take it out. More than that, she even appeared grateful to him for being told he would only spank her three times. He'd never had that sort of power over any woman.

He rubbed her bottom encouragingly, delighting in fullness of her fleshy cheeks and their perfect smoothness, all the time aware of the humid warmth emanating from their deep inrolling cleft and the

49

valley of her upper thighs. His cock was like a tentpole under his trousers.

'I'll just spank you hard enough to put a blush on your cheeks,' her told her. 'The others will probably be getting much worse. But you don't have to tell them how many you got.'

He drew back his hand and delivered the first slap. Her buttocks shivered and she gave a tiny muffled yip as the soft heavy clap of flesh rang out.

'There, that wasn't so bad, was it?' he asked, rubbing her bottom to massage in the blushing heat the blow had raised. 'Nothing you can't take . . .'

He delivered the second spank slightly harder than the first. She made no sound but squirmed in his lap. The brush head rubbed against his thigh. Was she deliberately working the shaft of the brush about inside her? He felt the warm slickness of her lubrication dripping from her vulva onto his trousers.

Tom rubbed her bottom once more, noting the pink blush spreading across the pale hemispheres. 'You've very wet. I can smell your juices. Do you want to come?' He delivered the final smack as he spoke, making a firm, meaty sound as it landed.

She jerked and whimpered, then nodded, twisting her head round as she did so. He saw a tear sparkling in the corner of her eyes that were full of need.

'Let's do it together,' he said.

He slid his fingers into her hot wet groin, gathering up her slippery exudation and rubbing it into the pucker of her anus. For a moment the ring of muscle clenched at his touch, then slowly relaxed; either in welcome or surrender to the inevitable he did not know and, at that moment, was beyond caring.

Lifting Hazel to her feet he twisted her round so that her bottom faced him and tore open his flies, releasing his straining erection. Clasping her by the hips he pulled her backwards so that she straddled his lap and then sat down. His cockhead found her tight little hole and forced its way inside. She let out a muffled wail as she was impaled by the length of his shaft, while he gloried in the hot, tight closeness of her rectum.

'Now you can come,' he said.

She began to jiggle up and down in his lap, her head thrown back, drool running down her cheeks from about her gag as the anti-static brush slapped and bobbed up and down between her thighs, its deeply buried handle stirring away within her vagina.

He clasped and squeezed her heavily bouncing breasts, controlling her increasingly wild gyrations as she desperately pumped up and down his shaft.

She came with a medley of throaty incoherent grunts and whimpers just a few seconds before his seed spurted hotly into her entrails.

As they sat together still coupled, letting the emotion slowly seep away, he whispered in her ear: 'Good girl . . .'

Stan and Louisa Jessop walked round Cassie, looking her up and down with calculated interest as she stood in the middle of their living room. Cassie glared back with nervous defiance. They both carried holly-tipped canes. She had assumed they would use her for sex as soon as they'd got her into the privacy of their own home, but they seemed in no hurry. Were they playing games with her?

'Nice tits,' Stan said. 'Bit small, maybe, but they stand out well.'

'I wonder how much punishment her bum can take?' Louisa speculated. 'Looks hard to me.'

Louisa Jessop was a bosomy dyed-blonde. Cassie thought her jaw was too heavy and her brilliant curls looked cheap. She hated everything about her and her husband; more than anything the fact that at that moment she was their helpless plaything.

'She'll take what we give her and be grateful for it, won't you, girl?' Stan said with a mischievous grin.

Cassie fought back a shiver, chewing at her gag and trying not to show her fear. She knew what they were trying to do by discussing her looks like she was a dumb animal, but she refused to be humbled. She was beautiful and she knew it.

She had blue eyes topped by fine brows and straight blonde hair. Her lips, when not stretched wide by a gag, formed classic butterfly bows. She had good high cheekbones and a neat nose with pinched nostrils. Her body was slim with shapely legs, firm round buttocks and a pop-up navel. Her breasts were small and neatly rounded, with brown, strongly marked and distinctly uptilted nipples. Her pubic delta was dark blonde, thick and fluffy.

'Well, let's get her started on the housework,' Stan said. 'A bit of hoovering for you, girl. We want everywhere looking spotless.'

Smiling brightly, Louisa brought in a cylinder vacuum cleaner trundling along on its casters. It was perfectly normal except for one addition that made Cassie's eyes bulge. Just where the metal tube curved over, after the socket that connected it to the hose, a large, flesh-coloured vibrator stood stiffly upright. It was held in place by wire and tape and glistened with freshly applied oil.

Cassie started to back away from it, shaking her head. Stan caught hold of her by a fistful of hair. 'You agreed to anything we chose to do with you as long as it wasn't harmful. And this isn't going to hurt. You might even enjoy it. But whether you do or not, we certainly will. And for the next week that's all that matters.'

While Stan held her, Louisa buckled a belt with lengths of string trailing from it about Cassie's waist. It took a couple of flicks of the holly cane across her thighs to make Cassie spread her legs and straddle the hose. Louisa guided the vibrator between the tight lips of Cassie's sex and pushed it home. Cassie gave a muffled grunt as the sculptured length of pliant oiled plastic slid up her vaginal sheath, plugging her tightly. The cords trailing from her belt were tied about the vacuum hose in front and behind her, holding the vibrator firmly in place. Cassie could only stand with awkwardly splayed legs while the hose trailed tail-like behind her and the tube and cleaner head jutted out before her in the manner of some bizarre phallus.

Stan Jessop turned on the machine and Cassie shivered as the whine of the motor was transmitted up the hose to her groin. Before she could come to terms with the disturbing sensation, Louisa switched on the vibrator. Cassie moaned as it came to buzzing life inside her. It was impossible to ignore and in seconds she felt her vagina growing slick with lubrication while her nipples began to swell and harden. Jessop noticed this and flicked the blossoming buds with his finger. 'I told you you'd enjoy it,' he said with a chuckle. 'Now start sweeping.'

Cassie pushed forward half-heartedly, rubbing the brush head over the carpet. Louisa swiped her cane across Cassie's backside, making her jerk her hips convulsively, sending the buzzing vibrator gouging even deeper into her.

'Haven't you ever used a Hoover before?' Louisa said. 'Do it properly!'

Wretchedly, Cassie jerked her hips forward and back, working the brush into the carpet pile. Then she took a splay-legged step forward, dragging the cylinder after her, and cleaned the next section. And with every move she made, the vibrator churned about within her, letting no part of her insides escape its insidious stimulation.

As she worked her way across the room Cassie began to feel a familiar sense of anticipation growing in her loins. She would have thought her circumstances would have made arousal impossible, but it seemed instead to have heightened her senses. The metal tube between her thighs was getting slick with her juices. Blushing furiously she lowered her head, trying to focus only on the carpet, but it was impossible to conceal what was happening.

Cassie snatched a sidelong glance at the Jessops to see Stan with a camera in one hand while his other arm was about his wife. Even as she glanced at them she saw Stan slip his hand inside Louisa's blouse and fondle her breast, while whispering something in her ear which made her smile. Tara had said these people were too stupid and repressed to be inventive about sex. How could she have been so wrong?

Despite her shame, reflex was taking over now. Cassie was grinding the brush head ever harder into the floor to work the vibrator about within her, surrendering to her natural urges. She just made it into the hall when she convulsed in the throws of an orgasm, grunting and gasping, sinking to her knees and bucking her hips frantically before collapsing onto her side with the vibrator still buzzing inside her.

As though from a great distance she heard Stan Jessop saying: 'We'll give you five minutes to get over that. Then you've got the stairs to do . . .'

Sian squatted on the scarred wooden top of the heavy workbench in Jim Curry's shed. A chain fastened to a beam overhead was hooked to the back of her

54

collar, ensuring she held her position. Her left hand was still cuffed behind her back, its partner locked to a belt Jim had fastened about her waist. Her right arm was free, but her hand had been taped about the handle of a dustpan brush so that she could not release it. Her knees were spread wide, concealing nothing. Jim had earlier taken some satisfaction in arranging Sian's posture so that this should be so, then examining and photographing her at his leisure.

She had a black, shoulder-length mop of hair, matching dark intense eyes and straight brows. Her neat slightly uptilted nose was set in a heart-shaped face. She had a slim body, a tiny waist and a small pale rounded bottom. Her breasts were apple-like in their firm rotundity, with nipples that Jim had been interested to discover resembled little more than crinkled buds at rest but under handling swelled to plump rounded cones. The pubic hair between her thighs was as dark and thick as that on her head.

Physically she was undeniably a pretty girl, Jim conceded, though when he had seen her in the past he thought there was something a shade calculating and aloof about her eyes. At this moment, however, her eyes communicated only discomfort, uncertainty and a wordless plea for mercy.

Jim enjoyed the feeling that look gave him. For the first time in her life, however reluctantly, what he thought and felt mattered to Sian Llwellyn-Finch.

As he fitted his devices to her he chatted cheerfully. The ball-gag stretching her lips into a helpless gape necessarily limited her responses.

'I've always been good with my hands,' he confided. 'When I more or less retired I set myself up here the way I'd always wanted. I can make pretty well anything in wood or metal. I was really happy, you know . . .' His mood darkened. 'Then you and your friends started your nasty games. Remember the night you broke that window over there and sprayed everything you could reach with red paint? That ruined a really fine walnut-veneered table I'd been restoring. That wasn't very nice, was it?'

Sian shook her head while making small whines in the back of her throat.

'Was that an apology?'

Sian nodded vigorously.

'You mean you did the spraying?'

Desperate head shaking and what might have been a gurgled: 'No, no . . .'

'I suppose it doesn't matter now. You're all going to get the same treatment, after all. I've got plenty of ideas I want to try out on you lot.' He chuckled. 'It's going to be an interesting week.'

Sian whimpered, dropping her chin to her chest. Jim caught her by the scruff of the neck and pulled her head back up so she looked him in the eye.

'Feeling sorry for yourself, are you? Well, can you really blame me for wanting a bit of revenge? And what better way than starting with you tidying up my workshop.'

He unclipped her collar chain and bodily lifted her down onto the floor. She could not have climbed down herself. Jim walked round her, admiring his handiwork.

Straps circled Sian's upper thighs and ankles, making it impossible for her to straighten her legs and forcing her to remain in a squatting position. She did not fall over because she was sitting on the head of an old stiff-bristled yard broom with casters screwed to each end. All but a short section of its handle had been cut off and the remainder had then been encased in a sleeve of waterpipe insulating foam and bound with tape. This stump had then been forced into Sian's tight little bottom hole and now, somewhat uncomfortably, plugged her rectum. Between her slim splayed thighs a large metal dustpan faced forward. Its handle, which Jim had bent upwards and also bound with foam and tape for grip, was buried in the depths of the pink cleft that peeped from Sian's pubic bush. Wires secured through holes drilled in the rim of the pan ran up to Sian's nipples, where the ends were twisted about the fleshy nubs, which seemed to remain swollen under their stimulus, much to their owner's evident dismay.

'Now do your job, my little sweeping machine,' her told her.

With a miserable whimper, Sian began shuffling forward on her intimately mounted casters as well as her doubled-up legs allowed, sweeping dust and woodshavings with her brush hand into her pan. A couple of times the leading edge of the pan caught in a crack between the floorboards, unexpectedly digging its handle deeper into her. Turning required a lot of awkward shuffling which, from the expressions that passed across her face, clearly worked the broom handle uncomfortably about inside her.

When the pan was full Sian trundled over to the shallow cardboard box Jim had put out for rubbish. Getting as close as she could she bent her supple body backwards. The wires linking her small breasts to the pan grew taut, lifting its front end over the rim of the box. Tears came to her eyes as her nipples stretched painfully under the load, the pan handle turning within her vagina. She brushed the pan clean, then shuffled gratefully backwards. The pan slid off the box rim and dropped suddenly back down between her thighs. Sian shrieked behind her gag at the agonising jerk her nipples received.

'You should have realised that would happen,' Jim said unsympathetically. 'Be more careful next time.'

Tears were trickling down her cheeks as she looked up at him, mutely imploring to be released from her mechanical torment.

'I'll be having you for a whole night later in the week,' Jim told her. 'You can talk then. If you plead really well then maybe I'll be kind to you. But right now, you keep sweeping.'

Roberta Pemberton looked a trembling Daniela over with delighted anticipation. It had been a long time since she'd had such a pretty creature to play with. Perhaps it was just reward for all she had suffered.

Daniela had smooth clear skin with a delicate olive-gold sheen. Her face was narrow and frank, her nose slightly prominent, balanced by her naturally full but well shaped brows. Her eyes were deep brown and rather shy. Dark hair fell to the middle of her back. Daniela's buttocks were full and deeply cleft without being overheavy, accentuated by the supple inward curve of her back. Her thighs were strong and nicely tapered. At their apex sprouted a fluffy delta of dark brown curls.

But Daniela's outstanding feature, Roberta decided, was her breasts. Though not large they had a convex swell to their upper slopes, hinting at a pneumatic ripeness that made them stand out from her chest, forming the neatest of creases where their undersides flowed into the skin of her ribcage. They were crowned with well-defined brown areolae tapering to sharply conical nipples crinkled with nervous apprehension.

Curious, Roberta reached out and rolled the small brown domes between her fingers. Daniela shivered and closed her eyes. Roberta continued her ministrations, knowing how and where to touch, circling her fingertips around the sensitive rim of the girl's areolae. As they blossomed into plump bulbous cones Daniela's head sank lower and her eyes closed in shame.

'Don't worry,' she told the young woman. 'We can't always help putting on a show. Like men's cocks, our nipples sometimes stand up at the most embarrassing times.' She lifted Daniela's chin and looked her in the eye. 'I know you've only recently joined Tara's gang so all this doesn't seem fair, but you did make the choice and now you've got to suffer the consequences.'

Daniela nodded sadly.

'The best thing you can do is take whatever comes and make it clear you're truly sorry,' Roberta advised. 'I think it'll go easier for you with the other residents that way. Some of it won't be very pleasant, of course, but we really do want to see you properly punished. You can't really blame us.'

Daniela shook her head.

'So we might as well get on with it. Now, what I have in mind for you will hurt a little and it's certainly meant to be humiliating, but you might find a bit of pleasure in it if you try . . .'

From a side table Roberta brought over several items which she placed before Daniela, who gazed at them in dismay. There was an aerosol can of spray furniture polish with a dildo taped to its cap, a tube of KY jelly, a fluffy duster the handle end of which had been embedded in a hard rubber ball, a pair of frilly garters and a couple of long elastic bands.

'When we were discussing how to start you off on domestic tasks earlier this morning, we all came up with similar ideas about the most demeaning way for a girl to be made to do housework. We had great fun making up these little devices. Maybe you'll compare notes with the rest of the gang as to who had it the hardest. Or of course you could decide to say nothing. Nobody can force you to do anything for the next week, except us. Now be a good girl and bend over.'

Numbly, Daniela turned and bent, spreading her legs without being told. Roberta patted and stroked the smooth tan hills of her pretty bottom. 'That's right. Now I'll just put a little jelly on this . . .' She greased the ball handle of the duster, then pried apart Daniela's buttock cleft and pressed the glistening ball into the bronze-rimmed pucker of her anus. Her little bottom mouth was reluctant to open at first but spread under increasing pressure, gaping to swallow the ball. Suddenly it popped inside, bringing forth a squeak from Daniela, and the ring of muscle closed around it. Roberta slid about a third of the wooden shaft up Daniela's rectum then gave it an experimental wiggle, eliciting a muffled gasp. It was like having a handle attached to the girl's most intimate parts.

'Stand up and turn around,' she commanded and gingerly Daniela did so, the duster sticking out of her rear like a drooping tail.

Roberta held up the can of polish with its bizarre embellishment so her captive could see it clearly. 'The only way to press the spray nozzle, when you can't use your hands, is to push down on the dildo while the base of the can is resting on something.' Daniela nodded. 'Do you also see there are drawing pins taped over the base of the dildo?' Daniela gulped, her eyes widening, and then nodded again. Roberta smiled. 'Now they won't touch you unless the dildo goes all the way up inside. So, the harder you grip it with your inner muscles when you spray, the less the pins will prick. Understand?'

Daniela nodded miserably.

'Think of it as exercise for your pussy,' Roberta advised with a grin. 'Now, on with the garters.'

Daniela lifted up her legs so Roberta could slide the garters high up her thighs. The long rubber bands Roberta then doubled over the inside of each garter, threading one end through the other and left the loops dangling. She applied more jelly to the dildo and then slowly slid it up into Daniela's vagina, watching the girl screw up her eyes as she was penetrated and noting the tremble of her lovely breasts as her breathing quickened. Her nipples, which had shrunk back to crinkled cones, erected once again.

'You're nice and tight,' Roberta said, as the dildo met some resistance. 'Is that nerves or is it natural? I bet your boyfriend likes that ...' She saw the expression briefly change on Daniela's mortified face. 'What, don't you have a boyfriend at the moment?' She twirled the dildo round in its new sheath of flesh, making Daniela gasp and shake her head. 'Do you like girls instead?' Daniela looked horribly confused. 'I see ...'

Roberta stopped when the dildo was lodged almost to its fullest extent inside Daniela, with the polish can dangling from it between her thighs. Taking up the rubber bands Roberta twisted them tight and snapped them round the can, ensuring it would not slip out of place, then stood back to admire the result.

Daniela stood trembling before her, gartered and plugged, with her thighs clenched about the polish can and the duster sticking out of her rear.

'Every home should have a maid like you,' Roberta said wistfully. 'Now, I want you to polish every bit of woodwork in the house. Start on the coffee table.'

Chewing anxiously at her gag, Daniela shuffled over to the corner of the table and squatted down until the base of the polish can rested on it. Screwing up her eyes she pushed downwards. A cloud of spray misted the table while Daniela gave a choked yelp as the pin-studded base of the dildo ground into her soft lovelips.

'That's a very good try,' Roberta assured her. 'Don't worry. Next time you'll squeeze harder. Or maybe you'll get used to a little pain . . .'

Blinking tears from her eyes, Daniela turned round and bent her knees. Sticking out her bottom and wiggling her hips, she began to rub the duster over the tabletop.

Hilary and Rachel grinned at each other and then at Gail, who was kneeling on the floor of the small conservatory that had been built onto the back of their house. Gail looked from one to the other of them with apprehension contorting her pretty features.

She had thick dark shoulder-length wavy hair which framed a heart-shaped face that still retained a certain childish aspect. Her eyes were dark as were her strongly marked brows. Her upper lip was sensuously uplifted and slightly rolled back. Girlishly slender legs and a narrow waist contrasted with wide hips, framing a dark pubic triangle, and prominent breasts standing out with melon-like firmness. These were capped by large areolae, shaded around their circumference, with small nipple domes in their centres.

'Don't worry, dear,' Hilary said. 'We're not going to take you to bed for a lesbian threesome. We'll save that for another day. This morning we're going to break you in gently. Well, fairly gently.' Her face grew darker as she gestured at their surroundings. 'Remember the filthy words your gang painted all over this place a few months ago? Do you know how long it took us just to scrape down the glass? We're still finding flakes of paint in the corners. Well, today you're going to give the windows another cleaning.'

'But we thought simply rubbing a cloth over a few panes of glass was too easy, so we've make it a bit more of a challenge,' Rachel added.

They drew Gail to her feet and ushered her out through the double doors. A garden table and chairs were set out on the small patio that flanked the conservatory. On the table was a plastic pressure bottle of the sort used for spraying plants, fitted with a length of green tubing and a spring trigger-activated nozzle. Taped vertically to the crosspiece of the bottle's pump handle was a small plastic roll-on deodorant container, with a conical cap which glistened with vaseline. Also laid out on the table was a camera, cleaning cloths, a reel of garden wire, a pack of thick rubber bands and, oddly, a pair of nutcrackers.

Before Gail could take it all in, Hilary clasped her breasts in both hands, kneading and squeezing the heavy globes. 'Lovely boobs you've got,' Hilary said, bending and kissing their bulging upper slopes. 'We're going to have fun with them when it's our turn to have you for the night. But today we're putting them to work.'

Handling Gail gently but firmly between them, they wrapped the cloths over her breasts and secured them in place with several rubber bands each, making her mammaries bulge into even more melon-like forms as their roots were squeezed ever tighter. Gail whimpered at this painful manipulation of her flesh but Hilary and Rachel just stroked and petted her and continued with their task.

The jaws of the nutcrackers were closed about the nozzle trigger of the spray head and held in place with another rubber band. More bands were looped about the handles, pulling them together until only a small amount of extra pressure was needed to activate the spray.

'Spread your legs,' Hilary commanded. Closing her eyes, Gail obeyed.

Hilary rubbed her hand up and down Gail's furrow, then slipped first one, then two and three fingers into her vagina, gently teasing the elastic tunnel wider. When she withdrew her hand it was coated with a glistening exudation. Hilary sniffed her fingers then held them out for Rachel, who inhaled the intimate scent they bore with a smile.

'Nobody who smells this nice could be really bad,' Hilary told Gail. 'Why on earth did you get mixed up with Tara's gang?'

Gail could only shake her head helplessly.

Hilary slid the ends of the nutcrackers up into Gail, whose eyes went wide as she felt the strange object penetrate her, until only the spray nozzle was visible, jutting upwards from Gail's cleft like a small metal penis. With garden wire they bound it in place, looping it tight about Gail's waist and following the creases of her buttocks at her rear until it and the tube connecting it to the pressure bottle could not come loose however Gail moved about.

'The bottle's full of water and glass cleaner,' Hilary told Gail. 'All you have to do is to pump it up. You'll probably need to do that a few times as there's plenty to do. You can see how you've got to pump it, can't you?'

Gail nodded, looking as though she could not quite believe what she was doing. She straddled the pump with its novel adornment and gingerly squatted down over it, opening her buttocks. The bullet-shaped deodorant cap nuzzled into the ring of her anus.

Screwing up her eyes she sat down harder. Suddenly the cap popped inside her and she was impaled on the pump handle. She straightened her legs, drawing the handle up with her, then squatted once more, driving the air into the pressure bottle. After a dozen thrusts she rose, straining until she expelled her anal plug.

Walking awkwardly up to the nearest window pane, trailing the plastic tube after her, she pointed the nozzle and clenched her thighs together. A jet of water sprayed over the glass, bringing forth a muffled gasp of surprise from Gail. She wiggled her hips, thoroughly drenching the glass, then relaxed, causing the spray to reduce to a dribble, looking round at Hilary and Rachel with an expression of surprise and wonder on her face.

'Good girl,' Hilary said, holding her camera at the ready. 'Now wipe it clean.'

Pressing her face almost to the glass, Gail began to rub her cloth-bound breasts over the pane, her supple back flexing, her perfectly rounded buttocks tensing, her slender legs braced as she moved from side to side.

Rachel and Hilary exchanged smiles of delight as they arranged the garden chairs to watch their lovely naked slave at work. This was going to be fun.

'Who would have thought one day we would have Tara Ashwell cleaning our kitchen floor?' Narinda Khan said in mock wonder.

'And stripped down to her bare skin to do the job,' Raj added in kind.

'You must remember the expensive clothes she wears,' Narinda pointed out. 'She would not want to get them dirty.'

'Of course!' Raj clutched his brow. 'How stupid of me not to realise.' He prodded Tara with his toe, the bantering tone in his voice melting into bitterness as he added: 'But then that is all I am to you. A stupid brown-skinned man you enjoy persecuting and insulting. But who is kneeling on whose floor now, eh?'

Tara glowered defiantly up at him, willing herself not to show any fear. It was necessary to endure the Khans' mockery, knowing they were secretly in awe of her naked beauty, which was saving her from an even worse fate. She knew what they were seeing. It was what her mirror had shown her often enough.

Clear golden skin, long dark wavy honey-blonde hair and a perfectly proportioned oval face with high cheekbones. Her brows were dark and expressive and set over sparkling warm brown eyes. Her nose was very slightly uptilted, her lips full and generously wide. There was a proud outward thrust to her full breasts, which were crowned with large rosy pink nipple cones. This pneumasticity contrasted with her hourglass waist and wide hips. Her bottom was perfectly pale and rounded, her dark pubic hair neatly trimmed. Regular riding sessions had given her strong shapely legs.

Yes, she must be proud of what she was, Tara told herself once again. Nothing they could do to her could take that away from – Her thoughts were cut short by the sight of the objects Narinda had just brought out of a cupboard.

There was more of the hateful binding tape they had used last night, plus floor cloths, a new wooden scrubbing brush with a rubber ball screwed to its back, and a mophead fitted to a short length of old broom handle with a small empty plastic bottle taped close to its end. Into the bottle's open mouth had been stuffed the tail-end of a large carrot. But most alarming of all was a plastic bucket of soapy water with what looked like a wreath of holly sprigs taped to the outside of its rim.

'We thought it would be properly demeaning if you held the brush in your mouth to scrub our floor,' Narinda said, beaming down at Tara. 'You'll have to put your face into the bucket to wet the brush. It's only plain soap in there, but as the water gets dirtier you will find it less pleasant. Also, each time those big titties of yours will rub against the holly, which should hurt quite a lot . . .' her face hardened, 'though not so much as the pain you have caused us over all these months.'

Tara cringed from the sudden force of her anger. Then the moment had passed and Narinda smiled again.

One at a time, they lifted her legs and taped the folded cloths over her knees and shins. Then Narinda pushed the ball screwed to the back of the scrubbing brush into her mouth. It pressed her tongue flat and jammed behind her teeth so she could not spit it out. The brush stuck out in front of her lips, just touching the tip of her nose.

'Now, how did we decide to make sure she stayed properly bent over with her nose to the floor?' Raj asked his wife with a grin.

'By sticking this little mop and carrot up her private passages.'

'But will that not be most uncomfortable for her?'

Narinda grinned wickedly. 'Very uncomfortable, yet also I think a little teasing. I wonder which she will feel most?'

'There's only one way to find out.'

Tara's eyes had widened in horror. The carrot was huge, its thick end facing forward. By being mounted in the bottle it was held clear of the mop handle. In effect it was double-pronged.

As Raj Khan held her hips steady, Narinda pushed the end of the wooden mop handle into her anus, at the same time feeding the carrot-head into her vagina.

'She's already very slippery,' Narinda observed.

'The Major had some fun with them before you came,' Raj explained. 'I think they got excited.'

Tara groaned as the handle seemed to butt up against her spine, forcing her rectum to conform to its unyielding presence, while the carrot filled her vagina. As her sheath automatically clenched about the carrot it seemed to squeeze its tapering shape even further up inside her. When both her passages were plugged to the hilt, her leash, which they had not unclipped, was passed down between her legs and the end tied to the shaft of the mop handle just above its head, ensuring it would not slip out of her.

'Now start scrubbing,' Raj commanded.

Miserably, Tara shuffled over to the bucket, feeling both the handle and carrot working about inside her as she trailed the mop head grotesquely after her. She tried to stretch her neck and dip the brush into the water without touching the ring of holly round the bucket rim, but her full globes hung too heavily and she winced as needle-pointed spines jabbed into them. Desperately she made a lunge with the brush, dunking it into the water, getting bubbles up her nose and in her eyes in the process. Jerking away she also ground the brush handle into her. The swaying hemispheres of her breasts were now peppered with dozens of stinging red pinpricks.

Snuffling and blinking her streaming eyes, acutely aware of the spectacle she presented to her captors, Tara spread her knees wider and bowed her head. Her nipples scraped across the floor and then her breasts made fat pancakes about them before the brush touched the tiles. How utterly humiliating! She would have to drag them all over the floor as she cleaned. Resolutely she began to scrub, closing her eyes as she swung her head from side to side, trying to make one brushload of water go as far as possible. It was not in fact a big kitchen, but from her current viewpoint it looked huge.

The flash of a camera told her the Khans were recording her shame for posterity.

Gradually the swaying of her upper body rolled her breasts over the tiles. That, together with the small but insistent sliding twisting motion of the mop handle and carrot, made her nipples began to harden. For a moment she felt appalled at her arousal under the Khans' watching eyes. Then she quashed her instinctive disgust. Had she forgotten the lesson she had learned in the garden? Even this could be turned on its head. She'd show them.

She shuffled forward and deliberately swung her hips from side to side, wiping the dry mop over the patch of floor she had just scrubbed, savouring the way the improvised dildos moved inside her, aware of the slick wetness beginning to flow about the carrot. Over at the bucket, she didn't try to avoid the holly ring, but pressed her swollen nipples into the spines as she neatly re-wetted the brush, glorying in the hot pinpoint pain on such sensitive flesh.

Returning to the next patch of floor she began to rock slightly forward and back as she scrubbed, pumping the mop handle and carrot deeper into her. She'd never tried anal sex. Perhaps she'd been missing out on something. It's just a game, she told herself.

Scrub, rinse, more burning pricks to her breasts, the water growing increasingly dirty, splashing over her as she worked making her feel soiled and menial as she never had before, which only roused her senses further. She was dripping juices from her vagina and rubbing them into the floor.

Tara came hunched over, rubbing the scrubbing brush to and fro in a frenzy to grind her burning nipples harder into the floor, even as her anal ring clenched the mop shaft in an iron grip and she gave the carrot stuffing her vagina a dressing of her most intimate discharge.

For a few moments the Khans were silent, then Narinda said dismissively: 'These spoilt brats are all the same. Anything for a new thrill.'

Four

At one o'clock, again concealed within bins and barrows, they were taken to Number 9: Gerald Spooner's house. Their named bowls had been set out in a circle on the back lawn and filled with a mash of potatoes and chopped vegetables. Water was provided in bottles with straws. From his chair under the shade of an apple tree, Spooner watched them eat, as before, with their bare bottoms in the air. Out of the corner of her eye Tara glimpsed him beaming at them in satisfaction and congratulating the other residents on their handling of the girls.

Tara turned her attention back to her food. Exertion and nervous tension had genuinely left her ravenously hungry, but also, with her gag removed, eating steadily excused her from answering questions about what she had undergone that morning.

Tara's brief sense of triumph had melted away with the afterglow of her orgasm, leaving sullen resentment in its place as a sense of reality returned. She still hated these people and feared what they might do to her. For the next week she was their slave and the shame of that would linger all her life.

Fortunately the other girls seemed equally preoccupied with their food and few words were spoken during the meal apart from the odd mumbled 'You okay?', which received non-committal grunts in response. But their eyes were busier than their mouths, searching for any clues as to how they had been used. Were they all so embarrassed by what had been done to them? Tara wondered, hoping the pinpricks the holly had left across her breasts were not noticeable. Perhaps she should speak up while she had the chance and be open about what she had suffered and how she had coped. It could be made to sound like a perverse sort of victory. But what if the others had undergone even worse indignities? In the end she said nothing.

After lunch they were allowed a brief rest and then put to work. Their confiscated footwear was returned and they were provided with gardening gloves and tools. Their gags remained off but they were warned not to speak, which suited Tara.

'You're all going to do a proper afternoon's work,' Warwick told them. 'Mr Spooner's garden needs some attention and it seems appropriate that you supply the labour, since in the past you've been responsible for tearing up his plants and desecrating his lawn. If this week achieves nothing else you will have performed, however unwillingly, one worthwhile service ... and perhaps learned what honest work feels like.'

Hazel and Daniela had their wrists cuffed to the handlebars of a push-mower and were started mowing the lawn. Sian, with her ankles hobbled by a short length of chain, shuttled between them and the compost heap at the bottom of the garden emptying the grass box. Tara and Cassie, their left and right ankles joined by a long chain, were set digging and weeding, while a hobbled Gail took the buckets of weed away. When in due course they needed to pee, they were each made to squat on the compost heap and do it before the watching residents, encouraged by flicks from holly canes. Gerald Spooner cheerfully applauded each display.

Tara felt assailed by a renewed sense of deep shame and indignation, but this time without any means of arousing herself as a diversion. But at least gardening was straightforward and less unpleasant than she had imagined. If she could ignore the chain round her ankle only her nudity was out of place, and in the enclosed garden in the warm summer air even that seemed less unnatural than it had at first. She vaguely recalled hearing of people who regularly gardened in the nude. Perhaps there was something in it.

At teatime they were fed again, then taken back to Number 2.

Six blankets had been laid out on the living room floor. On each of them had been placed a pillow and two thick planks of timber standing on their edges, connected at their ends by two longer but thinner battens to form roughly bed-sized frames. The battens were secured to the lower plank by a metal sleeve and pegs so that the separation of the top and bottom planks could be adjusted. These planks had been sawn lengthwise and the two halves joined by hinges at one end and a latch and padlock at the other. Large circular holes had been drilled through them in the manner of medieval stocks. The top plank had a larger hole in the middle to accommodate the neck and two smaller ones at each end for the wrists, while the lower one had a pair of intermediate-sized holes at each end for the ankles.

These horizontal stocks were hinged open and the girls laid down in the lower halves with their heads on the pillows, legs spread and arms bent at the elbows so that their wrists were level with their necks. The side battens were adjusted to suit their individual heights and then the top halves were swung back and locked into place.

In momentary panic Tara strained against the woodwork that had close about her neck, wrists and ankles. The edges of the holes had all been carefully bevelled and sanded, but it was impossible to slip her wrists free. She was almost completely immobilised and helpless, with her legs spread as though in invitation. If anybody wanted to use her right now she could do nothing to stop them . . .

Tara forced herself to relax. Her new position made no difference to the likelihood of sex, and it seemed they were going to be allowed to rest ungagged. The imprisoning frame and blanket it rested upon was no feather bed, but it was less uncomfortable than she would have imagined. After her labours in the Khans' kitchen and then the garden, it was actually a relief to lie on a firm surface with her back straight. Of course it did not allow her to touch herself or any of the others, which presumably was the idea. Only their captors had that privilege.

'I suggest you try to get a few hours' rest,' Warwick told them when they were all secured. 'We've devised a rota to ensure everybody who wishes can have the use of each of you in turn through the week, from 8 p.m. to 8 a.m. This is going to be the first of six long nights for all of you.'

He went out, turning off the light and locking the door behind him. Daylight filtered in around the boarded window, dimly illuminating the six naked bodies splayed out in their stock-beds.

For some moments nobody spoke. Then Sian said quietly but passionately: 'I hate you, Tara! I want you to know that. Really hate you!'

Tara flinched at the venom in her words, suddenly grateful for the solidity of the frames confining them. She had nothing to lose by asking: 'Why do you hate me, Sian? I thought we were friends.'

Sian almost shrieked: 'After the way Warwick handled me in the garden, after what Curry made me do ... what they're going to do tonight!'

'And what did Curry make you do?' Tara asked.

'It – it doesn't matter.'

'I didn't have a picnic either, but I'm not complaining,' Tara countered.

'But it's all your fault we're in this shitty mess!' Sian shouted.

'She's right,' Cassie interjected. 'You said Fanning was just some electronics nerd. You didn't say he was a fucking surveillance expert!'

'Nobody said anything about that when I asked about him,' Tara countered. 'Maybe he was just being modest or had to keep it secret. It doesn't matter now.'

'No, 'cos we're all screwed ... or going to be screwed,' Sian said wildly. 'But when we get out of this, I'm going to – to –'

'Do what?' Tara said. 'Tell everybody what happened to us? The police'll ask why and then you'd be in as much trouble as me. I didn't force you to raid the Close. You enjoyed everything we did to these people.'

'And now they're doing this to us,' Cassie hissed, rattling her frame futilely. 'We're the Elite, the best. It's not fair!'

'We did do some pretty nasty things to them,' Gail said quietly.

'Shut up!' Cassie snapped.

'I hate Cheyner Close and all the people in it, but most of all I hate you, Tara!' Sian persisted. 'I'll get even with all of you somehow.'

'That goes for me too,' Cassie added.

Tara was beginning to wonder if she had misjudged Sian and Cassie. She'd always thought of them as stronger-willed than Hazel, Gail or Daniela, but now they didn't seem to be able to handle a setback.

'And how're you going to do that?' she asked sarcastically. 'Run me down in the street? Wait for a dark night with an iron bar? Of course, if you really hate me that much you can always hire a hit man . . .'

In the gloom she heard Hazel sniggering at the idea. The absurdity of it briefly silenced Sian and Cassie.

Tara continued: 'Anything you do to hurt me in public, people will want to know why. Then what'll you say? You'll get no sympathy doing it for a reason you can't give, and you can bet I'll say nothing. And before you try to get back at the residents, remember they've got us on camera admitting what we did and begging to serve them. What will that make all of us look like if it gets out?'

There was a long silence as Sian and Cassie digested this possibility. Then Sian said, beginning to sound more worried than angry: 'Can we trust them not to show it around?'

'You can trust Warwick, and he'll make sure the rest of them stick to the deal,' Tara said.

'But you said he was a stupid prick of an old soldier –'

'Maybe he is, but I never said he wasn't honest,' Tara cut in, a little surprised at her certainty. 'His sort never break their word.'

There was another silence, then Daniela said: 'So you're saying we're safe if we stick to the agreement and let them do what they want with us.'

'Don't talk about it,' Cassie groaned miserably.

'Daniela's right,' Tara said. 'If you two haven't got the sense or guts to see this through, that's your problem. You know what I'm going to do? I'm going to show them I can take it by getting pleasure anyhow and any way I can!' She hadn't planned to say more but she was getting carried away with the desire to put Sian and Cassie in their place. 'You know what the Khans made me do? They stuffed a mop handle up my bum, a carrot up my cunt, put a brush in my mouth and made me scrub the floor with water from a bucket surrounded by holly, so I stabbed my tits on it every time I used it. And you know what I did? I worked myself off on it all and came right in front of their eyes!' She was high on perverse elation. Her nipples were erect and she was feeling almost boastful about her ordeal, savouring their awed attention. 'So you see they won't break me. Why don't you try it?'

'I came too,' Cassie blurted out, then choked off in silence.

Tara sensed they were all twisting their heads round trying to see Cassie, as she herself was.

'You what?' Sian said, her voice edged with incredulous contempt.

'It's true!' Cassie snapped. 'The Jessops made me hoover with a vibrator stuck up me. I couldn't help it.'

'Oh,' said Gail quietly. 'Didn't you enjoy it at all?'

'No . . . well, a bit . . .' Cassie sounded confused. 'I don't know.'

'Next time try to enjoy it,' Tara advised.

'Are you a masochist or what?' Sian said. 'None of this is any fun!'

'Well, what did Curry do to you?' Tara asked.

'I don't want to talk about it,' Sian replied defensively.

'Come on. Cassie and I have owned up. Or are you too embarrassed?'

Sian realised she was trapped. 'He – he made me sweep out his workshop . . .' Haltingly she described how she was turned into a living dustpan. 'There was no way doing that could get me excited,' she concluded defensively. 'It was just humiliating and painful. My nipples are still sore.'

'You had a hand free,' Gail said. 'You could have wiggled the dustpan about in your slot. That might have got you going.'

'With him watching?' Sian said aghast.

Gail surprised Tara by persisting. 'It might even have been more exciting that way. I mean, there's no prize for feeling worse than we have to. I'm still scared about what they're going to do to us, but I think it makes sense not to fight it. They're trying to humiliate us sexually, right, so there'll probably be something – intimate we can use for pleasure, if we let it.'

'So what did you have to do?' Sian demanded. 'I suppose you came ten times!'

'No . . . but it wasn't so bad after I got used to it. Even sort of fun . . .' She described washing the conservatory windows for Hilary and Rachel, and how she had to work the pump. 'Of course my boobs were like prunes when they took the cloths and bands off, and they really smarted as the blood came back, but they massaged them better.'

'You had your tits rubbed by a pair of dykes!' Sian said contemptuously.

'They weren't nasty,' Gail said. 'Yes, they wanted to see me suffer a bit. I understand that now. But they could have made it a lot worse.'

'You wait till it's their turn to have you in their bed, then see how much you like them,' Sian said.

'Well, we'll just have to compare notes on that after they've had you,' Gail riposted neatly, reducing Sian to fuming silence.

Tara heard both Hazel and Daniela chuckle. Enslavement seemed to have given the normally meeker Elite girls a perverse sense of freedom. Now they could speak their minds without any chance of reprisal, except verbally. They were also natural followers. Perhaps, as they got over their initial shock, that made the situation easier for them to accept.

'I had to clean Roberta Pemberton's house with a duster stick up my bottom and a can of spray polish between my legs,' Daniela said suddenly.

They listened with interest as she related her experience in detail. 'After a while I did get a bit excited. I mean, every time I took a step the garters pulled the dildo about inside me. Even getting pricked by the drawing pins didn't feel so bad. Eventually I started dripping, from my pussy, you know, onto the furniture, but Roberta just told me to polish it up.'

'So you're on first name terms with her now,' Cassie said scathingly.

'Well, it's her name. And she was quite nice, really.'

'You call her nice after doing that to you?'

'Like Gail said, she could have been much worse. I think it's best if we do what they want and let them know we're sorry.'

'You're crazy!' Cassie exclaimed. 'What about you, Hazel? Are you going soft as well? What did Fanning get you to do?'

'I had to dust off his computers with a special anti-static brush,' Hazel said in a small voice. 'He's got stacks of electronic stuff in his office.'

'That sounds easy enough,' Cassie said.

'Well, I had to hold the brush in my pussy,' Hazel explained. 'Then, when I'd finished he spanked me, just three times because I'd been good.'

'Did it hurt?' Gail asked.

'Not much. I was getting pretty excited by then. And so was he . . .'

'Yes?'

Hazel took a deep breath and said in a rush: 'So he sat me on his lap and put his cock up my bottom and he came inside me and I came as well!'

There was a stunned, perversely impressed silence. Hazel had been the first to have actual sex with their captors. Then curiosity took hold.

'What did it feel like, having a cock up your bottom?' Daniela asked in awed tones.

'Sort of odd but quite nice,' Hazel said, then added with a giggle: 'I actually felt his come spurt right up inside me. It trickled out of my bottom after he'd pulled his thing out. He wiped me clean with a tissue.'

'Was he any good?' Gail asked.

'I suppose so. I mean I came as well so he must have been OK.'

'Did he have a big cock?' Sian asked, sounding helplessly fascinated despite herself, perhaps wondering when it would be her turn to serve Tom Fanning.

'I never saw it . . . but it felt big enough!'

Tara thought she almost sounded proud of the fact. There was no resentment about what she had endured, but instead a strange sense of wonder.

It was then that Tara knew change was overtaking them all. They would be different people when this was over, for better or worse. It was also the end of the Elite Society. Maintaining its existence through this ordeal had been a futile fantasy, she realised. It had really been a juvenile creation and they were now being forced to grow beyond it. Her influence over the girls was also dwindling, which she resented more. The trouble was that no diversion she could contrive would rival what they had undergone in this last last day, nor what was yet to come. Well, she consoled herself, she'd been getting bored with it anyway. Besides, she now had more pressing things to think about.

The residents came for them with their bins and barrows at eight. By then Tara had become aware of a distinct scent pervading Number 2's living room. It was the female odour of arousal and readiness emanating from half a dozen captive, exposed and expectant vaginas. They all knew that by morning Hazel would no longer be unique amongst them.

Apparently somebody had been busy with a sewing machine, because the residents brought with them strips of cloth to serve as blindfolds. Before the girls were released from the frames their ball-gags were replaced and the blindfolds tied over their eyes. The stocks securing their neck and wrists were opened and they were sat up so that their hands could be cuffed behind them. Only then were their ankles freed and they were allowed to stand.

Tara understood the function of the blindfolds. They made them more easy to control, having to accept the guidance of unseen hands clasping their arms or pulling on leashes, reducing them to helpless stumbling inferior beings. Her ego raged at the new indignity even as her loins stirred perversely at the knowledge of what was to come. Yes, it's a sick thrill, she told herself desperately, so go with it. They want to see you suffer so defy them by enjoying it, like you did this morning. But that had been with a mop handle and a carrot, not a middle-aged man she despised.

Major Warwick loaded Tara into a wheelbarrow, threw a piece of sack over her and wheeled it across the road to his house. At the back door he helped her out and guided her inside, through the kitchen and into the sitting room, where he made her kneel.

'Display!' he said. Tara shuffled her knees wider and sat up straight. He undid the blindfold, then, to her obvious surprise, removed her gag. Then he sat on his comfortably worn green leather armchair before her, so that her open thighs faced him and he could see her labia peeping through her pubic bush.

Tara kept her gaze low, perhaps not wanting to make direct eye contact, her eyes flicking about the neat room with its many pictures hanging from the walls, bookcase and glass-fronted display cabinet.

'Look at me, Tara Ashwell,' he said.

She lifted her eyes to his. He read the fear behind them, and, perhaps, the wish to get whatever he had planned for her over with. If so she would just have to be patient. He was in charge now.

'I removed your gag because I've wanted us to have a private conversation for some time. Perhaps I also want to hear you cry out in pain later . . .' Tara trembled visibly '. . . but for the moment we shall just talk. I will not punish you for telling the truth, only if I think you are lying or you refuse to answer. You may speak perfectly freely, but you will always, I repeat, always do so respectfully, or else . . .' He picked up his holly cane, which had been resting on the small side table beside his chair and laid it across his knees at the ready. Tara gulped at the sight. 'Tonight I am your master. That's how you will address me. Do you understand?

'Yes . . . Master,' Tara replied, emphasising the last word, trying to make it clear it was something she said because she had to, nothing more.

'Do you remember how this all started?' he asked. 'A year and a half ago? You and your boyfriend, Peter Tucker, with his new sports car, which he took to driving you round the local roads in late at night and ridiculously fast. I suppose you thought you were having fun.'

'We were, Master,' Tara replied simply.

'But then you started doing handbrake turns in the Close. Did you think it was amusing being woken night after night by screeching tyres, blaring horns and blazing headlights, especially if you had a job to go to the next morning?'

'We didn't think about you at all, Master,' she said bluntly. 'We were just enjoying ourselves.'

'But you thought about us soon enough when we finally got your number and called the police. To his credit, Tucker took their warning to heart and never bothered us again. Why weren't you as reasonable?'

'Because you'd stopped me having fun, Master. The police came to my house because of you, and that was very embarrassing. The police are there to protect Fernleigh Rise, not to question us like common criminals.'

'You think it's your inalienable right to have fun?'

'Why not, Master?'

'And in your eyes I suppose we were being petty bourgeoisie spoilsports by not letting you.'

'Yes, Master. After that Pete started being careful and – and boring.'

'So you blamed us.'

'Yes, Master. You'd taken away something I enjoyed . . . so I made all of you in the Close my new entertainment.'

'Are you really so short of stimulation?'

'This was something different, Master. I like excitement and danger and doing things that are new.'

'And you roped in your gang of girlfriends to help.'

'They did what I told them, Master, not like Pete. Anyway, they thought it was fun as well.'

'And what do they think now?'

Tara hesitated. He raised his cane and she said quickly: 'Cassie and Sian hate me, Master. The others act almost like they believe they deserve to be punished. Gail goes on about understanding why you want to see us suffer.'

'And do you understand why, Tara?'

Tara shrugged, as though the answer was obvious. 'You want revenge, Master. And to make sure we don't bother you again.'

'Anything else, do you think?'

Tara frowned. 'I don't know what you mean, Master.'

'To hear you say you're sorry, of course. Are you sorry, Tara?'

For a moment Tara seemed at a loss. Then she licked her lips. 'No, Master. I did what I wanted to do. I feel sorry you caught us ... a bit sorry for myself now, maybe, but not for doing what we did.' She flinched back, as though fearing a swipe from his cane.

'Sit straight, you stupid girl,' he said sharply. 'I told you I wouldn't punish honest answers and I don't go back on my word.' He sighed. 'So, if you won't repent, it looks like I'll have to be content with simply redressing the balance and getting some satisfaction out of seeing you suffer.'

To his surprise Tara smiled. 'Why not, Master? That's what I was doing to you.'

Warwick found himself smiling back. 'So, we understand each other at last. I don't think I'm a naturally cruel man, but I believe I'm going to enjoy myself tonight.'

Tara gulped, but maintained her poise. 'You'd be stupid not to, Master. You won't have anybody as beautiful as me like this ever again.'

'Think a lot of yourself, don't you?'

'I know what I am, Master.'

'Your friends are also quite attractive. I'll be having them as well.'

'But I'm the best, because I'm the strongest, Master,' Tara said proudly. As though emboldened, or perhaps believing she had nothing to lose, she added, 'Can I ask a question, Master?'

'Go on.'

'How did you know how to handle us so well in the garden this morning? That wasn't army drill. You knew all the right buttons to press to make us do just what you wanted.'

He chose his words with care. 'In the past I have done work with certain units of the armed forces, where knowledge of interrogation techniques and how to resist them was required. As some brave young women are now part of these units, it was necessary to understand female psychology as it related to such situations. I simply applied what I knew to the current circumstances.'

Tara looked impressed despite herself. Glibly she said: 'I suppose you know ten different ways to kill people with your bare hands, Master.'

'Oh, I know many more than ten,' Warwick said simply. 'I also know how to set the most unpleasant traps for uninvited guests you can imagine . . .' Tara had gone pale but could not look away from his now stony face. 'But we're not meant to use such things in Home Counties back gardens, so I was trying to fight you by regular means first. By civilian rules. Still, it's probably a good thing Tom Fanning came along when he did, or I might have lost patience. Privately called in some favours from old comrades, perhaps. Then you'd have got a visit from people far less welcome than the police. Be grateful you're getting off this lightly, Tara Ashwell.'

'I am, Master,' Tara said faintly. She took a deep breath, seeming to gather her courage. 'You can probably make me say or do anything you want tonight, Master, but that won't mean I'm really sorry for what I did ... just sorry that I underestimated you, and the other residents.'

The statement seemed to be perfectly honest and without any artifice. He smiled. 'An admission that Tara Ashwell is not perfect. I suppose that's all I can expect for now. But it's a beginning.'

With that he took up her leash and led her upstairs. She followed obediently.

In the bathroom he sat her on the toilet. A length of hose with a spray nozzle was already plugged into the bath taps. Without being told, Tara parted her legs and peed, staring down at the floor but obviously aware that Warwick was watching the stream of urine issue from her cleft. Then she strained to empty her bowels. When she had done what she could he turned the hose on her open groin, sluicing her off. Then, kneeling between her spread legs, he slid the long tapering spray nozzle into her anus and flushed her insides out, watching her face contort as the warm stream swirled through her entrails.

Only when he was quite satisfied she was clean did he dry her off with toilet paper and towel. Then he led her through to the spare bedroom where he had made his preparations.

On a rug in the middle of the room was a small sturdy four-legged footstool with a cushion taped to its seat. Jutting up at an angle of about 45 degrees from under the stool, and fastened to its frame by 'G' clamps, was a stringless badminton racket. Sitting on the rug at the same end of the stool was a large round shaving mirror on a tilting base. Beside this was a collection of leather straps, a reel of tape and a jar of vaseline.

Warwick pushed Tara down so that she knelt over the stool with her middle resting on the cushion and her head lying against the empty racket face. Pulling her legs wide and bending her knees further, he made her clasp the stool between her thighs, exposing her rear even further. He passed a strap under the stool and round her thighs just above her knees and buckled it tight. A second strap went over the small of her back and under the stool, pulling her face down until it was pressed into the rim of the racket with her breasts dangling on either side of the handle which touched her sternum. Unlocking the handcuffs he then taped her wrists to the sides of the stool legs. A final strip of tape went across the back of her head, binding it tightly to the racket rim so that she could not lift or turn it and was forced to stare straight ahead.

Warwick stepped back to admire his handiwork for a moment, then said: 'I must change. I'll be back shortly . . .'

Briefly left unattended, Tara tugged at her bonds by reflex, even though she knew it was futile. She was even more completely immobilised than in her bed stocks. As her stomach did flip-flops of fear, the simmering heat lower in her loins grew, pumping out a slick wetness that seeped through to the lips of her vulva. She was simultaneously dismayed at the intensity of her arousal yet comforted by its presence. It was her shield and refuge. Through it she would find pleasure in whatever he did to her.

In his bedroom Warwick quickly slipped off his clothes and put on slippers and a robe, very aware of his tumescent manhood as he did so. Tara Ashwell was such a delicious creature, yet so self-centred. He had imagined various ways she might be brought to justice, or else forced to cease her vendetta against the Close, but never having her helpless in his house at his mercy. And he was going to enjoy every minute of it.

He went back to the spare room.

'It's unexpectedly satisfying seeing you like this,' he said, walking round her tightly bound body as she hugged the stool in an unwilling embrace, examining her from every angle. She tried to turn her head to follow him but her face was too tightly secured to the racket frame.

'You, like your friends, will know what it is like to suffer helplessly tonight,' he continued. 'Then you may begin to understand a little of what we went through ever since you started your vile campaign. I should thank you for talking us into this. It's far better than official justice. Or would you disagree?'

Tara shivered, but said in a remarkably level voice: 'I chose this, Master. I'm not changing my mind now. Do what you want with me. That's the deal.'

Warwick squatted down, stroking her bottom, sliding his hand round to cup the fleshy undercurve of her buttocks, testing their warmth and weight. 'You have guts, girl, I'll say that for you.'

His fingertips ran down the pouting cleft of her pudenda and he felt her slippery wetness.

'Your juices came quickly this morning as well,' he said. 'Does all this excite you?'

He thought he might have to threaten her with the holly cane to get an answer, but with only the slightest hesitation she replied: 'Yes . . . it does, Master. I think it's the danger. And, in a sick way, the shame of being here like this. It's perverted but it's getting me hot.'

Warwick felt oddly slighted. 'Not the thought of sex?'

'It helps, but I've never had a thing for older men. I don't like you, Master, but if I can get off on having your cock up me I will.'

The frankness of her reply surprised him. 'You don't hold anything back, do you?'

'You told me to be honest, Master. That's the truth. How else should I feel about somebody who's going to beat and rape me?'

'Not rape!' Warwick said sharply. 'You offered yourselves to us, remember. If you really believe this is rape then it stops now.'

'No, Master!' Tara said quickly. 'That wasn't the right word. But it feels like that. Which is all right because that makes it feel more dangerous.'

'And as you said, you like danger.'

'Yes, Master. But what I said about you is still the truth. You wouldn't believe anything else anyway, so why should I lie?'

Despite her utter helplessness, he realised she was still defying him. She had such a stubborn streak in her.

'No, I've had enough of your lies in the past,' he said. 'I'd rather you were honest. At least then we know where we stand . . .'

His hand had moved to the heavy bells of her breasts, squeezing and fondling, giving them light slaps that sent them swaying and bouncing off each other. Her nipples, already semi-hard, blossomed into full erection.

'Talking of which, I see these haven't forgotten how to stand to attention,' Warwick said.

Tara drew in her breath with a shudder.

He adjusted the angle of the mirror, putting it to one side of and a little in front of her head, then crouched down behind her. He would be able to see her face in it while he used her.

'First I'm going to give your bottom a good strapping, then I'm going to sodomise you,' Warwick told her, matching her own forthrightness. 'Of course I won't try to be gentle. I want to give you something tangible to remember me by, even if only temporarily. A rosy hot bum and a few bruises round your rear entrance. I think that's the most undignified way to treat you, giving me the maximum pleasure while putting you in your place. The marks will fade soon enough, but perhaps the memory will linger to some effect. Have you ever had anal intercourse before?'

'No, Master,' she admitted, her voice trembling now. 'I always thought it was – dirty.'

'I'll try not to disappoint you.' He held the tub of vaseline out for her to see. 'This will make it a little more comfortable, but you'll have to beg me to use it.'

He saw her face in the mirror. Her pupils were huge now, as though trying to take in every detail of what was happening to her. She licked her lips. 'Use the strap on me first, Master. Make me beg.'

'I see,' Warwick said slowly. Now he understood perfectly. 'Well, if that's the way you want it . . .'

He stood up and slipped off his robe. His penis was harder and angled higher than it had been for many years. He'd never felt so potent. He coiled the end of a strap round his fist. 'I'll stop when you beg to be greased,' he said.

The strap swished through the air and smacked crisply across Tara's smooth posterior hemispheres.

Tara yelped as the blow made her flesh jump, and a broad crimson strip flared across her backside. The strap cut less deeply than the bamboo he had used on her the night before, but it stung nonetheless fiercely. In the mirror he saw her face pinch into a grimace of pain. Good . . . He drew back his arm and laid down another stripe parallel with the first.

90

Tara yelped and moaned and whimpered freely as he systematically chastised her, jerking and squirming in her bonds and holding nothing back. She'd contained herself better when she'd been bent over the Close sign. But then her gang had been watching. Now she was free to wallow in her shame and suffering.

Her bottom was a solid blaze of red, though her flesh was not broken anywhere, and she was sobbing and gasping loudly. Her vulva was swollen with excitement and her glistening inner labia pouted from her cleft like an impudently stuck-out tongue. His chosen goal, the starburst-ringed pit of her anus, was contracting and gaping with every clench of her abused buttocks. Warwick thought he had never seen anything so primally desirable.

He was wondering how long he could hold on when she suddenly cried: 'Stop, stop! Please stop . . . I can't take any more. Have me, Master, I beg you. Use the vaseline, please, shove it up my bumhole. I'll be good. I'm hot and tight. I'll try to please you . . . I'll do anything, but don't use the strap again . . .'

Warwick had already dropped the strap. Scooping up a dollop of the clear grease he rammed it into her anus, twisting his stiff fingers round inside her rectum.

'Yes, yes, thank you, Master,' Tara sobbed. 'Now put your cock up me . . . I want it in me, all the way. I'm so empty inside!'

Was this part of an act or was it genuine? He didn't care . . .

Warwick took hold of her hips and jabbed his straining erection into her anus, forcing open her guardian ring of muscle, which slid up the length of his shaft as it plunged into her hot elastic depths which pulsed and contracted about him. He thrust into her so that the stool rocked, slamming against her haunches and driving a harsh grunt from her lungs each time. Then he hunched over her back and clasped her heavy swaying breasts, squeezing and kneading them, feeling their hard points pressing into his palms.

She came before him, bucking and straining at her bindings, her face in the mirror contorted in a strange rictus of pleasure, and then her eyes going wide in unfocused astonishment. He spouted inside her seconds later, pumping himself dry in an effort to fill her depths, then slowly collapsed over her, letting her bear his full weight.

A timeless interval passed. Eventually Tara felt Warwick stir and rise, drawing his now flaccid penis from her rear. A trickle of sperm followed it and began to run down the inside of her thigh.

He took a glass of water from the bedside table and held it so she could drink, which she did automatically. Then he threw a blanket over her as one might a horse after a hard race.

'I'll rest for a bit, then I might come back and use you again,' he told her. 'Perhaps I'll try your front passage next time. I haven't decided . . .'

He walked out, closing the door after him, leaving Tara alone with her throbbing anus, simmering bottom and tumbling, confused thoughts.

Five

Warwick pulled the blanket off Tara, then drew back the curtains to let daylight into the spare room.

Tara groaned as he freed the straps binding her to the stool and feeling began to return to her numbed limbs.

'We said all we needed last night,' Warwick told her. 'While you are ungagged you will not speak a word. If you have to express yourself, you will do so in animal noises, as a dog might. Do you understand?'

Tara nodded meekly, for the moment not wondering about the oddity of his instructions. The memory of his hard cock in her rectum was still strong, the ache where he had pounded deep into her lingered. It had been an act of domination both real and symbolic. Until she recovered her normal independence responses, she told herself, it seemed easier to obey without dissent. Besides, she had nothing more she could think that needed saying. They really had little in common, except for the most intimate and peculiar understanding a master and slave could share . . .

She started, mentally pinching herself. She had actually thought of herself as a slave! Well, for all practical purposes, much as she detested the idea, she was a slave; at least for the next week. Temporary slave, then, she amended.

Warwick cuffed her wrists in front of her. She did not know why but it was a relief, as she doubted she could have bent her arms behind her back at that moment. Her neck felt like a board and her legs were so stiff they hardly supported her as she shuffled unsteadily though to the bathroom. Being flushed out with the hose was both balm and torment: her vagina felt almost as sore as her anus. Warwick had used her a second time the previous night, this time sampling the delights of her lovemouth. He had not needed to use the strap on her again. Being broken once in a night was enough. She had pleaded with him in the most degrading terms to use her, offering up the intimate delights of her pussy to him, and he had accepted. Her shameful words and the sensation of his pelvis grinding against her tender bottom had been quite sufficient to bring her to a second orgasm.

Tara was next made to stand in the bath. A chain and hook had been added to the mounting of the shower head. Warwick secured her wrists to the hook and then gave her a brisk wetting down, soaping over and rinsing off. While she stood there he also had her open her mouth wide while he cleaned her teeth. She felt like a child not yet being trusted to brush properly, yet at the same time receiving such considerate attention was oddly reassuring. It was followed by a vigorous towelling dry.

Warwick then wrapped repair tape round her hands, binding her fingers and thumb to her palm into one paw-like extremity. Then he released her handcuffs and led her down to the kitchen. There Tara saw her named bowls were laid out in a corner on a sheet of newspaper.

'You'll stay on all fours until I tell you otherwise,' he said.

Tara ate resting on her knees and elbows, cradling the bowl between her forearms but not touching the food with her taped hands. Her red-raw bottom stuck up in the air. Warwick sat at the kitchen table reading the Sunday paper and munching toast.

Halfway though her cereal Tara was struck by how weirdly peaceful, even routine, everything felt at that moment. How normal for a bachelor to eat his breakfast and read his paper on a Sunday, with his dog for company. Except she was not a dog, only for the moment playing the part of a dog; a pet, an owned thing. Was that the reason for binding her hands? Was this another of his psychological tricks?

Tara finished, licking her bowl clean, then looked round at Warwick. He appeared to be engrossed in his paper. What should she do now? Lie down in the corner or defy his order and stand up and face the likely consequences? Shame or pain? But direct disobedience was not her chosen course . . . and her bottom still stung. Very well, if he wanted her to act like a dog she would do so. Dogs got bored, didn't they?

Moving in a half-crouch, careful not to actually stand, she padded over to the table on her taped palms and toes. Reaching Warwick she laid her head on his knee and made a dog-like whimper for attention in the back of her throat.

Almost absent-mindedly, Warwick patted her head and ruffled her hair. What sort of game was he playing now? Tara wondered. But having begun to play the role she could not simply abandon it, so she whined again and contrived to look up at him with soulful eyes.

'Do you want to go outside then, girl?' Warwick checked his watch and then looked out of the window. Mist shrouded the garden, though a brightening in the sky suggested it would turn into a fine day. 'I think we can walk over to Number 2, rather than use the wheelbarrow. Would you like that?'

Without thinking of the implications, and pleased to avoid the discomfort of the wheelbarrow, Tara nodded her head and even threw in a couple of eager panting breaths with lolling tongue.

'Then fetch your leash. It's on the chair in the hall.'

Crestfallen, Tara shuffled though to the hall, suddenly feeling ever more closely trapped in her perverse role. The leash was neatly folded on the chair. She knew what was expected of her next. Still, it was better than a holly-caning. Carefully she picked it up in her teeth and took it back to Warwick, sitting back on her haunches, splaying her knees, and offering the leash to him with another whine.

'Good girl.' He patted her head, took the leash and clipped it onto her collar.

There was a carrier bag resting by the back door. Warwick took something from it and held it out to Tara. 'Open wide,' he ordered. She obeyed without thinking and found a red rubber toy bone thrust between her teeth.

As she followed at his heel out through the back door she realised that with the bone in her mouth she was both demeaning and gagging herself at the same time. She could spit it out . . . but she didn't.

The misty air was cool and opalescent as Warwick led Tara up the side path and opened the front gate. Only when they had passed through did Tara suddenly become aware of her exposure. She was crouched naked on a pubic pavement. At least the junction with the main road at bottom of the Close was hidden by mist, though Tara could hear a car going by. It was Sunday morning and papers had already been delivered, so any other callers were unlikely at this hour. But there was just a chance somebody might unexpectedly turn into the Close. And what would they see at that moment? A man leading a naked girl on a leash like a dog.

Tara realised her nipples were erect. She would have liked to believe it was the cool air, but she knew otherwise. The fear of being discovered and her humiliating position were insidiously thrilling.

Warwick sauntered unhurriedly across the road with Tara shuffling nervously along at his heel, crouched down on all fours as low as she could. Only when they had passed through the gate of Number 2 did she breathe a sigh of relief. Once inside the house Warwick held out his hand and Tara carefully dropped the bone into it.

'Good girl,' he said, patting her head once more.

Again she was being subjected to praise and humiliation. She didn't underestimate Warwick now. Had it been a test of obedience or subtle indoctrination? Perhaps it was both.

Over the next ten minutes the other girls arrived. They also had their hands bound with tape.

Tara began to appreciate how well organised and coordinated the residents were. How many messages were being passed between them and how many decisions were being taken about the fate of herself and the others, that they knew nothing about? What had they planned for them next?

As they crouched on all fours in a row as ordered, Tara glanced sidelong at her companions, wondering if their nights had been as eventful as hers. She glimpsed a few telltale blushes on breasts and buttocks, binding marks on wrist and ankles, the awkward way they squatted that hinted at aching groins and above all eyes lowered in shyness or shame. Briefly she met the gaze of Daniela, who smiled uncertainly then turned her attention back to the floor once more. Sian shook her head as though in weary resignation. Tara had no means of learning any more, for though they were all ungagged, they had been told not to speak and none of them seemed inclined to disobey.

Once again Warwick took them through drill in the back garden, assisted by Tom Fanning and Rachel Villiers. They went over the postures they had learned the previous day, then Warwick added some vigorous exercises such as star-jumps, touching toes and push-ups. Those with fuller breasts had no advantage.

'They don't count unless you touch the ground with your chests,' Warwick informed them curtly, walking up and down the line of prostrate and straining girls while swishing his holly cane menacing-ly. 'Just brushing the grass with your teats will not do, Gail. I want to see those big tits of yours properly squashed against it, do you understand?'

Then, unexpectedly, came a game.

Six cards marked with coloured spots were shuffled and dealt out in front of them. The colours matched those of what were revealed to be half a dozen assorted rubber bones that Warwick had brought in his bag. These he tossed into the air all at once so that they scattered about the garden. The girls had to find and retrieve the bone matching their assigned colour, picking it up in their teeth. A small chocolate drop was awarded as a prize for the first girl back with the right bone. The cards were re-dealt and they had to chase bones of different colours.

After a few rounds they had almost forgotten where they were. It was almost as though they were children again, playing about innocently naked. Even Sian and Cassie seemed to lose themselves in the game, laughing when they tumbled over each other as they chased after their respective bones. It took an effort for Tara to recall that they were naked collared slaves, playing the game only because their masters wished it.

They were allowed a brief drink and rest after the bone game, then they were sent back into the living room on all fours. The bed-frames had been stacked in one corner, leaving the floor clear. Gerald Spooner and Narinda and Raj Khan were waiting for them. Spooner sat by Narinda who had a CD player set up on a chair, while Raj was standing by a slightly battered-looking male shop window dummy, posed with his hands on his hips and legs spread. But where a normal dummy had only a suggestive bulge, this one had been fitted with a startlingly lifelike flesh-coloured rubber dildo, complete with false testicles.

'I am here to give you a lesson in how to dance provocatively,' Narinda said, beaming at them as they knelt in a semi-circle facing her, thighs obediently spread in their display postures. 'Of course India is famous for its exotic dancing, with its sensuous rhythms and highly symbolic movements and gestures.' She grinned even wider. 'But as those take years to learn properly, they have nothing to do with what you're going to do today.'

Hazel stifled a nervous laugh.

'Today you will behave like the little sluts you are,' Narinda continued. 'You cannot use your hands so you must use your bodies. You will be dancing for Fred, here . . .' Raj bobbed the dummy forward in a mock bow. 'You will bump and grind yourself shamelessly for his pleasure, just as though he was your master and you were a slave girl trying to please him. You will make love to him with your dance, and you will finish by giving him the best screw ever.'

The girls gaped at the well-endowed dummy doubtfully. Over his shoulder Raj grinned back at them. 'And I'll be watching to make sure you do it properly,' he said cheerfully.

'Now, just to make it a little bit authentic, we have some things for you to wear . . .' Narinda began to pull out an assortment of jingling metallic items from her bag. 'We have bell bracelets and ankle bands and, oh yes, clip-on bells for your nipples and pussy tongues. These, you see, have little rings of carpet tacks taped to them. Very small and sharp, just to make sure you don't get bored.'

There was a moment of dead silence in the room as the girls unhappily contemplated the deceptively innocent-looking ornaments.

'I suggest you remember as much as you can from this lesson,' Narinda said mysteriously, 'because it may come in very useful at the end of your week with us. Anybody I don't think is trying hard enough will get a taste of my cane . . .'

She picked up a long bamboo which had been lying against the wall and swished it through the air. Taped to the last third of its length was a spiral of holly-leaves. Bells dangled from its handle which tinkled merrily as she waved it in front of them.

'Oh, yes,' Narinda added. 'As a further incentive you will be marked on your efforts –' a smiling Gerald Spooner held up a set of numbered cards for them to see '– for style, passion and originality. The girl who scores the least points will be suitably punished. Now up on your feet, spread your legs and put your hands behind your necks.'

Narinda and Raj went along the line tying the strings of bells about their wrists and ankles, then clipping the single bells onto their nipples and one of their labia. 'We don't want anything to get in the way of you pleasing Fred, do we?' Narinda said cheerfully. Tara had no idea where they had obtained the small spring clips from which the bells hung, but they pinched tightly enough to make her eyes water. The labial bell dangled between her spread legs so that for the moment its ring of tacks was not touching her, but the pin-like spikes on her nipple bells were already making themselves felt as they rested against the undercurve of her breasts. How much more uncomfortable would they be when she had to move?

'How you dance is up to you, but the more excited you make yourselves the easier it will be,' Narinda advised them when they were fully decked out. 'Licking Fred's big rubber dick first will also help. Remember where it's got to go in the end and make it part of your performance.' She went over to the CD player. 'Now, who shall go first? Any volunteers?'

Tara hesitated, unsure if it would be an advantage to go first or not. Then to her surprise she saw Daniela nervously hold up a taped hand. 'I'll go first, Mistress . . .'

'Very well. On your feet . . . ready . . . begin.' The sound of drums and sitars issued from the speakers, filling the room with a swirling exotic rhythm.

Daniela was very good. She swayed and twirled sensuously, bells jangling as she circled Fred and Raj, making them the focus of her dance. At first her face contorted as the spikes on her bobbing nipple and labial bells pricked her, but she seemed to ride the pain and turn it into passion. She began rolling her shoulders like a burlesque dancer, setting the nipple bells spinning round like tiny propellers on the bosses of her firm pointed breasts. Hazel, Gail, Rachel

101

Villiers and Tom Fanning spontaneously applauded this feat of mammarial dexterity.

Daniela swayed closer to Fred, wiggling her hips and thrusting out her pubes provocatively. She went down on her hands and knees and began licking the dildo from base to tip, looking up at the impassive face above her as though hoping for some response. Getting none, she tried harder. She took the head of the rubber cock into her mouth, sucking on its plum while slowly shaking her lovely bottom at her audience, her labial bell chiming as it swung from under the cleft peach of her pudenda, its spikes pricking the soft flesh of her inner thighs.

Still Fred seemed to ignore her efforts. Daniela turned about, resting her taped palms on the floor, splaying her legs and thrusting out her mound of Venus so that it made its own damp furry hillock between the taut rises of her buttocks; offering herself totally. Peering over the dummy's shoulder, Raj's eyes bulged in delight at the sight before him.

Weaving her hips, Daniela shuffled and swayed backwards, her nipple-bells hanging free. The tip of the dildo pressed against her cleft. With a moan Daniela pushed with her hips, impaling herself on the dildo. Her eyes went wide as she began to ride the rubber shaft, setting her bells jingling as she worked her hips steadily faster. Raj jerked Fred back and forth to meet her thrusts, plunging the dildo deeper into her. Sweat beaded on her forehead. Suddenly Daniela gasped aloud, her legs straining, and then she sank to the floor. The dildo came out of her with a soft pop and sprung back upright, its shaft gleaming with her juices.

Everybody broke into applause, which she greeted with a blushing smile as she slowly recovered her senses.

Spooner awarded her 25 out of a possible 30.

Having had a chance to think it over, Tara quickly put her hand up. 'May I go next, Mistress?'

Going now meant she would only have to lick Daniela's juices off the dildo. Also she reasoned that her dance would seem fresher if Spooner had seen fewer girls before her, and that meant more points. Apart from the risk of punishment, Tara Ashwell never came last in anything.

Tara knew she was no great dancer, but she could at least show plenty of uninhibited enthusiasm. After all, it wasn't as though she was coupling with a real man. If she pretended it was her own vibrator she was going to shaft herself with for her own pleasure, she could give Fred the dummy a good time. She was actually going to be marked on how well she performed, which was gross but also exciting.

So as the music played she bumped and ground her heart out, proudly showing off her body. She rubbed her taped hands through her crotch, glorying in her brazenness, until they came away wet. She cupped and jiggled her breasts to set her bells bouncing wildly, heedless of the stinging pricks they delivered in return. Steeling herself she moved right up close to Fred, ignoring Raj Khan's hungry eyes, and bent to lick the dildo, splaying her legs so the audience all got a good view up her backside. As she did so she caught the lingering scent of Daniela's juices; musky, raw and exciting. Don't pull back, use it, she told herself. Lovingly she licked the shaft, marvelling at her own responses, savouring its flavour, slobbering over it until it was lubricated afresh.

Then she twisted round to face her audience, arching her back to thrust out her breasts while pushing her hips back against the wet rubber penis. Reaching behind her she hooked her taped hands through the dummy's crooked arms and pulled herself hard back onto the dildo. She grunted as it filled her, rotating her hips, grinding into her synthetic lover. Raj Khan was rocking Fred to and fro by the shoulders, enjoying driving the dildo into her, but she didn't care. She was shaking her shoulders and tossing her breasts about wildly, drawing rings of tiny smarting pinpoints about her nipples as the spiked bells pricked her. Her loins were full to the brim with liquid sex . . .

She orgasmed lustily and sank to the floor, panting for breath, to the sound of applause. Later she might cringe at the thought of what she had done before so many eyes, but at that moment it simply felt like her just reward.

Spooner gave her 23 points.

Gail went next, blushing and hesitant, but looking curiously determined. She didn't try any fancy steps but undulated gracefully in time with the music, the flexing of her supple waist contrasting with the sway of her full hips. The spikes on her jingling nipple-bells were making their mark on her tautly-domed breasts, but she bore it nobly. As though being drawn helplessly forward to her fate, the look on her sweetly suffering face was captivating.

Going down on her knees before Fred she looked up at the dummy as though he really were her master. She licked its dildo, then cupping her breasts as though offering up her most precious gift, she rubbed the length of it along the deep fleshy valley between them. It was intensely sensuous. As she rose to take the dildo inside her she kissed Fred's chest. With a little groan she stood on tiptoe, peeling back her labia with her taped hands and sliding the fake penis up into the pink-rimmed hole they framed between them.

With a wondering glassy look in her eyes, as though she could not quite believe what she was doing, Gail embraced the dummy and deliberately pressed her boobs into its chest, digging the spiked bells into her own flesh. They heard her whimper then sigh. She began to undulate her hips in time with the music while brushing her breasts from side to side across Fred's torso, using pain and pleasure to work herself into a state of helpless ecstasy.

Tara was impressed, never having suspected the girl had it in her. Daniela and Hazel's jaws were hanging open in horrified yet admiring fascination. Cassie looked disgusted while Sian was tight-lipped and intense.

Gail came with a series of yelps and gasps, then slumped onto her back to a round of applause, streaks of sweat smeared across her reddened and heaving breasts. Narinda wiped them clean with a damp tissue, checked she had in fact suffered no more than pinpricks, and helped her back to her place.

Gail was awarded 27 points. Tara bit her lip. At the moment she was still last.

Sian went next, a determined expression on her face. Tara recalled that Sian had been quite serious about ballet until a few years ago, and she used everything she had learned in her routine.

The muscles stood out on her slender body as she sprang and twirled gracefully on her toes, nipple-bells swinging freely from the jiggling apples of her breasts. She did a splits before Fred the dummy, exposing her cleft bush and giving her labial bell a teasing flick. Sian's dance ended with her copulating elegantly while standing on one leg with the other crooked round Fred's waist, her small round buttocks clenching as she jerked her hips.

Her score of 24 brought a brief but genuine smile to her flushed face, even as it made Tara frown.

Hazel put her hand up before a hesitant Cassie. She was not a very rhythmic dancer, but she made up for it by a display of·sheer wanton abandon, writhing about the floor heedless of the pricks from her bells. She finished by mounting Fred and wrapping both legs round his waist, her pale chubby bottom trembling as she gleefully rode his rubber dildo. Raj Khan had to hold the dummy steady to prevent it falling over.

She got 26 points.

Now only Cassie was left. As she rose she looked both nervous and disdainful. She danced half-heartedly, wincing as the bells pricked her, and needed a flick from Narinda's cane to impale herself on Fred's now glistening and well lubricated rubber phallus. Even as Tara's hopes rose she felt Cassie was being stupid. She must have realised by now that it was easier to accept their situation and make the best of it, or else refuse to perform and take the consequences. But she was letting her pride get in the way of common sense. Tara thought she did eventually have a genuine orgasm, after much effort, but her performance was too grudging to be very entertaining.

Cassie got just 19 points. Tara breathed a sigh of relief.

'You should have tried harder,' Narinda told Cassie.

Fanning and Warwick bent Cassie over double and backed her onto the dummy's dildo. Rachel prised apart Cassie's unwilling buttocks to expose her anus and they forced the rubber shaft into her tight rear passage, bringing forth a dismayed groan. Then they pulled her arms behind the dummy's back and tied her wrists together so she could not pull herself free. Spreading her legs they tied her ankles to the outsides of the dummy's ankles. A final length of rope was looped about her neck and the ends drawn over the dummy's back and tied to her wrists, pulling her head back so that it rested on Fred's shoulder and making it look as though she was locked in some strange embrace with her plastic lover. Her taut breasts rose and fell tremulously while the pressure of the sodomising phallus forced her hips blatantly forward. The anger in her eyes was beginning to turn to alarm.

Narinda swished her long holly cane through the air in front of Cassie. 'Now, I'm going to give you six strokes,' she said. 'And after each you will say loudly: "I must try harder to please you." If you don't it won't count and I'll do it again.'

She drew back her arm and slashed the cane across Cassie's midriff, making her yelp and leaving a ragged line of red pinpricks in her skin. Narinda looked questioningly at Cassie who gasped wretchedly: 'I – must try harder to please you . . .'

By the sixth stroke Cassie's breasts, stomach and thighs were crisscrossed by swathes of reddened pinpricked flesh and she was sobbing 'I must try harder to please you . . . I must try harder . . .' over and over again.

Their captors left Cassie impaled and bound while they laid out the girls' food bowls in a semi-circle about her. While they had a proper meal Cassie was fed on bread and water. They all sneaked curious glances up at her as they ate, conscious that she had been left there as both a punishment and a warning.

That afternoon they were harnessed in pairs to a garden roller and made to pull it up and down Gerald Spooner's lawn. It was not a contest, merely hard sweaty work. When they were done Warwick turned the garden hose on them and they squealed like children as its cold spray washed over them. By the time they were returned to their stock-beds to rest before the coming night's exertions, they were so tired that the imprisoning frames and meagre bedding almost seemed comfortable.

The residents locked the door behind them and for the first time that day the girls were free to talk together. For a minute there was an awkward silence, then Hazel asked Daniela:

'Where did you learn to dance like that? You looked really hot.'

'I did study dance for a few years,' Daniela admitted. 'Just for fun we did some belly dancing.'

'Is that where you learned to spin your tassels like old-fashioned strippers?' Gail wondered.

Daniela giggled. 'Me and a few other girls in my class had a go at that secretly. I never guessed I'd ever do it for real. Did I really look sexy?'

'I bet you even had old Spooner creaming his pants,' Hazel said.

'Well, I thought I just had to forget being embarrassed and do my best. It was – fun, in a weird sort of way. Oh . . . does that sound sick?'

Hazel sniggered. 'Like this whole thing is not sick already?'

'Well, what about you?' Gail said. 'You went at it like a sex-starved bunny!'

'I was only doing what Daniela did,' Hazel said defensively. 'I thought: shit, why not go all the way? I've nothing left to hide. They want a show, I'll give 'em a show. Anyway, what about what you did to your tits with those nipple-bells? That really was pervy! Didn't it hurt?'

'I didn't think about it really,' Gail replied, sounding curiously uncertain. 'Narinda said the more excited we got the better, and it was true in an odd way. I thought if I was a real slave trying hard to please her master, I'd show I was ready to suffer for him. Everybody looks at my boobs so I used them. It hurt at first, but once I got that rubber cock inside me it seemed to make the pleasure stronger.'

'Did you both really come?' Daniela asked hesitantly. 'I wondered if it was only me.'

'Of course I did,' Hazel said. 'That's what made it fun.'

'I did too,' Gail admitted. 'In the end I couldn't help it. I didn't have to pretend.'

Listening to their chatter Tara was both amazed and disconcerted by the adaptability of human nature. What had happened to the three trembling, terrified figures she had seen bent over the Cheyner Close sign and caned not two days ago? Did last night's one-to-one sessions with the residents have anything to do with it? For that matter, had she been changed by her experience at Warwick's hands?

'Did you come too, Sian?' Daniela asked. 'You danced so beautifully and you looked like you were enjoying yourself.'

'It was all just an act, right?' Sian said quickly.

'But it was a great dance,' Gail added.

'All right, so I put on a good show,' Sian replied, sounding embarrassed.

'You did come,' Hazel insisted. 'I saw your face.'

'All right, so I came,' Sian snapped. 'That was the idea, wasn't it? That was how we we're meant to get through this. Anything wrong with that?'

'Nothing,' Daniela said gently. 'We just wanted to know if you enjoyed yourself.' She added quickly: 'What I mean is, getting yourself worked up while you were dancing and then hearing that applause when you finished, not everything else.'

Sian sighed. 'I suppose, just for a few seconds, that did feel good,' she admitted grudgingly.

Tara realised none of them felt they needed to compliment her performance. Coming second to last was nothing special, of course, but it showed how her power over them had melted away.

'Isn't anybody going to say anything to me?' Cassie said suddenly. 'Are you going to ask me if I enjoyed screwing up my dance and getting caned and buggered by a fucking window dummy?'

There was an awkward silence. After a moment Sian said: 'Sorry, Cassie. I thought you didn't want to talk about it.'

'Well, just so you all know, it hurt,' Cassie said miserably. 'Gail'd probably get off on having her tits beaten with holly while she had a rubber dildo stuck up her backside, but I didn't.'

'I think,' Gail said slowly, 'that if they did that to me, I would try to get as much pleasure out of it as I could. Maybe I'd beg one of them to use my front passage at the same time.'

'You'd beg for that?' Cassie said, aghast.

'Why not? It might stop them from doing something worse. And maybe, with my bottom plugged, it would feel special.'

'You're sick, all of you!' Cassie exclaimed.

Tara could not stay silent any longer. 'Cassie, stop feeling so bloody sorry for yourself! We're all in the same situation. Gail's right. We get whatever pleasure we can in any way we can. If you'd worked at enjoying your dance more, it would've been me on that dummy instead of you.'

There came a long sigh from Cassie, then she said in a small voice: 'You're right. I will try harder.' Then she added: 'But I still hate you, Tara.'

Cassie's resolve was soon tested. According to Warwick's rota Hilary Beck and Rachel Villiers had the use of her that night. Tara saw the look in Cassie's eyes and her teeth clamped tight on her ball-gag as the two women tied the blindfold round her head.

When the blindfold was next removed, Cassie found herself looking up into the smiling faces of Rachel and Hilary. She was bound spreadeagled to the gleaming brass frame of a double bed by leather cuffs and chains. The deep soft purple sheets and pillow under her carried a lingering trace of perfume, mingled with the more intimate scent of female bodies.

'She doesn't look happy,' Hilary observed.

'Maybe because she knows she's about to get ravished by two filthy dykes,' Rachel said. 'That's what you called us in one of those anonymous letters you sent to half of Styenfold.'

'I think I was a "bull-dyke",' Hilary added. 'No young girl was safe when I was around . . .' her face darkened. 'What do you think that felt like? Why do you hate us so much?'

Cassie was moaning and chewing on her gag.

'You want to say something?' Hilary pulled the rubber ball from Cassie's mouth.

'It was all Tara's doing,' Cassie babbled desperately. 'She said both of you deserved it and we believed her – ahh!'

Rachel had slashed her holly cane across the underside of Cassie's firm upstanding breasts. 'You will speak to us respectfully,' she warned. 'You've never shown us any in the past but while you're in our house you'll bloody-well behave properly, understand?'

Cassie spluttered: 'Yes, Mistress . . . sorry, Mistress.'

'So, Tara said we were wicked lesbians and you didn't think to disagree with her at all?' Hilary

111

continued. 'We complained to the police because of Tara and her boyfriend driving round the Close like nutters in the middle of the night. So did the rest of the residents. Anybody would have done that.' She tapped her chest. 'What harm did we do you personally? Or was that just an excuse? Be honest!'

Cassie licked her lips, then said hesitantly: 'I don't like – your type, Mistress.'

'And what other "types" don't you like besides us lezzy queers? What about the Khans? Or Jews or blacks?'

Shocked at the insinuation Cassie exclaimed: 'I'm not racist, Mistress –'

'Just homophobic.'

'I feel – uncomfortable – near people like you, Mistress.' It was the best way she could express her feeling. Was that why it had been so easy to join in Tara's revenge in the Close?

Rachel smiled mischievously. 'You know what they say. People who are strongly anti-gay are often secretly gay themselves.' She beamed at Hilary. 'Shall we give it a test?'

'Let's.'

Smiling at Cassie, they each began a mocking striptease, blowing her kisses and licking their lips suggestively as they shed their garments. Soon they stood naked, one on each side of the bed, taunting her with their bare bodies. It was impossible not to look at them.

Hilary must have been in her early thirties. Her skin was clear and tinted with a light golden tan. A mass of fluffy blonde hair framed a firm-jawed face set with serious brown eyes and, in Cassie's opinion, a slightly overlarge nose. Her hips were a little fleshy but compensated for by heavy double-'D' cup breasts. A fluffy triangle of dyed-blonde pubic hair sprouted from between her thighs. As Cassie's gaze fell upon her pubes Hilary ran a finger sensuously through her slit, then turned round and wiggled her bottom suggestively at Cassie. Her buttocks were deeply cleft, smooth and full-cheeked.

Rachel was slimmer, perhaps a year or two younger than her lover, and, Cassie had to concede, very pretty. Curling brunette hair tumbled over her shoulders, matching the thick bush between her thighs. Her face was well proportioned and friendly, her blue eyes set under neat brows. Mature but still shapely breasts capped by distinct brown nipples rose from her slender chest, accentuated by a narrow waist, smoothly curving but not overfull hips and shapely legs. Like Hilary she gave Cassie a twirl. Her bottom was neatly rounded and, like the rest of her, warmly tanned.

'So, are we as hideous as you expected?'

Cassie swallowed hard, fearing what was to come. 'No, Mistress . . . but I still don't want to – to make love . . .' She felt her resolve draining away with her pride. By just standing there naked before her they were breaking her down. 'Please don't make me do this,' she begged.

'But we want to enjoy ourselves while making you suffer,' Hilary said, sounding sweetly reasonable. 'And to predator-dykes like us you look very tasty . . .'

Cassie tugged at her bonds, trying to squeeze her thighs together.

'Are her nipples perking up just a little bit?' Rachel wondered aloud. 'I think she's really excited by the thought of us having her but doesn't want to admit it.'

'Well, let's give her the same choice she and her friends have given us all these months: none at all!'

They flopped down onto the bed on either side of Cassie and put their arms about her. She felt their breasts pressing against her, their legs crooked negligently over her outstretched limbs. The warm scent of their bodies invaded her nostrils as their hands ran freely over her body, stroking and caressing. They knew just where to touch her ...

Cassie moaned wretchedly, unable to control her responses.

'Her nips are like rubber now,' Hilary said, pinching the bulb of blood-filled flesh. 'And she has such firm tits ...' She bent her head and sucked and nibbled on Cassie's right teat while Rachel did the same to the left. After a minute they lifted their flushed faces and grinned at each other.

'She's a lovely little toy,' said Rachel, and they leaned across Cassie's bound body and kissed each other passionately.

Then they fell hungrily upon Cassie, each grasping a handful of her hair, turning her head to one side and then the other so they could take turns to kiss her fiercely, raping her mouth with their tongues. Meanwhile their free hands were busy playing with her nether mouth, now a gaping pink gash of flesh surrounded by a matted tangle of damp curls. Both women were slipping their fingers into the mouth of her vagina while their thumbs rolled the hard bud of her clitoris between them. Cassie groaned as she felt herself yielding to their probing, their stiff fingers going deeper as her passage expanded with a primitive growing need she could not quell.

A sudden amazing sensation of being plugged fuller than she ever had before made Cassie cry out loud. Rachel's slim hand had slid into her vagina up to the wrist, turning and flexing inside her tight-stretched sheath while Hilary continued to torment her clitoris from without. It was frightening and amazing and gross and wonderful. Her muscles went into orgasmic spasm clenching about the fist inside her, then she slumped, half insensible, trembling and helpless in their embrace.

For an unknown time they petted and stroked her, telling her she had been a good girl, while Rachel's hand remained buried inside her. Part of her detested what they had made her do even as the rest perversely basked in their praise.

When Cassie had recovered her senses, Hilary said: 'Now it's your turn to pleasure us. Rachel tells me you didn't try hard enough in Narinda's dance class and what it got you.' she stroked a trail of pinpricks that ran across Cassie's now sweat-sheened breasts. 'It's a pity to spoil such smooth golden skin, but we'll do it if you need the encouragement. Say twenty strokes of the cane to start with.'

'No, please,' Cassie gasped, thrilling at her own grovelling response. 'I'll try harder, Mistress. I'll do anything you want!'

Hilary smiled and kissed her. 'That's what we want to hear. And we'll make it as easy as we can for you. Do you like honey?'

Cassie blinked in surprise. 'Er, yes, Mistress.'

'Good. Then maybe you'll enjoy yourself . . .'

Rachel slid her hand out of Cassie's vagina. It came free with a sucking sensation that made Cassie squirm and shiver. Her empty passage seemed to gape obscenely wide for long moments before its natural elasticity began to close up.

The women uncuffed her ankles only to re-fasten them to a wooden rod with eyebolts screwed into its ends which held them nearly as far apart as before. They then freed her arms from the bedhead and cuffed them behind her back. Between them they dragged Cassie round until she knelt facing the head of the bed.

Hilary laid herself down in the position Cassie had occupied, bending and spreading her legs so that the lips of her full plump pudenda opened wide beneath its blonde pubic thatch. She took an open jar of clear honey from the bedside table, dipped in a finger and, smiling broadly at Cassie, began to work the heavy golden fluid into her cleft.

'You'll lap it all up like a good little pet until I come,' she told Cassie. 'Then you'll do the same for Rachel.'

Cassie gulped.

'Your pussy's had enough use for one night,' Rachel said, positioning herself behind Cassie, 'but you should be able to take this up your bum . . .' She held out a shocking pink translucent double-headed dildo nearly as long as Cassie's forearm. It glistened with oil and was made of a pliant plastic so soft that it bobbed and swayed in Rachel's grasp almost as though it was alive. 'This is Sid the Snake,' Rachel explained. 'We've had a lot of fun with him. You'll be amazed how far he can go. Now bend forward like a good girl . . .'

Cassie laid her head between Hilary's fleshy thighs, her nose almost bushing her pubic hair. She smelt honey mingling with the woman's own arousal, she could see the swelling bud of her clitoris and the crinkled lips of the mouth of her vaginal tunnel. Cassie felt the head of the dildo forced into her anus and then slide into her rectum with amazing ease, sensuous and slippery . . . and in, and in . . . Oh God! It was filling her her rear as Rachel's hand had filled her front passage earlier. She was being used like a glove puppet by the two women for whatever they cared to stuff up her.

116

And like a puppet she could only obey the orders of her controllers.

Rachel sighed happily as she fed the other half of Sid into her vagina until her pubic bush pressed against Cassie's bottom cleft and they were joined by the length of phallic plastic. Then she bent forward and embraced Cassie from behind, reaching round to cup and squeeze her breasts. 'Now, lick out that lovely honeypot . . .'

Trapped between her two mistresses, Cassie meekly buried her face in the glistening cleft of flesh before her and lapped and sucked its honeydew as though she was a hummingbird feeding from a rare flower blossom. Hilary stroked her hair while Rachel began to rock gently back and forth, grinding Cassie's face deeper into Hilary's vulva while she enjoyed Sid's slippery attentions.

The horrible thing was that Cassie could feel a tingling warmth growing in her own loins. She was becoming aroused by lesbian sex. They were forcing her to enjoy her own degradation!

The last fragile remnants of her pride and certainty were finally shattered when Rachel whispered in her ear: 'For the rest of your life, every time you eat honey, you're going to think of this moment and what we did to you.'

And she knew it was true.

Six

It was Monday morning.

To Tara, and, she suspected, the other girls, it felt as though a month had passed since Friday night instead of only a weekend. They had been subjected to so many intense emotions and bizarre experiences compressed into such a short space of time that, by comparison, their normal lives seemed like a pallid memory. And there were still five days of their ordeal remaining.

They had been brought to Number 2 early as some of the residents had to go to work. Tara wondered how they could possibly endure a typical day in some little grey office, or wherever it was they scraped a living, knowing they had six slavegirls at their mercy back home. Would any other race but the British do such a thing? It almost felt like an insult.

But apparently necessity and routine won out over carnal desire and revenge, at least between nine and five on weekdays. Tom Fanning, Stan Jessop and Raj Khan left to catch the train up to town, while Roberta Pemberton went to work in a shop in Styenfold. Meanwhile Rachel Villiers and Hilary Beck set off for their jobs at a local nursery garden.

This left the girls in the care of Warwick, Narinda Khan and Louisa Jessop. Jim Curry was apparently busy in his workshop and would be with them as soon as he finished his latest creation. When this last item of news was relayed to them they were all struck by stomach-churning apprehension, yet also a certain dark curiosity.

After they had eaten breakfast, the tape bound about their hands was removed and remnants of adhesive cleaned off with white spirit. They had gone 24 hours without being able to use their fingers and these felt stiff and strange when they tried to flex them. It had been a demonstration of their helplessness and the residents' power over them. The use of their hands could be denied to them at any time, reducing them once again to the level of helpless pets.

After the usual exercises in the garden under Major Warwick's supervision, their arms were once more cuffed behind them. Then they were marched back into the living room where they found a new humiliation had been prepared.

Six kitchen or footstools of different types and sizes had been arranged in a circle in the middle of the room. On each rested a solid square of blockboard. To these were variously taped and screwed vertically the dildo that had adorned 'Fred' the previous day, a polished metal vibrator, a bottle brush, an oiled dishmop, a cucumber and a small empty plastic spring water bottle.

The girls were positioned in the gaps between the stools. Lengths of light chain were clipped to their collar rings and taken forward over the shoulder of the girl ahead and clipped to her ring in turn, linking them in a closed circle with a little slack between each. Then short lengths of clothesline were threaded through the chains midway along each length. The ends of the clothesline were taped to more of the little spring clamps that had fastened the spiked bells to their teats the day before. These were now clipped to them in the same way, so that if the chains were pulled tight, their nipples would be jerked painfully upward.

When they were arranged to their captors' satisfaction, Louisa Jessop produced a video camera and began walking round shooting them from different angles.

'This is to show Stan and the others when they come back from work,' she explained with a smile.

Tara felt a sense of numb resignation. The images would join the residents' growing archive of similar material recording their degradation. She would have to live with the shameful knowledge of its existence for the rest of her life. Then she caught sight of Hazel actually smiling foolishly into the camera. Of course it might not feel that way for some, she conceded.

Narinda had taken up position by a small side table on which rested a metronome. 'You will move in time to the beat,' she told them. 'Starting from a standing position, you will squat on the first beat and rise on the second. You will repeat this three times. On the seventh beat you will all step forward to the next object and repeat the sequence. The only pause will be when you come. You will continue round until you have all done so or the batteries on the vibrator run down.' On cue Louisa Jessop switched on the vibrator, which began to hum softly, then she resumed filming. 'Position yourselves . . . and begin.'

The arm of the metronome ticked over. Tara squatted down over the cucumber, feeling her lips part as the vegetable drove up deep into her vagina, accompanied by a soft chorus of gasps and moans as the others impaled themselves in time with her. Another tick and she rose. She skewered herself twice more on the cucumber, then moved forward in time

121

with the rest to stand with legs splayed over the bottle brush which Sian had just vacated.

At first there were a few yelps from girls who did not keep in step with the others and got their nipples jerked, but surprisingly soon they were all moving in time with the steady tick-tock of the metronome. They had not even needed the threat of a holly cane to start them off, Tara realised. They had simply done what they were told and now, like living automatons, they were endlessly circling round until turned off.

Each phallic substitute produced a distinctly different sensation as Tara took it inside her. The cucumber was cool and not unpleasant, the bristles of the bottle brush made her shiver, the vibrator deeply stimulating, the oiled dishmop soft but odd and the dildo virtually an old friend. The hardest to take, at least at first, was the small plastic bottle. It had a greater girth than any of the other devices, with chunky moulded contours for grip and a nobbled surface. It had no cap, which puzzled Tara at first until she realised it was slowly filling with trickles of translucent fluid. It was milking their juices as they squatted and strained over it, their lovemouths stretching about its unnatural form.

Yes, they were inexorably getting aroused, and an intimate spicy scent was filling the air of the closed room. Their vaginas were clinging more tightly to the dildo, vibrator and cucumber as they got slicker with their exudations. Their insides were thoroughly coated with each others' outpourings by now, surely the most intimate of sharing. The knowledge made Tara squirm, yet her erect nipples were straining against their imprisoning clips. How could such a repetitious mechanical process be so arousing?

At least she was not alone. Sweat was beading on the other girls' bodies, their breathing was getting faster and the squatting thrusts they made to impale themselves more desperate.

Daniela, who was riding the vibrator, suddenly cried out aloud and hunched over the buzzing silver spike of metal, her hips jerking and hard-tipped breasts jiggling as the spasms of orgasm overcame her, her animal motions startling by contrast with the fixed rhythm they had been obeying. The rest of them came to a painful halt as their linking chains jerked on their nipple clips. Louisa Jessop moved in closer with her camera to record Daniela's flushed features and the trickles oozing from her pudendal lips as they sucked on the metal shaft on which she rode.

A terrible need was gripping them all and it was hard to hold still on whatever item they were impaled on until Daniela recovered sufficiently to set off once more. They had only just completed another circuit when Gail came. As though determined not to be last this time, Cassie followed moments after. Tara surrendered to nature and spent herself over the uncomfortable contours of the plastic bottle, even as Hazel did the same on the dildo. Sian completed the set by bringing herself off on the cucumber while they were still recovering. Needless to say, her orgasmic writhings were minutely recorded by the hungry camera lens to join those of all the rest.

They were allowed to rest in the garden before lunch, but with their gags in place. They could only stare mutely at each other and their matted pubic hair and the drying streaks of discharge that smeared their thighs and wonder what they were becoming. Hazel, Gail and Daniela looked quite relaxed in the bonds, Tara thought, as though content with what they had done. She could almost believe there were smiles hidden behind their gags.

After lunch Gerald Spooner came round to Number 2 in his wheelchair. Two lengths of rope were tied to the chair frame just above the front wheels. The ropes had then been tied round the ends of three wooden rods, rather like the rungs of a rope ladder. There was space between each rod for two girls to kneel side by side. The rods were pushed into their mouths and held in place by strips of tape bound around the backs of their heads. By this means they were both gagged and simply but effectively harnessed to the wheelchair in three tandem pairs.

Spooner had the long holly cane Narinda had used on them the previous day, and this he flicked across their backs and buttocks to control them. They made several circuits of the lawn, scrabbling along on their hands and knees as they drew him after them. Neck straining and drool dribbling round the rod clamped between her teeth, Tara was acutely aware of the spectacle they were giving Spooner as they shuffled along. He could look right up their backsides and see the split peaches of their sexes peek-a-booing between their rolling thighs. Well, he was an old man, she conceded. Looking was all he could do now. He couldn't have many more thrills as good as this to come. If he enjoyed it then . . .

God! Was she beginning to feel sorry for him?

Then Spooner swished his holly cane across her bottom and the pain put everything back into context. It didn't matter who was doing what to her, she would simply concentrate on getting her own perverse pleasure out of being used like a sledge dog. A sledge bitch, she corrected herself.

They were locked into their bed frames to rest earlier than usual, as they were to be alert for when the workers returned. Tara gathered they would then feature in some activity at Gerald Spooner's house for the whole Close to enjoy before being separated for the night. As soon as they were alone Hazel, Gail and Daniela once again began talking excitedly about their experiences of the previous night, which they had been unable to share until now. Unexpectedly Cassie cut through their chatter.

'Isn't anybody wondering how I got on with Hilary and Rachel?' she asked brightly.

'How was it?' Hazel asked tentatively.

'They finger-fucked and fisted me, then I had to lick their cunts out while they took turns buggering me with an extra-long dildo,' Cassie said lightly. 'But I just pretended it was all a crazy sex-dream and I even came a couple of times. No problem.'

To Tara's ears that last remark sounded forced. But Gail seemed to take it at face value.

'I'm glad you enjoyed it,' she said sincerely. 'I'm sure that's the best way to get through this.'

'They used that snakey-dildo on me on Saturday night,' Daniela admitted. 'I was frightened at first, with it going in so far I mean, but after a bit it –'

'So don't you worry when it's your turn with them, Sian,' Cassie continued loudly, silencing Daniela. 'Just let them play with you and come when you can.' She gave an evil chuckle. 'But I told them it was Tara who wrote all those anonymous letters about them, so I think they're going to give her a real hard time when they get their hands on her!'

After tea they were readied to be taken across to Number 9. Their gags were reinserted, their hands were cuffed behind them and their collars linked by chains. In a coffle they were marched out into the side alley of Number 2, with Tom Fanning leading them and Louisa Jessop bringing up the rear, ready if necessary to urge them on with her holy cane.

Because of the time of day and being in a single group they could do without barrows or wheelie-bins. Warwick went to the end of the Close and signalled the main road was clear. Tara felt a renewed thrill of exposure as they were marched briskly across to Number 9 in the still-bright sunlight. Narinda Khan evidently thought the scene was special as well. She was standing in the road and took a picture of them as they crossed, framing their column of naked and chained bodies against the backdrop of mundane houses: proof they really were the captives of Cheyner Close.

It was almost a relief to have the garden gate of Number 9 close behind them and be back in its comfortable enclosure. But the sensation was short-lived. As Tara took in the devices laid out on Gerald Spooner's now well rolled lawn and the grinning faces of the other residents, she once again revised upwards their capacity for perverse invention.

The golf ball plopped into Tara's gaping vagina.

'Hole in one!' Stan Jessop cried cheerfully.

Those residents not in the process of swinging golf clubs themselves at that moment applauded his efforts. Tara clenched her inner muscles and with an effort popped the ball out of her so that it rolled back onto the grass.

It was clock golf with a difference.

They had staked out the girls in a neat ring on the lawn. Tara, like Hazel opposite her, was lying spread-eagled flat on her back with her open legs facing the centre of the ring. A shallow V-shaped wooden ramp, painted green, was wedged between her thighs, its apex pressed against the undercurve of the pouch of her vulva. Projecting horizontally from the narrow lip of the wedge were two lengths of wooden dowel. These had been forced into the mouth of her vaginal passage so as to hold it stretched wide in a mocking rictus of a smile. This grimace had been turned into an 'O' of surprise by a hook curling round the upper rim of her passage and held under tension by a chain running up between her sex lips to a belt buckled about her waist. It left her lovemouth wide open to the air, to inquisitive flies, to anybody who cared to look up into her secret depths ... and of course to golf balls.

It was a new low (or did she mean high?) on the scale of degradation to which they had so far been subjected. So why did her hard clitoris bulge against the hook chain as it cut through her cleft, and her juices seep down the cleft of her buttocks? Could she get aroused no matter what they did to her?

On her left, Sian was staked out in a different fashion.

Her slender body was doubled over so that her knees almost touched her shoulders, while her arms were folded and cuffed under her bent back. Ropes crossing between two stakes on either side of her neck ensured she held her head steady, while her ankles were tied to two more widely spaced stakes, which helped to brace her in position so she could not squirm about. This left her smooth tight buttocks and groin exposed to the sky. A large translucent plastic funnel had been plugged into her vagina, held in place by garden wire running from holes drilled through its rim to encircle her doubled-back thighs. An accurate chip shot would land a ball into the funnel where it would bounce around until it finally dropped into her warm moist living cup. A simple mask made of aluminium mesh of the kind used in car bodywork repairs protected her face from balls that overshot their intended target.

Sian flinched each time a ball was directed at her and an occasional throaty whine escaped her gag. But the tangle of dark hair ringing the neck of the implanted funnel glistened wetly and her small nipples rose up in hard points. Tara wished she could see her face properly to judge how well she was coping with this latest humiliation.

It was easier to tell with Daniela, who was positioned on Tara's right. She was bent over on her spread knees so that her chest rested on the ground, and her face was turned towards Tara. Her arms were drawn out straight back down between her knees and tied to the middle pair of a row of four stakes, the outer ones of which secured her ankles. Another large plastic funnel had been slipped between the flawless tan hemispheres of her buttocks and into her anus, forcing it wide enough for a golf ball to enter her. The funnel projected bizarrely from her rear like a strange sort of tail, held at the desired angle by a wire running back down from its rim to her collar.

Tara could see Daniela's face was alive with anticipation, flinching as a ball struck her bottom or thighs, but seeming as though she was willing the player to succeed; to feel a ball roll into her open rectum. It was a tricky shot and most missed altogether or rebounded from the sides of the funnel. But as the players got their eye in a few began to land in the dark pit between her haunches. And when they did Daniela gave a little moan and briefly closed her eyes, though not, Tara thought, in shame.

After all the residents had played a round, Major Warwick said: 'Right, let's swap them over and give them a taste of the other positions . . .'

Half an hour later Tara was squatting down straining to expel the last golf ball from her rectum. They had all been hosed out and greased before the game had started, so the balls came out quite cleanly. I'm being made to shit golf balls, she thought dizzily. Who'd have thought it?

With a disturbingly exciting sensation the last ball finally popped out into the bowl placed under her for the purpose, which was then removed. With a leash clipped to her collar, Tara was led over to where the other girls knelt in a line, waiting for Warwick to announce who would have the use of them that night.

Gail was assigned to Jim Curry, while Hazel, eyes wide with nervous anticipation, was given to Tom Fanning. Then Warwick said: 'And Tara Ashwell goes with Hilary and Roberta . . .'

As the women took hold of Tara's leash, she saw Cassie's face light up with malicious delight. Nerving herself to show no apprehension, Tara simply smiled back at Cassie, then stood proudly and allowed herself to be led away.

Gail dangled from a beam in Jim Curry's workshop.

A pulley chain was hooked through a heavy ringbolt set in the middle of a horizontal tubular metal bar. Gail's ankles were enclosed in broad leather cuffs and clipped to the ends of the bar, pulling her legs out and up into a broad V. Her arms were drawn straight up from her shoulders and similarly cuffed to the bar on either side of its central mount. This posture left her groin totally exposed. The centre of gravity of her body caused her hips to swing forward slightly, as though offering the open maw of her lovemouth to his gaze. Her anus was a little crinkled starburst ring below the swell of her pubes.

A touch on the bar made Gail turn slowly, allowing him to examine every detail of her lovely form. He drank in her girlishly innocent face, her wide round eyes nervously meeting his gaze and her wonderfully ripe body. A few days ago he would never have imagined he could have possessed such a beautiful creature, and yet now she was his alone for the night to do with virtually as he wished. He picked up his camera and snapped away, wanting to record the moment forever. He felt his manhood stirring in anticipation. Steady, he told himself. No need to rush.

Gail was making plaintive noises from behind her gag while her eyes pleaded for attention.

'You want to say something?' he asked.

Gail nodded.

'You know it's no good begging for mercy or anything, because you aren't going to get it. You deserve all that's coming to you, along with the rest of your gang.'

Gail was still nodding. Intrigued, Jim pulled the rubber ball from her mouth.

'I know I deserve to be punished, Master,' she said meekly, her voice low and tremulous. 'I just wanted you to know I'm so sorry for everything I did. I never imagined how it was hurting you. It all seemed like a big game at the time . . .' She trailed off, chewing her lip mournfully. 'Anyway, that's all I wanted to say.' And she opened her mouth again ready for the gag to be reinserted.

Jim's eyes narrowed. She seemed too good to be true. 'Do you think this'll make me go easier on you?'

Her round eyes appeared completely guileless. 'No, Master.' She took a deep breath. 'You do whatever you want to me. That was the agreement. And I should be punished for being so nasty to you. As long as my parents never find out.'

She seemed utterly candid, but could it be an act? He took her melon-breasts in his hands, feeling their warmth and weight and resilience, rolling and squeezing them together. Her hardening nipples pressed into his palms. She trembled and her eyelids fluttered.

'Do you like that?' he asked.

She gulped. 'Yes, Master.'

'You've got lovely big tits.'

A shy fleeting smile crossed Gail's lips. 'Thank you, Master. Boys always want to play with them.'

'But what if I did more than play with them?' He caught hold of the thick cones of her nipples and gave them a warning tweak.

Gail gave a little shiver and licked her lips. 'I understand if you want to – to torture them. It's probably a good way to punish me because they're quite sensitive . . . especially my nipples.'

'Is that all you've got to say for yourself?'

Gail looked genuinely puzzled. 'I – I'll probably make a lot of noise when you punish me, Master. You might want to put my gag back in.'

'You really are ready to let me do anything I want with you?'

'Yes, Master.'

'Don't you want to escape if you could?'

Briefly her fists clenched as she tugged on her cuffs as though by reflex, but then she relaxed again: looking utterly helpless and perfectly passive once more. A troubled expression crossed her face as she sought for the right words. 'I suppose I do in a way, but at the same time I know I shouldn't. I deserve to be here.'

'Even tied up like this?'

'Yes, Master.'

'But you can't be comfortable.'

'I'm not, Master . . . but it feels right.'

Jim dropped his hands from her breasts down to her gaping vulva. He ran a finger though the slippery cleft, its lips already engorged with blood, feeling its wet warmth and smelling her arousal.

Gail gasped at his touch. The tendons on the backs of her splayed legs contracted in response, setting her swaying in her bonds.

'The truth is all this excites you, isn't that it?' he said.

She was breathing faster now. 'Y – yes, Master.'

'Are you a masochist?'

Gail took a deep breath, chewing her lip again in an innocently childish display of uncertainty. 'I . . . I don't know, Master. I never thought so before now. I was terribly afraid at first. But I can't help getting excited and – and coming, even when I'm being hurt. As long as it's sexy as well.'

'Is that what this is for you? A sex game?'

'No – a bit, maybe . . . but I am really sorry for what I did, Master. I deserve to be punished.'

He slipped a finger into the mouth of her vagina, now gaping in anticipation. 'You mean you want to be punished?'

'Yes, Master!' she gasped.

'Then say it.'

'Please punish me, Master! Do anything you like to me!'

Jim felt a glow of satisfaction grow within him in keeping with his mounting lust for Gail's body. Here at last was his perfect reward; a beautiful willing victim begging him to take his just revenge upon her.

From his workbench he took up a pair of metal screw clamps. 'Because of their shape these are called G clamps,' he told her. 'G for Gail. That's appropriate, don't you think? But where should I put them?'

There was a strange light in Gail's eyes now. 'On my nipples, Master. Put them on my nipples!'

Jim screwed the clamps tight about her plump nubs of flesh until Gail whimpered in pain, then he let them dangle. Such was the firmness of her breasts that they hung clear of her body, their weight stretching her nipples into tongues of pink and purple flesh. Gail's eyes were misty with tears, but she looked at him without fear; patiently waiting for the next indignity to be laid upon her.

He placed a chair in front of Gail so that when he sat down his head was level with her blatantly displayed groin. On an impulse he cupped her taut buttocks in his hands and bent forward and kissed her vertical smile, savouring its warm wet promise and exciting perfume. Gail squirmed in delight.

'That doesn't mean I've gone soft on you,' he warned her.

'I know, Master,' she replied, as though it was the most obvious thing in the world. 'Do whatever you want with me.'

He unrolled a long plastic wallet on the bench beside him. It held a gleaming set of small spanners, each in its own pouch. He took the largest out, wiped it with a cloth already coated with vaseline, peeled back Gail's thick outer labia and slid the spanner up into her hot dark depths. She shivered as the strangely shaped piece of cold metal lodged inside her. Jim selected the next largest spanner from the set and repeated the process.

By the time he reached the last few he was forcing them into gaps between the others, while Gail was groaning with their weight and the cruel way they stretched her vaginal passage and made her pudenda bulge unnaturally. The bright metal heads of the spanners projected from her cleft like the blooms of strange flowers, made shinier still by the exudation that flowed past them and dripped onto the workshop floor.

When Gail was stuffed full, Jim reversed his chair so that its back was directly underneath Gail's dangling backside. To this he clamped a variable-speed power drill with its bit pointing upwards. Into the chuck he fitted a short length of soft rubber hose. The other end of the hose he greased with vaseline and then fed into Gail's anus.

Turning on the drill at low speed set the greased hose twisting inside Gail's rectum, bringing forth a little yip of surprise. Gradually she began to rotate in the same direction as some of the torque transmitted itself through the friction between rubber and flesh into her body. The clamps on her nipples lifted outwards as she spun faster, pulling her nipples out into tormented cones.

Cautiously Jim activated the hammer action. The drill head began to judder up and down, sending ripples up the hose and into Gail. She yelled in horrified delight, jerking wildly on her straps. Her body went into spasm and she came copiously, spanners dropping out of her and jingling to the floor. Then her head dropped onto her chest and she hung limply in her straps, motionless except for the steady rise and fall of her chest.

While Gail was still half insensible, Jim removed the hose from her anus, pulled the remaining spanners from her vagina and lowered her to the floor. Unclipping her wrist and ankle cuffs from the bar he picked up her unresisting body as though she was a rag doll and laid her across his workbench, so that her legs overhung the side and her heels trailed on the floor. Her head he placed in the jaws of a large bench vice which he had padded with strips of foam rubber. Carefully he screwed the vice closed until it held her head, slightly tilted so that she could look down the length of her body, firmly in its unyielding grasp.

Laying out her limp arms along the length of the bench, he fed lengths of wire through the rings of her wrist cuffs. The wires were coiled round hooks screwed into the ends of the bench. Now he pulled the free ends of the wire tight, stretching Gail's arms straight out on either side of her, and wound them about the hooks until they were secure. He repeated the process with two more lengths of wire fastened to a second pair of hooks screwed into the lower corners of the bench ends, this time threading them through the rings of her ankle cuffs. He pulled her legs out into the widest splits he could force her supple young body to assume, until the big tendons of her inner thighs stood out starkly, then he made the wires secure.

Gail was now symmetrically arrayed before him; taut and immobile, her bottom just overhanging the scarred wooden edge of the bench, while her pouting pubic mount was open to his every whim. He unscrewed the G clamps and massaged the blood back into her abused purple nipples. The acute sensation of pins and needles as they filled out brought her back to full consciousness. She gasped in pain, then looked uncertainly up at him.

'Did – did I please you, Master?' she asked softly.

'You did, girl,' he assured her, bringing a smile to her face. 'But I'm not done with you yet ...' He undid his flies, releasing his erection which sprang up for her to see.

Gail grinned like a naughty schoolgirl. 'Oh, it's so big, Master! It's a good thing you've already stretched me.'

A brief pang of concern made him ask: 'Do you feel sore?'

'Yes, Master ... but that mustn't stop you.'

He stroked her lovemouth, feeling it pulse with life.

Resting his hands on the soft skin of her exposed inner thighs he slid into the bliss of her tight clinging haven, the force of his thrust setting her big breasts trembling. She gave a plaintive gasp and her face melted into a look of happy submission.

Seven

When they assembled the next morning for breakfast in Number 2, Tara went out of her way to appear at ease. She didn't want Cassie to think her scheming had made any difference to the treatment she had received at the hands of Hilary and Rachel.

She rehearsed what she would say when they were allowed to talk later. It could have been worse ... it wasn't what she would have chosen ... but, once she had let herself go, bits of it had been quite fun ... in a sick way, of course.

That last part was truer than she cared to admit, even to herself. Their perverted situation was doing things to her desires and emotions that she had yet to come to terms with. But she needed time to think it over. For the moment she had to continue following the logic she had used to convince the others this was preferable to facing official justice.

Defiant submission ... Play at being slaves ... Fool the residents into thinking you've had been broken ... Let them take their revenge but live to fight another day ... They'll have nothing to show for it and we'll still be the Elite ...

Well, that last aspiration was certainly dead and buried. The Elite was no more. And the residents would have something tangible besides memories as mementoes of their revenge: a library of high quality S&M images to enjoy during the long winter evenings. Would some of them be masturbating over a picture of her ten years from now? The idea made her stomach churn.

If that possibility had occurred to her on Friday night would it have made a difference? She was not sure. She was not sure of so many things now. Everything had changed.

There was Gail lapping up her food like a dog. She was holding herself stiffly but had a contented expression on her face. As she ate she was exchanging knowing smiles with Hazel and Daniela that clearly meant: 'Tell you about it later,' and was receiving similar glances in return. It was disturbing how readily the three of them had settled into slavery after the fear they had first shown. Even Sian looked relatively at ease. Or was she putting on an act? Only Cassie appeared morose, flashing accusing looks which Tara responded to with bland unconcern.

The Elite was finished and she no longer cared for what Cassie thought of her, except in so far as it affected her own circumstances. All that mattered was getting though the next four days.

After their morning exercise, Warwick announced that, as they were making so much use of the place, it only seemed right that they mow the back lawn of Number 2. But they would not be using a conventional mower. Louisa and Narinda had brought a curious selection of items out of the house while he had been speaking, and now they set about putting them to use.

The girls were arranged in a row shoulder to shoulder on their hands and knees. A long pole fitted with six regularly spaced snap hooks was then slung from their collar rings, ensuring they kept in line.

Their ankles were tied to those of the girls on either side and then spread with short lengths of bamboo. One end of a length of wire had been twisted round the middle of each of these bamboo spreader bars. The other end had been skewered through the middle of a rubber ball, folded back on itself and twisted tight. With the help of a little vaseline, these balls were pushed up the girls' rear passages.

It was an indignity to which they were becoming accustomed, and there were only a few muted grunts as the balls were forced inside them. But beyond encouraging them to shuffle forward on their knees in small increments, and not to stretch their legs out behind them, Tara could not see what other purpose they served. However the residents had not been lacking in ingenuity so far . . .

A garden glove was placed on their left hands and a pair of spring-handled clippers were taped to their right. Six black plastic bin bags were then produced. These had rings of wire taped to their mouths to hold them open. A loop of wire threaded through a short plastic sleeve was fastened to each ring. The sleeves went into the girls' mouths like horses' bits, leaving the bags to trail under their bodies.

The girls were shuffled into line facing down one side of the rough lawn and commanded to start cutting. Once again Louisa had her camera out to record their shame for those residents away at work.

While resting on her left hand, each girl clipped the patch of grass immediately in front of her with her clippers. Then she rested on her right hand while scooping the loose cuttings into the bin bag with her gloved hand. When they were all done they shuffled on to the next patch.

Now the true purpose of the wires running from their ankle spreaders to their anuses became clear. As the bags filled with grass cuttings they dragged more heavily against their ankle rods and the bulging ends started to roll over them. The wires held them in place, though the bags pressed with increasing force on their anal balls. But then it was not intended to be comfortable.

Neither was it the fastest way to cut grass, Tara thought, as the sweat began to pool on her back and trickle down the cleft of her buttocks, but in a perverse way it was ecologically sound and energy efficient. And who would not rather have a bevy of sweaty slavegirls on their hands and knees with their backsides on show than a roaring smelly petrol mower?

The grass was so thick and rough that their bags were almost full by the time they reached the end of the lawn. They were briefly allowed to straighten up while Warwick emptied the bags into a bin. Narinda took a bottle of water along the line and they drank from it gratefully, spilled drops falling onto their already glistening breasts. Then the bag handles were put back between their teeth and they were turned around and set off up the lawn to cut a second swathe.

Tara tried to estimate the rate they were going and doubted if they would be finished by lunchtime. Still, although it was uncomfortable it not the most humiliating thing they had been made to do, she decided. It must be one of those tasks the residents had concocted to teach their 'spoilt' captives the value of honest hard toil. Did they really think it was that simple? For Hazel, Gail and Daniela perhaps, she conceded, but then that trio were already so lost in playing at slaves they'd do anything they were told and probably enjoy it. But Sian and Cassie were unlikely converts to the work ethic. As for herself – well, it was giving her ideas . . .

With the heat and mechanical repetition of her task, her thoughts began to wander. The six of them did make a pretty sight. After this was over maybe she could find a few girls willing to cut her lawn naked and bound like this, while she watched over them. Hazel, Gail and Daniela, perhaps? She felt her juices begin to drip onto the bag between her legs at the exciting thought, then started in alarm.

She was getting excited about having naked girl-slaves in her garden! Worse, she was leaving a sign of her arousal on the sack where it would be seen when it was next changed! God, what was happening to her?

Then she thought: so what if she was getting excited? They were trapped in a weird sex game so it was perfectly natural to have pervy daydreams. And the residents couldn't know exactly what she was thinking. Besides, they'd already seen her do far more intimate things. Modesty was suspended for the duration. She was a slave and expected to act perversely. It was a sort of freedom, she supposed.

Tara slipped back into her happy fantasy . . .

What about the other games the residents had played with them? Could she do to those three what Hilary and Rachel had done to her the previous night?

Her daydream was cut short by a sudden commotion from the bottom of the garden.

Somebody was shouting loudly even as the timbers of the back fence shook. There was the sound of a body crashing though the overgrown shrubs in the lower boarder and then heavy feet pounding across the lawn.

'What have you done to them?' a man cried in horror as he ran into view. 'I'll save you, Miss Tara!'

It was Simon Pye.

* * *

It was absolutely the worst moment of Tara's life,

She thought she had plumbed the depths of shame and degradation over the last few days, but to have Simon Pye of all people see her like this was too much to bear. He was a simple-minded gardener who worked for her father, for God sake! Tara cringed, suddenly acutely aware of her nakedness, and futilely tried to cover her breasts and pubes by hugging the half-filled grass bag to her. On either side of her the other girls were doing the same. They had grown used to the residents seeing them naked, but Simon was an intruder from outside, a shocking reminder of their old life where what they were doing right now was unthinkable and degrading.

Simon Pye was arguing with Narinda and Major Warwick and pointing angrily at the girls, while trying not to actually look at their naked bodies. If they didn't let them go right now he'd call the police and –

All the time Louisa Jessop had been working the controls of her camera. Now she held its screen up in front of Simon's flushed face.

'. . . is Simon, you know, all right?'

From where they crouched on the grass they could hear the audio playback. It was Cassie's voice, and with sudden horrible clarity they all knew where and when the images to accompany it had been recorded. Tom Fanning had done his job all too well.

Tara winced and lowered her head out of a sense of shame even deeper than that she had felt only moments earlier. The absolute worse moment in her life had just been surpassed. One by one the others did the same, not wanting to meet Simon's eyes. Relentlessly the recording played on, and as it did so Simon's face turned from anger though confusion to misery.

'. . . that's what this week's for: to remind them exactly where they belong.'

Louisa turned off her camera. Warwick put a hand on Simon's shoulder and led the young man into the house, leaving the girls in the charge of the two women.

Narinda clapped her hand briskly. 'Back to work. You've a job to finish.'

They bent to their task without a murmur, grateful to have something to occupy them, happy not to have to look into each other's faces.

An hour later Warwick returned to the garden alone. The living mowing machine was halted and the girls permitted to sit back on their heels to listen to what he had to say.

'Simon Pye now understands why we've been treating you like this,' Warwick told them gravely. 'He's seen recordings of your confessions and knows everything you've done to us over the last eighteen months. Needless to say he will not be attempting to rescue you again. Being an honest young man he thought you should be turned over to the police –' Tara's heart skipped a beat and Gail drew in her breath in alarm '– but I have persuaded him that justice will be served if we continue our course of private punishment. On this understanding he has agreed to keep both your crimes and our retribution secret. He will also maintain the illusion that you are away on holiday and mind your camp and possessions.' His gaze lingered on Tara, Cassie and Sian as he added: 'Some of you must realise how badly you both insulted Simon and spurned his trust, apart from implicating him as a potential accessory to your activities, which could have got him into serious trouble had things worked out differently. At some time you'll have to make your peace with him, one way or another. But for the moment we shall continue as before.'

They went back to work again.

As they clipped their way across the seemingly endless lawn, Tara fought a silent battle with her conscience. Of course Simon wasn't important as such, but unlike the residents of the Close he had done nothing to harm her. He had been totally loyal and trusting, he'd known his place and had actually been worried enough to come looking for her when he thought she was in trouble. And in return she had used him rather callously. It had been a challenge to pursue her war against the Close, whereas wrapping Simon round her little finger had taken next to no effort or ingenuity at all. It was nothing of which to be proud.

It was mid-afternoon before they finished cutting the lawn, and a positive relief to be locked into their bed frames and rest their aching backs. But there was no swapping of stories between Gail, Daniela and Hazel, nor sniping from Sian and Cassie; just a long awkward silence, which Daniela eventually broke.

'It was nice of Simon to try to rescue us,' she said simply.

'Yeah, he's a real fuckin' white knight,' Cassie said scornfully. 'Now we've got to live with him knowing what we've been through.'

'He's not working in Fernleigh Rise ever again,' Sian said. 'How could we have him in our gardens after he's seen us like this? You can get rid of him, Tara. You must!'

'He was just doing what he thought was right,' Tara said impatiently. 'Warwick said he'd keep quiet and I believe him.'

'How can you be so sure?' Cassie exclaimed. 'What if he changes his mind and tells on us?'

'Buy him off,' Sian said desperately. 'Set him up somewhere else. You want to tear down his house anyway –'

'Shut up!' Tara snapped. 'I'll do whatever I choose about Simon when it comes to it, but for now I'm just thinking about getting through the next few days.'

There was another silence, then Gail said: 'Whatever anybody else does, I'm going to apologise to him. It wasn't right getting him involved in our business like this. He could have got into real trouble if the police had found out.'

Hazel and Daniela murmured their agreement, and Hazel asked: 'Tara, how much did you tell him about what we were doing?'

'I don't want to talk about it,' Tara said.

'But how much?' Hazel persisted.

Tara sighed. 'Just that we wanted to stay in the woods quietly for a week as a joke. He didn't ask anything else. He was good like that. He did what he was told.'

'He won't be so good in future,' Daniela observed.

'Do you think he'll, well, try to get his own back at us in some way?' Hazel wondered.

'Oh, God!' Cassie moaned. 'Don't say we've got to worry about him stalking us? Why couldn't you have found somebody normal, Tara?'

'It didn't help you and Sian calling him "simple" and "stupid",' Gail pointed out. 'Anybody might get angry after hearing that.'

'It's not our fault!' Sian snapped. 'All this is down to Tara and her stupid bloody war on Cheyner Close. That's what got us into this.'

'I didn't hear you complaining while we were having fun,' Tara said. 'You've had eighteen months to say something. Having regrets just because things have gone wrong and now you're feeling sorry for yourself?'

Sian didn't answer. After a moment Daniela asked quietly: 'Are you sorry about the things we've done to the people in the Close, Tara?'

There was a long silence before Tara said thoughtfully: 'I think I misjudged them . . .'

The soft tomato burst with a stinging smack against Tara's right breast, momentarily driving her hard nipple back into its fleshy resilience, and spraying pulp and seeds all over her. Its remains slithered down her body, mingling with the slimy streaks of egg and rotten apple that already plastered her. Tara swayed about on her treacherous mount, her thighs trying to clench. She was filthy and bedraggled and humiliated . . . and she was going to come at any moment.

The evening's entertainment was taking place in Gerald Spooner's garden once again. It was a variation on the old-fashioned pillory.

A heavy rope had been slung high up between two trees and drawn tight. Thinner ropes were slung over this and tied to the girls' wrists, which had been strapped in front of them, and then pulled tight, drawing them up until their toes dangled clear of the grass. Then the pogo sticks had been fitted.

They were not actual pogo sticks, of course, but wooden rods about the length of walking sticks with crosspieces screwed into place close to their lower ends. The upper ends of the rods were capped with fluorescent-coloured play balls, bristling with soft rubber prongs.

These had of course been forced up into their vaginas, making them gasp and shiver as the prongs worked their way into their tunnels of ribbed flesh.

Their ankles had then been spread and strapped to the crossbars. The lower ends of the rods dug into the ground, leaving the tops to sway about as they shifted their weight, half-supported by the sticks and half by their bound wrists. This motion stirred the pronged balls lodged in their warm wet elastic sheaths. The only way to minimise the torment was to hold as still as possible. But being suspended from the same rope meant they kept shaking each other off balance as they wobbled about comically, like counterweighted toys that never quite fell over however much they rocked and swayed.

If that was not enough, the residents had lined up before them with boxes of old tomatoes, eggs and apples, and started hurling them at them. Even old Spooner himself joined in. The impact of these missiles made them flinch and gyrate even more, as did their almost entirely futile but instinctive attempts to dodge, only adding to their perverse misery.

They were being used for malicious target practice, no better than some fairground coconut shy, Tara thought. It was mean and so utterly humiliating ... and still her juices were running down her thighs along with the other muck coating her.

Gail's buttocks twitched and clenched. She gave a long sigh and then sagged forward, her back bowed and her lovely big filth-streaked breasts hanging pendant like ripe fruits. The rain of eggs, tomatoes and rotten fruits turned to the remaining five girls.

So that was how it worked ...

Tara clenched her inner muscles tight about the pronged ball on which she was impaled and squirmed about desperately, willing herself to come. Panting and gasping she rode the rod until the blissful knot in her loins burst and flooded her with raw pleasure. Letting go she hung limp, not trying to dodge any more, surrendering herself in the hope the residents would obey the rules of the game. And they did.

The girls were in such a sticky smelly mess by the time the game finished that Stan Jessop unrolled a garden hose and sprayed them over to wash off the worst of the muck. Each resident was nevertheless advised to give their slave for the night a proper shower when they get them home. Still, everybody agreed it had been a good game.

It was only as she hung from her wrists dripping wet and shivering that Tara thought to wonder why she had not tried to fake an orgasm to remove herself from the firing line. After all the deceptions she had perpetrated, why not this most minor and excusable one to save herself unnecessary discomfort? Why had she become so determined to play the residents' games by their rules? Was she trying to prove something to herself?

Tom Fanning worked the shampoo well into Sian's thick black hair. She twisted her head about, screwing up her eyes as the lather rolled down her face.

'Don't squirm so much, girl,' he said, directing the jet from the shower to rinse the suds away. 'You want to get properly clean, don't you?'

Sian spluttered and blinked and gave a resentful nod.

Tom couldn't let her get away with that. He reached for his holly cane, which had never been far from hand in recent days even in the shower, and swished it across her lean stomach. She yelped and twisted away as far as her upstretched arms, which were cuffed to a large hook set high up the shower cubical, allowed. He caught her by the chin and turned her head back round to face him once more.

'I don't expect you to pretend to like this, but you will speak when you're spoken to and you will do it properly. Those are the rules, remember?'

'Yes, Master,' Sian said contritely. 'I'm sorry, Master.'

'That's better. I may be new to handling slavegirls but I'm learning fast. And one thing I expect is a proper show of subservience.'

Sian hung her head humbly. 'Yes, Master.'

Tom lifted her chin up again. 'That's the idea, but you can look me in the eye. You've got a nice face when you let yourself smile.' He looked her slim wet body up and down and grinned. 'A nice everything, in fact . . .'

This was the fourth naked and handcuffed girl he'd been in the shower with since Saturday. Even in his adolescent dreams he'd never imagined anything like this. He was pale and not in great shape, while she was tanned and supple, no doubt courtesy of an expensive health club. But for tonight she belonged to him. The shower water ran off the end of his joyfully tumescent penis.

He began playing with Sian's soapy body. Her little rounded breasts were wonderfully firm, tipped with hard nipples. Sian rested her head back against the tiles and bit her lip, but she kept her eyes on him as he had instructed.

'I had Hazel last night, and she was great fun to play with,' Tom said chattily. 'But so far you've been behaving like your friend Cassie. I had her on Saturday and she was a streak of misery, far worse than Tara, at least until I encouraged her to brighten up. Do you want to be bright or miserable?'

She licked her lips. 'I'll try to be bright, Master.'

'That's better. Of course we both know you'd rather not be here at all, but since you are you might as well make the best of it, even if it's only out of pure selfishness. As I said, Cassie took a lot of persuading to cheer up. If you're sensible you'll save yourself some unnecessary pain and at least act responsively . . .'

By now his hands had travelled down the curve of her stomach and slipped between her slender thighs into the still-soapy tangle of her pubic bush.

Sian gulped and spread her legs wider. 'I'll be sensible, Master.' She forced a smile. 'Will you – will you wash my pussy, please?'

Tom was glad to see that rather haughty and superior expression finally wiped from her face. She might learn in time. But whether she did or not, he'd have his fun with her. That was the bargain.

He worked her pubic hair into a lather, feeling her body trembling as he rubbed his fingers though her slit, then rinsed the soap away. He probed her labia again to test they were clean and found a slipperiness there that had nothing to do with soap. His cock was straining now, which Sian could see quite clearly. There was a wonderful inevitability about what came next.

Sian forced another smile, then, either wanting to get it over with or trying to further stimulate her own passion, she craned her neck upwards and kissed him. He stooped and so that his cockhead could connect with her lovemouth. Her tight cleft parted about his shaft as he slid into her. Tom straightened his legs so that Sian's back slid up the slippery tiles and her feet lifted from the floor.

Her slim legs scrabbled about for a moment, then reluctantly crooked about his waist, her ankles cross-ed in the small of his back, easing some of the strain on her wrists. He thrust into her again and again, driving the breath from her slim frame. He sensed her loosing her inhibitions as nature took over. The embrace of her legs tightened about him and she kissed him again with something approaching genuine passion. The analytical part of Tom's mind that never shut down was surprised. Sian had come only a couple of hours ago, unless she faked her orgasm on the pillory pole. Maybe a real cock turned her on more intensely; maybe there was a sensuous being under that slightly frosty exterior. Whatever the reason, she wanted to come now.

But he could not wait for her to catch up. Besides, his pleasure came first.

His sperm pumped into her hot tight depths, making her ride him with more desperate vigour. But after a moment to recover he firmly disentangled her legs from about his waist and pulled out of her sticky clinging maw. She was left swaying from her wrist cuffs, thrusting out her hips to him, the engorged pink lips of her cleft pouting from the nest of her pubic bush.

'No – finish me off!' she demanded angrily, her eyes filled with unfulfilled need. Then she added meekly: 'Please, Master.'

A week ago she would not have given him the time of day, now she needed him. That felt so good. 'Do you want me back inside you?' he asked.

'Yes!' she sobbed.

'Beg.'

'I beg you, Master – please bring me off!'

Tom grinned. 'Well, you'll just have to hold that thought. But I promise you'll get plenty of opportunity later. You see, Jim Curry's not the only inventor round here, and I've got a little device I want to try out on you.' He reached for a towel. 'But first, let's get you dry . . .'

* * *

Fifteen minutes later Sian was lying on her back on a sturdy square of blockboard resting on a table in Tom's study workroom.

Her upper arms were spread clear of her body, exposing the soft hollows of her armpits. Her elbows were bent at right angles so that her wrists were fastened to the board with buckled straps bolted close to the one that encircled her neck. Another strap crossed tightly over her waist. Her legs were pulled up and splayed wide, with straps holding down her thighs almost flat. Her knees were both bent and turned outward, so that the ankle straps holding them in place caused the sides of her feet to press against the board. This posture forced upon her slim body starkly displayed her mound of Venus, capped by its dark pubic forest. The acute spreading of her thighs caused its central valley to gape invitingly.

The open vulnerability of her groin was emphasised by a small electric motor connected to a crank wheel which was bolted to the board just below the cleft of her buttocks, with its reciprocating shaft pointing right at her vagina.

Sian's eyes had passed anxiously over the jumble of computers and electronic apparatus that packed the desks and shelves as he had strapped her down, and then fixed with growing alarm on the black box with its dials and switches and trailing cables which Tom was arranging beside her.

'I tried this out on Hazel last night,' he explained, uncoiling several coloured wires with crocodile clips on their ends. 'It'll be interesting to see how you make out.' He saw the expression on her face and added wryly: 'You know I'm good with electronics. It's quite safe. A lot of voltage but low current. It doesn't mean it won't be painful, of course, but you were expecting that anyway, right?'

'Yes, Master,' Sian said, trying to control the tremor in her voice.

'Don't worry, there's a way you can make it more pleasant for yourself. But I've got to open you up first . . .'

He had two pairs of sprung plastic clips tied to lengths of elastic cord. Pinching her thick outer labia between his fingers he snapped the clips about them, ignoring Sian's little whimpers, then pulled the cords tight and tied them round her thighs. The tension pulled the elastic fleshlips wide so her vulva seemed almost to blossom; exposing the crinkled crescents of her more delicate inner lips, the hood of clitoris, the tiny mouth of her urethra and below it the dark pit of her vagina. Tom paused for a moment to admire the result, deciding that the oft-made comparison between female genitalia and orchids was quite valid. Here before him was just such a pubic orchid, blooming in a bed of black moss.

He held up one of the crocodile clips for her to see. It had a double wire trailing from it. 'Each of these forms a complete circuit,' he explained. 'The halves of the jaw are insulated from each other so that the current flows directly between them. It'll probably feel like having a needle stuck through your skin, only there won't be any mark afterwards.'

Sian bit her lip, but said nothing.

Tom began fastening the metal crocodile clips to Sian's body: one each on the natural terminals of her nipples and two on each petal of her inner labia. Sian whimpered anew as the fine metal teeth bit into her tender flesh. He slid an electrode rod, with a rubber ring about its base to stop it being expelled, up her anus.

He then picked up a dildo-sized cylinder of blue foam rubber, with a single copper wire coiled in a spiral round its shaft and a separate bundle of insulated wires trailing from its base.

'This coil is the other half of the circuit terminating in the electrode up your rear,' he explained. 'When they're both in place the current will flow between them. But this also has a sensor inside linked to another circuit that will reduce the size of the shocks you get the wetter it becomes.' He grinned. 'And you know how to make it wetter, don't you?'

Sian nodded.

Tom mounted the dildo onto the shaft of the motor and slid its tip into the open mouth of her vagina.

'Hazel had a little accident when I used this on her last night,' he explained, putting a plastic sheet down on the floor. 'It might just be her nature, or it may be a side effect of the machine. Better safe than sorry . . .'

Tom took up position by the control box and grinned at Sian. 'As an incentive I'm setting the timing of the shocks, their strength and the speed of the motor to get steadily stronger and faster. The sooner you come and the wetter you get the less it'll hurt, you understand?'

'Yes, Master,' Sian said, pale-faced.

Tom pressed a button. The motor whirred, sending the dildo slowly into Sian. She gave a sharp gasp and her hips jerked as far as her straps allowed as a jolt of electricity passed through her labia. As the dildo plugged her completely its coil came alive, the current flowing though the narrow membrane separating her front and rear passages, making a circuit with the probe in her anus. Tom saw her bottom sphincter tighten about the metal rod skewered within her. As the dildo pulled out again her back arched and her small breasts heaved and jiggled as her nipples were shocked. Then the cycle started again, but a little faster.

'Talk to me,' Tom said, 'tell me what it feels like.'

Sian moaned and licked her lips, trying to talk even though her whole body was tensing in time with the shocks. 'Pins stabbing right through – ah! – my nipples, Master – aww! – stabbing my pubes – uhhh! – that was right inside . . . I never – aghh! – oh, God . . . please, Master . . . I'm trying – ahhah! – to come!'

He could see her vagina squeezing the wire-coiled dildo as it pumped into her. Already it was glistening with her slick secretion.

'You can do it,' he encouraged her.

'Aww! They're getting hotter . . . uhh! . . . I'm trying, I'm trying –'

Her peeled-back and twitching pubes were shiny with her exudations. A dark stain was growing on the board beneath them.

'Your juices should be reaching the sensor now,' he said. 'The shocks will feel less intense, more pleasure than pain. You're doing very well. I'll turn it off when you come.'

'Yes, Master,' Sian gasped. 'It's – aw! – better now . . .'

Her neat body was trembling with her exertions, sweat beading in the valley between her breasts. Her breathing was getting faster, the straining of her limbs more forceful as though she was driving herself forward to finish a race.

Suddenly she gave a loud yell, half of triumph, half of surprise. The dildo emerged streaming with her come while a fitful jet of pee spurted from her cleft onto the plastic sheet, pulsing in time with the shocks still galvanising her inner muscles.

Gasping from the force of her orgasm even as she blushed with shame at her display, Sian lay still, panting heavily.

Tom turned the machine off, wondering if it would have the same result on the next girl. Would she also believe the shocks were getting less intense the wetter she got, when in fact they did no such thing?

'What did you think of my little invention?' he asked. 'Tell me the truth.'

Sian struggled to speak coherently. 'It – it frightened me, Master. It was alive inside me. Being controlled . . . like a puppet.'

'But you did come. You must have enjoyed it a bit.'

'I couldn't help it . . . but please don't use it on me again, Master. I'll try to please you in any other way. I'll do anything you want.'

Tom savoured her desperate expression. 'Hmm. Is your bum as tight as your cunt?'

Almost eagerly, Sian replied: 'Oh yes, Master. You'll like using my bumhole. I've always been called a – a –'

'Tight-arsed little bitch?' Tom suggested.

A new blush was darkening Sian's cheeks. 'Yes, Master,' she said miserably.

'Then I'll try to loosen you up.'

Sian spent the rest of the night tied face down on Tom's bed, while he happily rode her hot tight rear to three more orgasms. When he released her the next morning she could hardly walk. Nevertheless she thanked him when he helped her along to the shower.

Could his machine generate better manners as well as orgasms?

Eight

There was something subtly different about Sian that morning, Tara thought. Her normally self-possessed and brittle expression had softened into something more introspective. Tara wondered if it was due to her night in Tom Fanning's charge or the unresolved matter of Simon Pye. It had been playing on Tara's mind as well, though for the moment she was trying to keep her worries at bay. That was a problem to be faced after they had served their time in the Close.

But as usual there was no opportunity to hear from Sian or any of the others about their experiences the previous night. After breakfast they were put through their regular hour of exercises by Warwick in the back garden. Tara happily lost herself in the vigorous activity, working out the kinks in her muscles and shaking off the aches, if not the soreness, left over from her demanding session with the Jessops. With the dew still lingering on the grass, it was almost enjoyable.

At the end of the session, breathing heavily and cheeks flushed, they were formed up into line so that their wrists could be cuffed behind them once again. Warwick then tied metal rings to the backs of their collars, with enough slack so they dangled free against their skin.

What were they planning now? Tara wondered.

Warwick ordered them into the 'Present' position. As they bent over with their legs spread and heads level with their knees, Narinda came out of the house with what looked like a bunch of toffee apples in her hand. She made her way along their line, forcing the bulbous ends of the toffee apples up their rears. They were in fact thick lengths of dowel with holes bored through up their shafts, and capped with rubber balls.

The balls had been vaselined, but even so Tara gasped as her anal ring was forced to expand to let it in. Once it was in place Narinda tugged at the shaft protruding from Tara's anus to check it was secure. Tara knew there was no way she could expel it on her own. But what were they for?

They were marched back inside the house, where Jim Curry, Louisa Jessop and Raj Khan were waiting beside a strange collection of items that had been assembled in their room. As she took it in Tara realised they were going to be on the receiving end of another display of the residents' perverse ingenuity.

Six plain wooden chairs, with their feet nailed to sheets of hardboard, had been arranged in a circle. In the centreline of each seat, and about a third the way in from the backrest, a hole had been drilled through the solid wood. Screwed vertically to the back of each chair was another length of the same thick wooden rod they had up their rears.

At the centre of the circle of chairs was a tyreless bicycle wheel, its axle perpendicular, suspended at about head height from a ceiling hook which had previously supported some heavy light fitting. Below the wheel, resting on a low stool, was a red plastic bucket to which six short lengths of black plastic guttering had been fastened with small brass hinges. The lip of each overhung the bucket rim and they

158

radiating symmetrically outward like the spokes of a wheel.

The outer ends of each length of gutter had been trimmed so that they tapered into flat plastic tongues. Sleeves of yellow foam pipe lagging had been slipped over these protrusions and taped in place. The ends of these rested one each on the seats of the chairs.

Lengths of cord were draped over the rim of the bicycle wheel and fastened to a large coil spring, the bottom of which was hooked to the bucket handle. The free ends of these cords were tied to crocodile clips. A second set of cords had been fastened to the bottom of the bucket, and these were tied to wooden pegs.

Stepping over the gutters, the girls were carefully positioned before they sat down. The dowels sticking out from between their buttocks were guided through the holes in the chairs, while their new neck rings were slipped over the upright rods rising from the chair backs. The cords attached to the bottom of the bucket were drawn out, threaded through rings screwed to the underside of their chair seats, and slotted into the holes in their projecting anal rods.

Their legs were spread, their feet pulled round to the outside of the front legs of the chairs and tied in place. They sat very straight-backed. Their collar rings did not permit them to bend forward and they could not rise to disengage the rings from the upright rods they were hooked over because of the pegs under their chairs holding their anal rods in place.

The residents then produced six two-litre plastic bottles of mineral water, which had each been bound round with slings of wire extending into two wing-like nooses. These they looped about the roots of the girls' breasts and drew tight. To prevent the nooses slipping off they clipped clothespegs to the bulging flesh just

159

below the wires. Sian's small globes got three on each, Tara and Gail six.

A chorus of moans and whimpers rose up when the bottles were allowed to hang free in their cleavages, their full weight supported by their stretched and pegged breasts. But none of the girls protested in words or begged to be excused the unfolding ordeal. They knew better than that by now.

Long bendable drinking straws were placed in the bottles. The ends of the straws passed through holes carefully punched in strips of repair tape. The straws were pushed between the girls' lips and the tape pressed down across their cheeks, holding the straws in place.

The residents edged the ring of chairs forward, feeding the yellow foam gutter tongues into the girls' vaginal passages until they were lodged halfway up them. Then they drew out the lines running over the rim of the suspended wheel to the bucket handle and fastened the crocodile clips on their ends to the girls' nipples. There were some grunts and whimpers as they were clipped to their swelling nubs of flesh, but no more than that. It did not add greatly to the sum of their discomfort.

Then the stool supporting the bucket was removed. The cords went taut as its weight and half that of the guttering drew their nipples out into distended cones. Now the whimpers and gasps were louder and prolonged and eyes began to water. They breasts were simultaneously strangled and pinched, while their nipples felt like they were being stretched like elastic.

But then an odd thing happened. Their captors set up three cameras spaced about the room to record their plight from every angle, set them running, and then walked out of the room without a word, locking the door behind them.

Tara saw the same puzzlement briefly rising above their mutual pain in the eyes of the others. Why had they been left alone? Was this meant in some way to increase their suffering?

Cassie was grunting through her gag. The tape held the straws in place but as their mouths were not otherwise filled it was possible to shape muffled words, like an amateur ventriloquist.

'Why ... the fuck ... did they ... leave us?' she said.

'We can't win,' Sian moaned. 'We drink to save our tits from being strangled ... then have to pee ... it goes into the bucket ... and we get our nipples torn off!'

Tara was trying to ignore the pain throbbing through her distorted breasts and staring at Daniela who was seated opposite her in the ring. Her lovely pointed breasts were already tinged with purple. But Tara was looking at the cord running to the peg holding her anal plug in place. Of course! They were meant to work it out for themselves without any prompting.

'Listen!' she said as clearly as her gag allowed. 'Drink ... all the water you can ... Then hold on as long as possible ... then pee together ...'

'It'll tear our ... tits off!' Cassie wailed.

'Not for long ... The bucket will go down ... far enough to pull pegs out ... Then we can stand up ... and our tit cords will be loose!'

They looked at each other helplessly, realising there was no other solution. If they did nothing and endured the existing pain they would have to pee eventually, adding to their misery. And that could take hours. But they had to do it all together or it would not work.

Gail, closely followed by Daniela and Hazel, began sucking at her bottle. Tara started as well. Sian looked at Cassie, shrugged, and then they joined them.

By the time her bottle was empty Tara felt horribly bloated, but at least her breasts were no longer being strangled. Now there was nothing else to do but wait.

Her thoughts wandered. How much would the bucket take? The residents must have tested it was enough to pull out the pegs, but did it have to be only half full? Two thirds? More? How quickly would the water pass through them? Fifteen minutes? Half an hour? There was no clock in the room and she suspected her time sense would deceive her in the circumstances.

Tara found herself staring at Daniela's groin and her pussy lips parted by the yellow foam plug. How much use had they been put to over the last few days? Could she see a gleam of moisture? It wasn't pee. She must be getting excited. She saw Daniela was looking back at her even as she realised her pudenda were also wet as they sucked at her foam dildo, despite the pain of her tortured nipples. Or did that make it easier? The plug up her backside probably helped as well. Were the others getting aroused? She examined them as they sat with their legs spread and nipples cruelly stretched. A ring of pretty, helpless toys.

'I'm going to have . . . to go soon,' Sian said.

'Hold on . . . as long as you can. We must do it . . . together,' Tara said.

After another ten minutes they were all squirming. It was pee or burst time.

'On three,' Tara said. 'One . . . two . . . three!'

Jets of clear pee hissed from between their gaping labia with surprising force, swirling and gurgling down the gutters like mill races. For a few seconds all Tara felt was the blessed relief of emptying her bladder, mingled with the strange thrill of doing it so openly before the others.

Then the six streams of pee began to pour into the bucket.

Their nipples stretched even further under its increasing weight. They whimpered in pain. But the bucket was sinking steadily as its spring lengthened, drawing on the cords that pegged them to their chairs.

As it did so the gutter tongues pivoted on the edges of the seats, something Tara had not foreseen, pressing the foam plugs up into the roofs of their vaginal tunnels. Wasn't that where her 'G' spot was supposed to be? Oh yes! Oh, God, that was good . . . but terrible timing!

The bucket was nearly touching the floor, but the flow from their pussies was slowing to mere dribbles. They were gasping and whining as their nipples were drawn out into tortured cones of flesh. It had to work!

One by one the pegs under their chairs popped out.

The others immediately tried to stand up, but Tara realised the last one up would have the whole weight of the bucket dragging on her tits.

'All together,' she grunted.

They slid their haunches forward, dragging the shafts of their anal plugs up through the seat holes, trying to get into balance to stand without being able to lean forward. The gutter tongues were sliding further into them as they rocked to and fro. They were shafting themselves now. Tara felt the motions of the others transmitted up her gutter tongue though the bucket. The pee was slopping about inside it, setting it swaying. It would tear their nipples off!

Tara clamped the plug inside her and hauled.

Suddenly she was on her feet and the terrible tension on her breasts vanished.

Daniela opposite her lost her counterbalancing tension and screeched in pain.

'Use your cunt!' Tara grunted, pulling her gutter to her. With a heave Daniela shot to her feet.

Suddenly the others were standing as well, panting from their exertions. The bucket was resting on the ground and their nipple cords were slack. By comparison the pinching of the crocodile clips and pegs still adorning their breasts seemed a minor irritation.

For some minutes they just stood quietly recovering, all deeply impaled on the gutter tongues which now angled up from the bucket rim into them. Their ankles were still tied to the chair legs so they could not pull themselves off. They would have to wait to be released.

Then Tara realised Hazel and Gail were gently rocking themselves back and forward on the yellow foam shafts, making their vulvas bulge as they slid into them. They were deliberately masturbating. And why not, Tara thought? It was some reward for their suffering and they were quite beyond shame now. She began to grind her hips about the plug inside her. One by one the others joined in. By the time she remembered everything they did was being recorded it was too late to stop.

Shortly afterwards female juices began to trickle down the gutters into the bucket to join the urine.

Tara was still wondering what the residents had hoped to get out of their elaborate contraption, beyond the obvious pain and humiliation of course, during their afternoon rest. Had it been meant as a lesson in cooperation, or had they hoped they would inflict unnecessary suffering on each other out of mutual spite?

Meanwhile Sian was being unexpectedly open about her session with Tom Fanning the previous night. She described her experience on his electrical machine, concluding: '... and I so lost control I actually peed as I came. I wish he'd had it ready when he had his turn with Tara. Then she'd really know about having to pee.'

Tara said nothing, not wanting to get into another argument.

'She's already the Queen of Pee after this morning,' Gail giggled.

'I don't think you can help it on that machine,' Hazel said seriously. 'I wet myself when he used it on me. It's so, well, intense. It gets right inside you.'

'It wouldn't work if you had more self-control,' Cassie said dismissively.

'Like you, I suppose,' Sian said sarcastically. 'Lucky you've had your session with Fanning so you don't have to prove it. Well, maybe I did wet myself, but at least I was fun. He said you were a streak of misery until he brightened you up. What did he do to you anyway?'

Cassie suddenly sounded defensive. 'It doesn't matter.'

'I bet he had you begging to please him,' Sian taunted. 'Was it up the bum? I think he likes that. Come on ...'

Tara lay back and let them argue.

The weather was still warm and dry, so the teatime entertainment was held in Gerald Spooner's garden again. The rest of the residents were there and smiled as the girls were marched in.

The rope strung between the trees was still in place, though now twelve sets of thinner ropes dangled from it, while directly underneath it six pegs had been driven into the ground, each trailing another length of rope. Five of the chairs they had used that morning were set out in a line facing the rope. A white-painted rope, rather like that marking the boundary of a cricket field, had been laid out in a large loop around the chairs, arcing wide of their backs but running close across the front of them. On a table to one side was a CD player, a long holly switch and, oddly, a Thermos flask.

'Have you ever played musical chairs?' Major Warwick asked rhetorically, as the girls were made to kneel in line, their hands still cuffed behind them. 'Well, we've made certain modifications to the traditional game to make it suitable for the occasion. For instance . . .'

He tilted one of the chairs forward to show them. Ten or a dozen holly leaves had been taped to the seat.

'As you can see the chairs will be somewhat uncomfortable,' Warwick continued, smiling at their expressions of dismay, 'but you might still decide they are preferable to the alternative. The girl who loses the first round will be hung up by her ankles, have six ice cubes pushed into her front passage and receive six strokes of the cane across her breasts. The loser of the second round will receive five cubes and five strokes, and so on. The winner will get just one cube and one stroke, though of course her bottom will be the most pricked.'

By this time the girls were looking horribly confused. Was that the intention, Tara wondered, or was it supposed to teach some deeper lesson? The challenge this morning was best solved by cooperation, whereas this perverted version of musical chairs was all about individual determination to succeed at the expense of others. Perhaps it was just about choosing the lesser of two evils . . . or simply another means of punishing and humiliating them. The residents had a lot of revenge to pack into a single week. That alone could explain everything they did.

Narinda took up position by the CD player. 'You will dance properly round outside the rope in a clockwise direction with plenty of skips and high steps. When the music stops you can go in any direction to reach a chair. In case you think you can save your bottoms a pricking by only pretending to sit, you must keep your feet outside the rope at all times while on the chairs. As you see there is a gap between it and the front legs, which means you sit with your feet in front of you. You will not get up again until the losing girl in each round has received her punishment. Do you all understand?'

'Yes, Mistress,' they chorused nervously.

The music began. It was some saccharine, remorselessly jangling, jolly children's party tune, which made the situation more bizarre. Round and round they skipped; six naked handcuffed young women, their breasts bouncing and bottoms swaying, nervously eyeing the chairs and each other. As they circled the backs of the chairs they speeded up in case the music cut and left them stranded, while they slowed when passing before them, snatching glances at Narinda's hand on the CD controls.

As she danced, Tara's mind was spinning. Which was the least unpleasant option? How much would sitting on holly hurt? What would it be like to have ice cubes up her fanny and her tits holly-caned? How long would she have to hang upside down? She'd have to sit on the holly five times to win . . . Oh, God, she couldn't decide. It was easier just being used or punished without having to make choices for herself – Oh no! Was that the hidden lesson?

The music stopped.

For a second they froze, then made a rush for the chairs. Tara was caught round the back of the loop with Cassie just in front of her. Hazel, Daniela and Sian were already finding their seats, accompanied by yelps and gasps as they sat. Tara and Cassie both darted forward to reach the corner chair where Gail, who had been better placed than they, was about to sit herself. Cassie wildly barged Gail aside, knocking her to the ground, and then poised her own bottom over the chair. She must be extra desperate, Tara thought, as she had already had her tits holly-caned while impaled on Fred the dummy and presumably didn't want a repeat.

This left one empty chair next to the end one. Gail was struggling to her feet between Tara and it, blocking her way. She could not get round to it in time.

But Cassie was not sitting down. Her bare bottom was trembling just above the holly-decorated seat, a fearful look on her face. She was too frightened to sit. Feeling sudden contempt, Tara slammed her shoulder into Cassie, sending her sprawling, turned round, gritted her teeth and sat herself down firmly.

Dozens of spines like little needles, driven by her full weight, stabbed into her buttocks, making her choke with surprise. But at least she had the courage to face the pain. Before Cassie could recover, Gail was on her feet and took the free chair beside Tara, sitting down on it with a squeak.

Tara instinctively wanted to squirm about, but she had already deduced what the other girls in the line were just discovering, to the accompaniment of many moans and gasps, that moving would only make the spines dig in deeper. So she sat rigidly still, her suffering alleviated only by the sight of Cassie glaring at her furiously as Warwick strode forward to take her by the arm.

Cassie made a pretty sight dangling from her spread ankles. They put her gag back in her mouth and then tied the rope from a ground peg to her hair, so she could not twist about and would remain facing her audience. Then they took six ice cubes from the Thermos flask and stuffed them into her cleft one by one. Cassie gasped and gurgled as they were inserted, her eyes bulging in horror as the chill began to radiate from her vagina. She gave another yelp as Warwick thoughtfully used a small bulldog clip to pinch her inner labia together to prevent her expelling the cubes.

Gerald Spooner had the honour of delivering the first holly-caning of the game, as Cassie was dangling at a convenient height. He used a backhand swing, and for an old man he had a good eye for a target. Cassie's firm breasts shivered under the swishing blows, her nipples growing perversely hard as the pale taut hemispheres blushed with pricks and scratches.

After the last stroke fell, leaving Cassie dangling shivering and red-eyed before them, Tara made a decision. She'd tried the chairs and seen Cassie punished and knew she'd prefer the ice cubes and the tit-lashing to grinding holly leaves into her bum again. The pain of rising for the next round and feeling the spines pulling out of her flesh convinced her. She would not be the first out of the game now, so her pride was saved, but she didn't want it to look like she was simply giving in.

And so, the next time the music stopped, Tara convincingly tripped over the ground rope as she dashed for the chairs and failed to get a seat. She was suspended beside Cassie, who twisted round to stare at her. Both their heads now being the same way up she could read the satisfaction in her face.

Having the ice stuffed into her was a surprising sensation, actually perversely exciting until the cold began to bite. The nip of the bulldog clip contrasted sharply with the dull chill it sealed within her. Her big breasts, hanging inverted and bobbing proudly free of her ribcage, made fine targets, of which Raj Khan made full use. She yelped and jerked against the rope that bound her hair to the ground, but that did not stop her bouncing globes being thoroughly scoured by the bristling cane. The painful highpoints came when her full hard nipples (she seemed unable to prevent them self-erecting any more) received a couple of blows full on, the spines tearing into her tender flesh. The resulting convulsions of her stomach forced meltwater out past the bulldog clip and to trick through her pubic hair. Just let it reach her burning tits and cool them down, she thought desperately.

But finally it was over, and all she had to endure then was the heavy sense of her head being bloated with blood and the cold of her ice-stuffed pussy. Through misty eyes she watched Gail, Hazel and Daniela suspended beside her in turn. It was strange to see them writhe in their bonds the right way up from her point of view, their breasts bulging upwards and outwards in apparent defiance of gravity, bouncing under their allotted cane strokes. There was something disturbingly exciting about the way the three of them suffered; seemingly unresentful that they were giving pleasure to their audience.

Sian won the game fairly enough as she was the most agile. She almost looked smug as she was hung up beside the others to receive her token punishment, though her small tight buttocks were a mass of red blotches and pinpricks.

They were being made to pay dear for all they had done to the residents of Cheyner Close. But at least their ordeal only had two days left to run.

Louisa Jessop was prettier naked than Daniela had imagined. Perhaps it was because she seemed to be enjoying herself so much.

Though her blonde curls might be artificial her bright blue eyes shone and her smile was warm and genuine. Her big breasts, capped by large pink nipples, bobbed and swayed cheerfully as she moved. Her waist was still trim, her hips full and her skin clear.

It was also evident, as she and Stan handled Daniela with a confidence no doubt born of recent practice, that they were very much in love. Stan Jessop had receding hair but his body was still trim and his erection of impressive proportions. Its prominence might have been due to his affection for his wife or a tribute to Daniela's beauty, or both. It didn't really matter, as Daniela was sure where it would end up.

Though nervous, Daniela did not feel frightened of the Jessops. Yes, they wanted to have their revenge on her for being part of Tara's gang, but they were not cruel. None of the residents she had served these last few nights had been cruel. Roberta Pemberton's advice had been sound. She had apologised for what she had done and accepted without complaint whatever humiliation or punishment they had meted out.

After all, it was only fair and proper. It was what she had agreed to . . . and it was also very exciting.

The Jessops had washed her inside and out, and now they had her in their bedroom, still cuffed and gagged. She felt like a toy as they discussed, stroked and fondled the best features of her body. Daniela knew they were playing with her and she was happy to be part of their game.

They decided how they wanted to use her first.

Laying her down on her back and reversed on their bed, they put a pillow under her head, then raised and spread her legs and tied her ankles to the corners of the headboard. Stan Jessop knelt over Daniela with a holly cane in his hand, and removed her gag.

'Now, girl, do you need a taste of this, or will you do as you're told?' he asked.

Daniela felt strangely calm as she responded, not because she was beyond feelings of anxiety, but because she was now certain of her feelings in a way she had not been just a few days earlier. 'You can cane me if you want, Master, if it gives you and the Mistress pleasure. But I'll try to please you both anyway.'

Louisa laughed, pinching the hard swollen cones of Daniela's nipples. Daniela closed her eyes and sighed blissfully at the gentle torment.

'Look how excited she is, Stan. I don't think this one's going to need any encouragement. She's going to enjoy this as much as we are.'

Louisa bent and kissed Daniela, then turned herself round so that she faced the bedhead, straddling Daniela's torso. Daniela found herself looking up into Louisa's thick dark pubic delta, with its long pink wet gash peeping out from its depths.

'You get Louisa nice and hot and ready, like a good girl,' Stan commanded.

Louisa spread her knees and lowered herself over Daniela. She smelt sweet, fleshy and exciting. Her plump cleft seemed to envelop Daniela. Happily she burrowed into its wet pulsing secret intricacies, nuzzling and exploring its folds and furrows. At the same time she felt Louisa's head lowering between her own spread thighs and her lips brushing over her open lovemouth. Their bodies merged, Louisa grinding her pubes deeper into Daniela's face, the heat growing between them as a slick sheen of sweat.

Stan knelt on either side of Daniela's pillow, clasped Louisa's hips and raised them slightly. The hard shaft of his penis passed over Daniela's head, his balls brushing her nose. She saw his purple cockhead part Louisa's thick wet labia. As it sank into the secret passage beyond, Daniela raised her head and kissed his ball-sack, then licked along the fast disappearing shaft. She felt Louisa's tongue probing the simmering depths of her own vulva.

Stan began to pump in and out of his wife with increasing vigour. Daniela ground her face into the slippery junction of flesh between her master and mistress, kissing and licking where she could, tasting Louisa's mounting excitement as her juices dripped onto her face.

The bed shook when Stan came, followed a moment later by Louisa, who collapsed onto Daniela. Daniela felt fireworks going off inside her own loins and gasped and shivered with delight.

Still infused with post-orgasmic bliss, Daniela recovered to find her face pressed against Stan and Louisa's still-coupled genitalia. Instinctively it seemed she knew what she should do. So, while her master and mistress sprawled on top of her, she dutifully licked both of them clean, lapping up sperm and female exudation alike.

Stan and Louisa held Daniela between them as they rested, playing with her nipples and fondling her pubes. Her hands were still cuffed behind her, but that seemed almost normal by now. She had shared in something adult and exciting that had pleased all three of them.

'How did a nice girl like you get mixed up with Tara's crowd?' Stan asked.

'I suppose it was mostly to help my father, Master,' Daniela explained. 'When we moved to Fernleigh Rise he said I should try to make friends, especially with the Ashwells. Really he thought it might help him do business with Tara's father. And also my mother, who's Portuguese, wanted to fit in with the local community. She did all the right things like going to church and coffee mornings and charity events, but she wanted to be accepted by the people who counted. I thought going about with Tara would mean being polite to people I didn't know, saying I liked music I secretly hated and perhaps going to silly parties and pretending to have a good time. Then they started talking about the Elite Club. It seemed like a bit of a joke at first. I never imagined it would come to this . . . and me being here right now.'

Louisa squeezed her sympathetically. 'It sounds like you got into this just to please your parents.'

'Oh, it's not their fault, Mistress. I wanted to do it. You see, I've been quite shy all my life. Passing the Elite initiation test was a way of proving I was grown up and could be brave and take risks. I'm so sorry it hurt anybody. The way Tara talked, what you felt didn't seem to matter. I didn't think . . .' She trailed off miserably.

Stan lifted her chin and smiled. 'Well, you're making up for it now. Are you ready to pay us back a bit more?'

Daniela grinned. 'Whatever you wish, Master . . .'

Stan knelt on the bed resting on his heels with Daniela's bottom in his lap and her ankles tied behind his back. His cock was firmly lodged inside her. Daniela lay back on the bed with Louisa

174

straddling her head, her engorged labia lathering Daniela's face with her juices, while she leaned forward and kissed her husband passionately.

Daniela squirmed happily under them, straining to pleasure both cock and vagina. Now I've passed the only test that really matters, she thought with joy. I know who I am at last.

Nine

The routine changed the next morning.

After breakfast and their exercises in the garden, they were lined up by the back door and sent into the house one by one. When it was Tara's turn she was taken into their room, where Narinda and Louisa Jessop reinserted her ball-gag, then put plugs of cotton wool in her ears and pads of it over her eyes. These they bound in place with a length of black repair tape that went right round her head, covering both her ears and eyes.

Mute, blind and almost deaf, Tara was led upstairs into what must have been one of the bedrooms. There she was hobbled and made to sit in a corner.

She remained alone in her dark and silent private world for what she guessed was twenty minutes, but which could have been longer. This muting of her senses was horribly disorientating and soon her mind began to wander. What had they done with the others? Mornings were for group punishment sessions. Was she being singled out specially for some reason? And why plug her ears? What new torment had the residents planned for her?

Somebody suddenly loosed her hobble and then lifted her to her feet, causing her to flinch violently. She hadn't even known anybody was in the room.

Whoever had charge of her was wearing gloves, so though she thought it was one of the women, she could not be sure which.

Tara stumbled down the stairs and into the living room. She felt plastic sheeting under her bare feet. What was that for? Her cuffs were removed and she was made to kneel down on all fours. Her hands and feet were pulled apart, brushing across what felt like flattish pieces of wood in the process, and then they were secured with straps.

A rubber-gloved finger covered with vaseline was poked into her anus to grease it, then a short metal sleeve or collar was pushed into the ring of muscle, holding it wide open. Clips were fastened to her nipples. The clips were attached to what felt like sprung cords, dragging her nipples slightly down and back. The other ends connected to the middle of the wooden object to which her ankles were strapped. The clips were uncomfortable but the drag on the cords was not painful as long as she remained still.

What seemed like a stiff rod was clipped to her dangling collar ring. From the way it moved the other end must have been hinged to the middle of the board to which her hands were strapped. As Tara swayed forward slightly, though not too much for fear of tugging on her nipple clips, she felt the resistance of a spring keeping the rod from bending freely.

Then came what she had expected, in some form or another. A slim dildo was fed through the metal ring holding her anus open and a little way up her rectum, at the same time as something rather fatter entered the mouth of her vagina. Tara froze, waiting for the things to be pushed all the way into her at any moment, but they remained as they were. After a minute or two Tara tentatively began to explore the objects as best she could, tensing her muscles so as virtually to suck on them with her rectum and vagina.

Could she have imagined using her private parts for such a task a week ago, she thought wryly?

The dildos, if that was what they were, had a pliancy suggesting rubber, but their tips seemed to be tingling slightly. At first it had seemed a minor irritation, but gradually it began to feel more like growing heat within her most intimate and sensitive sheaths of flesh. Instinctively she leaned forward a little against the resistance of her collar rod to slide the dildos as far out of her as possible and so reduce the sensation, though this pulled harder on her nipples.

Was this it, she wondered? How long would she have to stay like this waiting for something to happen?

The double dildos suddenly stabbed back into her. As their shafts slithered through her wet sheaths of flesh Tara gave a gag-smothered gasp at the jolt of pain she felt. Now she understood the tingling sensation. They had electric coils wound about them, and the deeper they were inside her the more they hurt.

By reflex her buttocks clenched, jerking her forward, only to flinch as her nipple clips pulled her back. But in that moment the dildos had at least withdrawn, leaving only their tingling tips inside her.

However she only had time to take a single relieved breath before they jabbed into her again, harder and deeper. She lunged forward to escape the pain, tearing on her nipples and then jerking backwards to escape their own torment, to find the dildos had once again, if only briefly, withdrawn.

After a while a relentless rhythm established itself. As long as she jerked herself forward the moment she felt the shock-dildos sliding up her it was not too bad, though her nipples were suffering by default. They were of course perversely responding by pulsing with erectile blood, which only made the pinching of the clips worse.

Hurt as it did, she could feel her loins also responding to the relentless shafting, the pain in her nipples and the shocks. She was dripping onto the plastic mat under her ... oh, that was what it was there for! Her body was doing just what she recklessly said she intended when their ordeal started; finding pleasure wherever she could despite the circumstances. Yesterday she had a choice about masturbating on the gutter tongues, but that was after the worst was over. Now she was in far greater pain and even more aroused. At what point did using pleasure to defy her captors and blunt the pain of their punishments become pleasure in the punishment itself? Was she, deep down, beginning to enjoy the whole perverse process? No, surely not. But at the very least, she was becoming a helpless puppet whose juices could be made to flow with little effort.

Her only consolation was that the other girls need never know.

Warwick, Narinda, Jim Curry and Louisa looked down with satisfaction at the ring of straining, bound and blindfolded girls who were unwittingly screwing and sodomising each other in turn. Cameras were ranged about them to record their disgrace.

The girls on their hands and knees alternated with six identical devices mounted on wedge-shaped wooden bases. The wrists of the girl behind were strapped to the corners of one side of the base, while the ankles of the girl ahead where strapped to the other. The cords from the nipples of the girl in front ran back to the baseboard behind her, while the rod fastened to her collar ran down to the board in front.

Rising from the centre of each board was a short length of timber with a pivot ring mounted on top. Through this was slotted a horizontal rod which at one end connected to the collar rod of one girl and on the other bore the electrified dildos which were partway lodged in the rectum and vagina of the girl ahead of her.

The beauty of it was that there had been no need to do anything except switch on Tom Fanning's transformer, which fed power to the dildos, and then wait. The slight twitchings the girls had made as the low-powered tips of the dildos began to irritate them had been transmitted through the rods to the next girl, who responded naturally by shifting forward herself, driving her dildo rod into the waiting orifices of the girl in front of her, before the painful tension of her sprung nipple cords drew her back. This response had been magnified and accelerated as it passed round the ring, causing the girls in turn to react a little more vigorously each time. Positive reinforcing feedback, Tom called it.

Now the impulse was travelling round the ring in under four seconds. The girls had become a living machine formed of sweating bodies, straining twitching buttocks, blushing dripping pudenda and jiggling swaying nipple-tethered breasts. The plastic sheets under them were speckled with drool from their gagged mouths, drops of perspiration and growing puddles of vaginal lubrication. The smell of sweat and helpless arousal filled the air.

The inevitable orgasms began to occur, but they hardly slowed the impulse. Gail came with a moan and a shudder, discharging her juices very prettily. But unknowingly she was being shafted from behind by Cassie, and so had to continue innocently thrusting into Tara to save her from worse shocks. Tara did not know she was screwing and buggering Hazel, who was blindly rogering Sian, who was in turn reaming out Daniela, who was pumping the dildos into Cassie's by now well used passages, and so on.

It was only after nearly an hour, when the girls began to tremble with sheer exhaustion, that the residents took pity and switched off the current to the dildos. Such was the strength of the thrusting reflex to which they had been subjected that it took a couple of minutes for the girls to realise the dildos were no longer shocking them. Only then did they hang their heads, let their backs sag and slowly give way to muffled gasps, sobs and snorting breaths.

Leaving their blindfolds and ear plugs in place, the girls were freed from their straps and clips only to have their wrists cuffed behind them once more. As limp and unresisting as rag dolls, they had to be virtually carried into the garden. Leashes tied to widely spaced stakes hammered into the grass ensured they did not move far. Here their gags were briefly removed so they could greedily gulp down water, and then replaced.

They sprawled almost motionless on the lawn, except for the rise and fall of their chests. Hazel and Gail were so exhausted that they could not find the strength to squat properly and peed down their legs.

By lunchtime they had all recovered sufficiently to eat, if rather unsteadily, bent over on their knees as normal; though their noses had first to be pushed into their bowls so they understood what was before them. When they were done they were taken back to their room, where their bed frames had been laid out once

182

again. Only when they were all secured in them were their blindfolds and ear plugs removed.

Even the dim light filtering through the shuttered living room window made Tara squint, while every slightest sound boomed in her ears. For some minutes after the residents departed she lay still, every muscle aching, grateful simply to lay flat and not have to move. She felt utterly drained and just wanted to luxuriate in the security of her bed-stocks, in which she was always allowed to rest easily with a straight back. She knew that the others were with her once more, but for the moment was too tired to care where they had been.

It was Hazel who asked in a faint voice: 'Is everybody there? What happened to you?'

Feebly they acknowledged their presence. They all sounded as exhausted as Tara was. After they had recovered a little, Gail began to recount her adventures.

'. . . so I was on my hands and knees with clips on my nipples and had these electric prod-things up my bottom and pussy.'

'That's what they did to me,' Sian interjected.

'Me too,' said Hazel.

Realisation slowly dawned.

'Shit!' Cassie said. 'They had us screwing each other!'

'Sorry,' Gail said.

'What are you being sorry for?' Cassie demanded.

'I don't know,' Gail admitted. 'You seemed angry.'

'Of course I'm fucking angry!'

'Did you come?' Hazel asked Gail, ignoring Cassie's rage.

'Oh yeah, though I'm sore now.'

'Me too. How many times?'

'Don't you understand?' Cassie shouted. 'They've got us doing it to each other now!'

Tara had to speak up. 'Get real, Cassie. It just proves what we already know. They can do anything they like with us.'

'But today was tougher than anything we've been made to do so far,' Sian pointed out. 'What's next?'

'Freedom!' Tara reminded them. 'Tomorrow's Friday. The week'll be up and we're quits. Midnight tomorrow it'll all be over and we'll be out of here.'

'If they let us go,' Cassie said gloomily.

'They will,' Tara assured her.

'I wonder if they've got any surprises for us?' Hazel asked innocently.

They felt so tired, Tara wondered if they were up to whatever evening event the residents had planned for them. Perhaps the residents realised the same thing or perhaps they just wanted to keep them off balance because, apart from being held in Gerald Spooner's garden once again, it turned out to be quite different from what she expected.

They were used as living furniture.

Before the other residents arrived, they were led round to Number 9, where it was obvious from the bustle in the kitchen that a garden party was planned. From a beaming Jim Curry standing beside a pile of straps, boards, rods and pieces of carefully cut perspex, it was also obvious he'd been busy in his workshop again. By the time the other residents arrived, the girls had been positioned about the garden and were, literally, ready to serve.

Tara stood very straight and erect. She had no choice. Her ankles were strapped together around a vertical metal rod set in a blockboard base. A second strap round her knees ensured they would not bend. The rod passed on up between her clenched thighs and vanished between the inrolling cleft of her buttocks. Its head was nestled deep in her rectum. She soon discovered that it was an excellent way of encouraging somebody to stand with their back straight.

A flat ring of clear perspex circled her middle just above her hips. It was made in two halves that had been screwed together, nipping her waist tight between them, and made an excellent table for bowls of party snacks or simply somewhere to rest a drink. It was braced by a slim rod running from its rim down to the cleft of her pubes, where its end made an angle up into her vagina and was capped by a rubber ball.

Tara's arms were folded behind her and strapped wrist to forearm. This both showed off the inward curve of her waist and kept them clear of the second tabletop she bore. This was formed out of a crescent of perspex slung hard up under her breasts, so their warm fullness actually rested on the cool clear surface as though being offered up for the delectation of the diners. A strap joined the tips of the crescent behind her back, while the front edge was supported by a short chain clipped to Tara's collar ring. Her mouth was of course filled with her ball gag. Living furniture was expected to remain silent.

So she stood mutely serving her captors, reduced almost as far as it was possible for a living being to be to an inanimate object. She burned softly inside with shame, yet perversely certain at the same time that she made a beautiful and elegant side table that would grace any party.

The other girls had been arrayed differently.

Gail was kneeling with her legs spread, showing off her pubic mound. Her body was bowed over backwards, her stomach outthrust. A rod rising from a blockboard base beneath her was plugged into her anus, helping support her hips. Her upper body was braced by her arms, which she held rigidly straight and vertical, so that her hands pressed to the ground close to her feet. Straps linked her wrists and ankles.

The upthrust double swell of her pneumatic breasts provided the perfect level support for the perspex table top slung about her neck and shoulders. Looking though the clear top you could see her erect pink nipples pressed against its underside. Even gagged her face was perfectly calm, almost dreamy.

Daniela was also on her knees, but with her body bent forward so that her level back provided support for an oval of perspex. Her hands rested on the ground just in front of her spread knees. A chain ran from the strap that bound her wrists together back between her legs to the rod that linked her ankles. A second rod ran up from this rod into the soft cleft of her vagina, ensuring she kept her bottom up. The table she carried was secured in place at the front end by a strap that went around her head and between her teeth, thereby serving also as a gag, and at the other by a spring and hook which curled its tip into the pucker of her anus.

A similar hook and strap method had been used to fasten the table to Cassie's back. She was standing with straight legs strapped to a wooden base and pole like that on which Tara was impaled, except Cassie's pole went up between her thighs into her pubes. She was bent over at right angles from the hip, braced by her arms with her palms resting on her knees. Straps bound her wrists to her lower thighs. Tara noted that Cassie's eyes remained closed most of the time she was serving, while her bared teeth showed very white about her gag strap, as though she would like to bite through it given the chance.

Hazel lay on her back with her legs in the air, wedges on either side of her baseboard preventing her rolling to one side. Her thighs were clenched and doubled up and her arms were clasped behind her knees, where her wrists were strapped together. A chain ran from this strap between her legs to her collar ring. Her shins were bent over so as to be level, and on this her table rested, strapped in place about her calves. A bracing rod from her ankle strap ran down to lodge in her anus. This enforced doubled-over posture exposed the pouting swell of her pudenda and their soft deep cleft to all who used her. Her eyes were bright and excited over her gag.

Sian also lay on her back, but in acknowledgement of her slender suppleness, her posture was more extreme. Her arms were strapped behind her back, which was sharply bent with her legs pulled up and over so her knees touched her shoulders on either side of her head. Her lower legs extended straight into the air, the soles of her feet flat and level. A bar held her ankles apart and from it a chain ran down to her collar ring, preventing her from uncoiling. The table top rested between her feet and her tight bottom, where a short ball-capped rod secured it to her anus.

Of course these living tables were stroked and handled in a casual manner, as one might examine an interesting ornament at a party. Breasts were squeezed, hair tousled, slits fondled, nipples tweaked, but for the most part they were effectively ignored; taken for granted and treated as, well, part of the furniture.

At first this was a relief to Tara. They didn't have to perform any more bizarre sex games and so they had more time to recover for their last night of solo service. All they had to do was stay still. Their various postures were not exactly comfortable, but the straps and rods did most of the work supporting them. They might be a little stiff afterwards, but that was better than riding pogo sticks or being used as golf holes or playing musical holly-chairs ... wasn't it?

The trouble was, even after less than a week, they had come to expect such treatment, like a conditioned reflex. Their present exposure was more than enough to trigger it. Tara could feel the growing excitement and readiness in herself and see it in the others

Expectation could be a terrible thing. Lapsing lyrical, their pussies were weeping; but was it out of shame at their humiliating exposure or sadness at not being used?

Tara hoped the party would end soon.

That night, Hazel knelt on a rug in Roberta Pemberton's bedroom. Her gag had been removed but her hands were still cuffed behind her. The loop at the end of her leash was hooked over a brass knob of the bedframe. Roberta, wearing a red and gold silk robe, was sitting on the silk-sheeted bed looking her up and down. Her intelligent face, framed by a fluffy mass of light brunette hair, held a thoughtful expression. Her lips were pursed, her warm brown eyes narrowed as though assessing Hazel.

As she waited to do her mistress's bidding, Hazel's eyes flicked round the room. It was smaller than her bedroom at home but much neater. A few tastefully framed nude sketches decorated the walls.

Hazel felt both nervous and excited but not afraid. A week ago she had been terrified, but no longer. She had discovered things about herself she had never suspected existed and knew there was even more to be revealed. When Tara had reminded them that it would all be over tomorrow, the first thought that had come into her mind was 'must it?'

'You're quite a little puppy, aren't you?' Roberta said unexpectedly.

Hazel focused her attention on her Mistress-for-the-night.

'Mistress?' she asked in surprise.

Roberta chuckled. 'Not just because you've still got a little puppy fat to lose. And don't worry, it's very appealing. But because I think you're quite easily led. Being the youngest member of Tara's gang, you wanted so much to fit in. And Tara is very persuasive and strong willed. You couldn't help going along with what she said. I bet it felt exciting taking part in all those raids on the Close, or even what you did while I was walking along the road to Styenfold. Remember how you came past on your bikes in a line, freewheeling so I couldn't hear you, then each of you called out some obscenity as you passed? But all the time you kept your faces perfectly straight and didn't even look at me. From a distance nobody would guess anything had happened.'

Hazel gulped. Roberta seem to know her so well. This was the bit she hated to think about. She had felt a kind of shame about being naked and humiliated at first, but that had quickly turned into a weird sort of thrill. This was different. This was the true shame you felt when you knew you'd done the wrong thing.

Roberta continued: 'Or the times you were helping at charity auctions and fetes, like such good little girls. You'd be behind a stall and smile sweetly right in my face. Then, when nobody else could hear, still smiling, call me a slut or dyke or worse. What it got you, of course, was the older girls' respect. Acting tough, even if you didn't mean it.'

By now Hazel was feeling sick and wretched. 'I'm so very sorry, Mistress,' she sobbed. 'I know it was wrong now. It was just like the way you said. I wanted to be part of the Elite. You people didn't seem to matter. Tara said you were only –' Hazel paused and took a deep breath, sniffing back tears. 'No, that sounds like I'm laying it all on her. I could have said no but I didn't. It was easier to go along, to pretend what we were doing was clever when it was really cruel and stupid and I know it's my fault ... and if you want to hurt me back, I'd understand.'

Roberta was smiling sympathetically at her. 'What I wanted above everything else was to hear you say sorry and mean it. And now you have. I understand how hard it can be. Sometimes there are pressures to do things you can't resist. I've done a bit of acting myself. Not that you'd have seen any of it and I wasn't very good, but I know about pretending to be something you aren't ... or not being something you are.' She studied Hazel closely for a moment. 'Would you like me to show you something secret?'

'If you want, Mistress.'

Roberta took a magazine from the side table and laid it out on the bed where Hazel could see. It was a men's magazine, and an old one by the look of the cover. Roberta flicked through the pages until she reached a particular photo set. Hazel goggled at it in amazement. The model's name was given as 'Samantha' and her hair was longer and darker, but it was unmistakably Roberta Pemberton, perhaps ten or fifteen years younger than she was now. Roberta smiling at the camera as she cupped her breasts, or sat with legs splayed holding her pussy wide, or knelt doggie-fashion with her rear to the lens showing everything.

'I needed the money, you see,' Roberta explained, 'and this seemed like an easy way of making it. I did a few photoshoots then I got into porn films. Some

190

of the things we've put you through the last few days were my idea. Now you can guess where I got them.'

Hazel looked at her with new respect. She'd never have imagined anybody living in Cheyner Close would have had the nerve to do something like that.

'You looked . . . lovely,' Hazel said. 'I mean, you look lovely now, Mistress, but even better then.'

'Thank you.' Roberta smiled. 'But the most important thing was that I got out of the business before I was in too deep and nasty. Best decision I ever made. Knowing when something is a game and when it isn't. When to play and when to be serious. When it might hurt you or somebody else, and when it's safe to have fun. That means taking responsibility for yourself and your actions. And that's being an adult, not a puppy.' She reached out and stroked Hazel's hair. 'Even a very sweet one.'

Hazel's heart thudded in her chest with delight at her touch, even as her loins turned liquid. Slowly she said: 'But puppies do need to be punished sometimes, if they've been bad, Mistress.'

Roberta raised an eyebrow. 'Yes, they do.'

Hazel felt a lump in her throat. She understood. It was going to be all right. 'This puppy needs to be punished,' she said meekly. 'To help her remember her lesson. Please, Mistress . . .'

'I see. Well, I have one memento of my porn years that might interest you. It's a prop from a very perverted but fun film I was in that I managed to acquire. Do you want to see it?'

Hazel nodded eagerly.

Unhooking her leash, Roberta led her though to the spare room. In the middle of the floor was a very large, brightly painted rocking horse, mounted on a sturdy frame. There were three or four slotted levers set in the horse's rump just behind the saddle. It was a moment before Hazel saw the horse was clearly male, as shown by the huge erection protruding from under his belly.

Hazel giggled at the sight. 'He's lovely, Mistress.'

'And there's more to him than meets the eye. Get on and see.'

Roberta helped Hazel onto the saddle, which was real leather. As she straddled it she saw there was a slot in the top of the saddle. When she sat down her vulva and the lower cleft of her buttocks hung over it. Roberta slid Hazel's feet into the stirrups, which were rigidly fixed to the horse's sides, and then buckled straps around her ankles to hold them in place. When she was done she slid her hand up Hazel's leg and thigh, across her lower stomach and down into the soft folds of her lovemouth.

As her fingers toyed with the bud of her clitoris, Hazel shivered and sighed with pleasure, her eyes half-closing.

'Happy?' Roberta asked.

'Perfectly, Mistress.'

Roberta unclipped Hazel's leash and reversed her collar. Smiling, she pulled out a hook which had been protruding from a hole under the horse's tail. The hook was connected to the end of an elastic cord which unreeled from some inner recess until Roberta could clip it to Hazel's collar ring, now dangling at the back of her neck. The cord resisted her leaning forward in the saddle, though she could stretch it a little. Roberta cupped Hazel's breasts, sending another shudder of pleasure through her, and rolled her reddened nipples thoughtfully under her thumbs.

'These still look a little sore,' she said. 'Perhaps they should have more rest.'

'Please, Mistress,' Hazel said. 'I'm here to be punished.'

'As you like.'

She lifted the reins from where they had been hung about the horse's neck. Hazel saw they had a pair of spring clips fastened to them. These Roberta snapped about Hazel's plump nipples, adjusting the slack on the reins until they began to lift Hazel's pale soft mammaries towards the bit rings in the horse's mouth. Now Hazel was confined by the tension of the elastic cord fastened to her collar and that of the natural elasticity of her stretched breasts. She could lean a little forwards by pulling on the rear cord, but leaning backwards would be torment for her breasts.

Roberta moved round to the levers behind the saddle. Hazel drew in her breath as she felt a thick rubber dildo pushing its way up through the slot in the saddle and into her anus. She squirmed by reflex, feeling her anal ring bulging under its girth, but of course she could not escape its impaling length. There was no choice, not that she wanted any, but to sit up even straighter in the saddle, her eyes watering.

'That will hold you steady,' Roberta told her, 'while this will please you . . .'

A second dildo rose up beside the first, this time nosing into her pudenda. But it stopped when it had barely breached her tunnel mouth.

'It's worked by pistons under the rockers,' Roberta explained with a smile. 'The more he rocks, the faster and deeper it goes . . .' As she spoke she slipped off her robe, leaving herself quite naked.

She still had a lovely body, Hazel saw with delight. Her hips might be slightly fleshier and breasts heavier than in the photographs, but her skin was clear, her legs were shapely and her waist still held an hourglass curve. And she was clearly aroused. Large brown nipples stood up firmly from their parent globes, while the swelling tongue of her inner labia pouted from her pubic cleft.

From a small wardrobe, Roberta took out a riding crop and swished it through the air a few times.

'Now, I want to see you ride until you come, young lady!' she told Hazel, flicking the crop across the soft swell of her stomach and causing her navel to pinch inwards.

Thrilling to the sudden pain, Hazel began to roll her hips to and fro, thrusting out her tingling belly in an effort to get the horse rocking. Slowly it responded. She found its rhythm and began to work with it.

Roberta swished her crop again, this time catching the underside of her breasts, making them bounce at the end of their nipple tethers. 'Harder!' she ordered.

Sobbing with joyous fear, Hazel strained to obey, her swaying upper body tugging on her clipped nipples, stretching them and her breasts. As the rocking motion of the horse increased, the phallus aligned with her vagina began to bore deeper into her. To her delight she realised it bore a collar of bristling rubber prongs which teased her clitoris as it sheathed itself again and again into her hot wet depths. As her wooden steed galloped faster her juices seeped from her gulping vulva to stain the polished leather of the saddle.

The crop flicked across her flank, coiling round her buttocks.

'This is the home straight,' Roberta said. 'I want to see you gallop over the finish line . . .'

Hazel rocked even further in her saddle, heedless of the torment she was causing her nipples, riding the plunging phallus to the end. She gave one last jerk and then shrieked with delight, dousing the shaft with her orgasmic exudation.

As she slumped in her bonds, panting from her exertions, Roberta whispered in her ear: 'Wait till I get you into bed, little puppy . . .'

Ten

Their final day of captivity in the Close began with the familiar routine.

They were brought to Number 2 from the other houses, stiff, sore and aching from last night's use. Breakfast was laid out on the floor and they ate it eagerly from their bowls, hardly troubled that their hands were cuffed behind them, or that they had to flatten their breasts to the ground to lick it all up. Then they were taken outside for a full hour's vigorous drill and exercise.

It was when they were brought back in, cheeks rosy from their exertions, that they saw today would be different.

A simple stage, built of wooden crates floored with sheets of hardboard, had been set up at one end of the room. Dustsheets pinned to the ceiling provided a backdrop and closed off a small backstage area. Two stacks of crates draped in blankets formed the sides of the tiny proscenium, while a beam resting between them supported a pair of full-length dark blue velvet curtains. The stage was lit by anglepoise lamps taped to simple stands set up on either side of the curtains.

Along one wall were piled several cardboard boxes. Some were packed with odds and ends of old clothing, while others contained rope, chains, belts and straps, a bundle of bamboos and thinner basket canes, assorted dildos and vibrators. On a side table were bottles of mineral water, a travelling clock, the CD player, a stack of cassettes and CDs, scissors, sticky tape and glue, a reel of garden wire, a jotter pad and pencils.

As the girls blinked at this strange assortment, Narinda explained.

'I said you should take note when you did those dances, because tonight you are going to put on an erotic variety show for us. It will start at nine o'clock and you have the whole day undisturbed to write and rehearse. There are old clothes and things here for you to use as props. If you want anything else, within reason, we can get it. You can do any sort of acts, even song and dance, as long as there's plenty of sex, punishment and humiliation involved. All of that's got to be genuine, of course. Basically, we want to see more of the sort of thing we've been doing to you this last week, except this time you'll be doing it to each other. And as an incentive for you to perform well . . .'

She pointed to the other side of the room, where two more of Jim Curry's constructions rested.

They were both identical. On lengths of timber fitted with splayed bracing feet, were mounted three thinner wooden rods fastened to heavy coil springs, so that they angled upwards a little off vertical. Bolted to the tops of these rods, one on each side, were pairs of translucent plastic food storage bowls with their open mouths facing upward. Dangling straps fastened to the outside of the paired bowls made them resemble surreal bra cups. The girls looked closer and shivered. Bras are not normally studded with carpet tacks. These had been hammered through the plastic from outside, so that the insides of the bowls bristled with a dozen or more tiny black metal spikes.

'The idea is that you are bent over them with your feet tied to the beam and your boobs dangling inside the bowls,' Narinda continued. 'They're different sizes to fit each of you nice and snugly, and they have the same number of tacks in each, so they should prick you just as much whether you're big or small. It won't hurt if your tits are not moving, but if you were to be caned really hard, for instance, everything will start bobbing around and then I think it would hurt quite a bit. Which is the idea, of course.'

She grinned at the expressions on their faces.

'It'll be our final judgement on you. This is how it works. You'll start off the performance marked down for 25 strokes each. The more entertaining you are the more points will be taken off that number. At the end of the evening what's left will be added together and divided amongst you. You won't get away without any punishment, of course, but you can make it as few strokes as possible if you've put on a good show. That should encourage you to work with each other and try really hard to please us.'

The girls were gaping at the fearsome devices and each other, still trying to take in the challenge facing them. They were hardly aware of Warwick undoing their handcuffs until they realised he and Narinda were standing by the door.

'We'll leave them there until this evening,' he said, pointing to the six ominous pairs of bowls mounted on their frames. 'It might help keep you focused. We'll bring you lunch at the usual time.'

And they went out, locking the door behind them.

The room was silent. Nobody appeared inclined to move. Tara felt unaccountably lost and helpless, as it seemed did the others. For the first time in a week they were ungagged and unbound, except for their collars, nor were any residents standing guard with a holey cane. They rubbed their wrists and looked about them, unsure of what to do with their sudden, relative, freedom. They were not secured to their bed frames and nobody was telling them what to do. They could walk about the room as they liked, pick up things with uncuffed hands using untapped fingers, stand up, sit down, almost anything . . . But instead they just stood there uncertainly, as though waiting for orders.

As the seconds dragged on Tara feared they had all forgotten how to think and act for themselves. Could the habits of freedom really be erased so easily and quickly? No, that was ridiculous. Then was it just them? She felt she should say something, make plans, but the possibilities seemed daunting.

Then Cassie broke the spell.

Moving stiffly at first but with gathering confidence, she walked over to the bundle of canes, selected one, and turned towards Tara with a murderous glint in her eyes.

'I said I'd get you for dumping us in this shitty mess,' she hissed, slashing the cane viciously though the air and catching Tara a stinging blow on the arm. As Tara stumbled backwards in surprise, Gail, Daniela and Hazel sprang on Cassie, trying to restrain her. Sian hovered in the background, as though uncertain which side to join. Such was the force of her anger that even the weight of the three girls clinging to her could not stop Cassie crashing into Tara. The five of them tumbled to the floor in a tangle of naked limbs.

The shock of Cassie's attack finally penetrated Tara's numbed mind, and she found herself bellowing: 'Stop it! Cassie – save it for the fucking show! You want revenge, then save it for later! When it can do us some good!'

Then Sian waded in and helped pull Cassie away from Tara, shouting: 'This is so stupid. Stop it, Cassie. What are we doing fighting each other?'

'I hate her!' Cassie snarled, red-faced and panting.

'Yeah, well I don't think much of her either, but kicking the shit out of each other is still crazy. The residents are the ones who're meant to be punishing us.'

'Please don't fight,' Hazel begged, her face distraught.

'Keep out of this,' Cassie spat. 'You may be a happy fucking slave, but I'm not. She deserves a slapping!'

'For what?' Gail said sharply. 'For getting us caught or making the residents' lives a misery for so long? Yes, Tara started it but we should have known better. I think you're still denying the truth by trying to lay all the blame on her. We're all guilty and it was right we should be punished.'

'Speak for yourself,' Cassie said, but without much conviction.

'I think ... we've all got grow up to and start behaving like adults,' Hazel said with quiet conviction.

'None of us are what we were a week ago,' Daniela added. 'Maybe you should accept that and move on.'

'They're right,' Sian told Cassie. 'You're just feeling sorry for yourself. I felt the same, but I think I'm getting over it. You've got to take things as they are. Let's just get today done, OK?'

The tension gradually drained from Cassie's body and she sagged in their grasp. Tentatively they let go, though still looking at her anxiously.

'Stop staring at me like that,' Cassie said. 'I won't do it again.' She looked at Tara. 'What did you mean, save it for the show?'

That paralysis of mind and body had left her now, and Tara found herself thinking and talking fluently once more.

'They want a show with lots of S&M, so we'll give it to them. You want to give me a good hiding, that'll be your chance. We'll write it into the script. And the better you do it the less we all get hurt later. Win win for you, right?' She felt the familiar warm fluttering in her loins as she spoke the words, but they were only the simple truth.

Cassie looked at her narrowly. 'You're a cold calculating pervy bitch, do you know that?'

Tara smiled as though it was a compliment. 'Yep.'

'I still won't talk to you ever again after this is over.'

'You can do what you like afterwards, as long as you do what you must to get through today. Well?'

'I haven't got any bloody choice, have I?'

'None of us have.'

'And I suppose you'll tell me to make the best of it and try to have fun?'

Tara shrugged. 'Why not? This'll be the last performance of the Elite Society. One night only. And then . . .' She took a deep breath, turning over strange possibilities in her mind, but contented herself by concluding: '. . . then we grow up and move on.'

'There's lots of stuff we can use in here,' Hazel called out.

While they had been talking, she, Daniela and Gail had begun rummaging in the props boxes.

'Somebody must have kept these for dressing up or charades or something,' she continued. As they watched she pulled out a long tasselled scarf and wrapped it round herself, giggling and flouncing about to show off. Gail tried on a battered woman's hat with a large floppy brim. Daniela was turning a vibrator on and off while smiling thoughtfully.

'Look at them,' Cassie exclaimed. 'You'd think they were looking forward to this.'

'At least they're enjoying themselves,' Tara said. 'Why don't we join them?'

Sian had picked up the jotter pad. Now she stood over Tara and Cassie looking purposeful. 'We've got about eleven hours to write, rehearse and design this perverted sex show, so let's get started. First: what do we call it?'

The large star-emblazoned felt-tip-drawn card propped up at the foot of the stage read: THE ELITE FOLLIES.

Cancan music stuck up and the curtains were drawn back to reveal the girls in a line arm in arm, minimally dressed in assorted boas and lengths of tinsel. The backdrop behind them was decorated with cut-out paper stars, balloons and musical notes.

The residents seated in the other half of the room applauded loudly. To one side Tom Fanning stood by his tripod-mounted video camera, recording the performance for posterity.

The girls began high-kicking in time, yipping and yelling, their breasts bouncing and jiggling merrily, showing off their glitter-dusted pubes. The line broke and Tara, Daniela and Gail twirled about, spread their legs and stuck out their bottoms, while Cassie, Sian and Hazel leaned over them and pulled their labia wide to expose their shiny pink clefts. Reaching into the dark pits of their fellow performers' vaginas they began pulling out lengths of coloured paper streamers and throwing their coils out into the audience, who laughed and clapped.

The line re-formed. In time with the rise and fall of the beat, they sang:

'We're so sad that
we gave you all so many tears.
As a sor-ry,
we hope you enjoy our pretty rears.
Let us show you
all our nooks and all our crannies,
By the end you'll
know every hair on our fannies!
Cane our tits!
Cream our slits!
We hope to keep you all in fits!'

They bowed and slipped away into their impromptu theatre's tiny wings. The curtains closed to loud applause.

A moment later Tara, now wearing a top hat and red-sequinned jacket unbuttoned to expose her breasts, pushed through the curtains to stand on the narrow strip of stage. The sound of bare feet scuffing on the boards and urgent whispers told of the scene being hastily reset behind her.

Tara took off her hat and bowed humbly. 'Ladies and gentlemen, welcome to the one and only performance of the Elite Follies, where six misguided young women are demeaned and degraded for your delight and delectation. Our first act this evening is a daring feat of distending vaginal dexterity. I give you Daniela the Dildo Swallower!'

Tara stepped aside and the curtain drew back to reveal Daniela resting upside down in a chair with her legs splayed wide in the air, so that the cleft mound of her pudenda rose like a little hill between them. A sheet of black card had been taped to the back of the chair to highlight her brightly lit pubes. On a table beside her were several dildos and vibrators. Background music started up with an eastern swirl, full of reedy pipes and jingling tambourines, of the kind more usually heard accompanying the Indian rope trick.

Daniela picked up a dildo, threw her head back and sensuously licked the rubber shaft, then reached up between her legs and slid it into her anus. She next picked up a vibrator, turned it on, and slipped it into her vagina, which she first spread wide with her fingers, showing off her dark passage to the audience. Then she took up another dildo and slid it into the passage beside its buzzing predecessor, stretching her vagina a little wider.

By the time she was forcing the third dildo in beside the humming vibrator, her splayed legs were trembling and she was sweating and gasping with effort, the lips of her labia stretched painfully taut about the bundle and her pubic hair glistening with lubrication. When she had finally forced it in she gripped the sides of the chair and orgasmed before their eyes, a trickle of her juices running down her belly to her navel.

The curtain closed on her to loud applause. This time Hazel came out in front wearing the top hat and sequinned jacket.

'And now a lesson to us all. The moral is: Do not behave badly in class, or else you'll come to a painful end. At least, your end will be painful. I give you Tara and Cassie in: The Naughty Schoolgirl.'

The curtain parted to reveal Cassie, wearing a long gown and mortar board, standing in front of a blackboard. Opposite her Tara slumped in a chair. Her hair was tied in bunches, she was dressed in a white shirt and short pleated grey skirt, and had a sulky expression on her face: the image of a petulant schoolgirl.

Cassie tried to teach but Tara kept interrupting, flicking paper pellets and calling Cassie names. Eventually Cassie took out a cane and ordered Tara to bend over with her rear to the audience. She lifted Tara's schoolgirl skirt to expose her bare bottom, and then, with evident relish, proceeded to give her six of the best. The blows sent shivers though her flesh and Tara's yelps of pain were clearly genuine, as was the blush that spread across her buttocks.

The curtain closed to particularly loud applause.

Daniela appeared in the hat and jacket to announce the next act. 'Is there no end to the disgraceful behaviour of young women today?' she asked. 'We hope not otherwise this show ends right here! We now bring you a government safety information film, featuring two disgraces for the price of one, really pissing each other off at high noon: Hazel and Gail!'

The curtain parted to reveal a wobbly painted cactus standing in front of the backdrop. A large plastic sheet had been laid across the stage. Background music from the climax of a spaghetti western came on. Hazel and Gail entered from opposite wings. They were naked except for large Mexican hats and toy gunbelts slung about their waists.

They circled each other warily, hands hovering over their gunbutts as they waited for the other to draw. As the music rose towards the inevitable climax they both suddenly squatted down, resting back on their hands. Lifting their hips and splaying their legs they squirted jets of pee onto each other's bodies, splashing it freely over groins and breasts, all the time shouting: 'Bang! Bang! Bang!' like children.

As their streams of pee died the pair kicked and shuddered comically, then lay still. An anonymous hand from the wings held a large sign out for the audience to read:

The curtain drew closed to the sound of laughter and Tara appeared as the compère once more, while there was a lot of rustling as the plastic sheet was hastily cleared away behind her.

'I'm sure we shall all take that important warning to heart the next time we shoot peas. And now, for your entertainment, we have a trial of strength between two of our tightest performers. Forget the football or the cricket, even beach volleyball doesn't get as good as this. It's the new sport that's bound to make the Olympic Games next time: a Tug-of-Pussies between Sian and Cassie!'

The curtain parted to reveal Sian and Cassie limbering up theatrically and flexing their biceps. Daniela stood between them holding a rope with two sets of three close-spaced rubber balls strung on it at each end.

The girls shook hands, then turned away from each other and bent over, spreading their legs wide. Daniela fed the sets of balls one by one deep into each girl's vagina, then stood back.

'Pussies, take the strain,' she said. Still bent forward with their bottoms raised, Sian and Cassie clenched their thighs, put their hands to the floor and edged apart until the rope was taut between them.

'Pull!' Daniela said.

The two girls began to tug, scrabbling at the floor for grip, leaning at impossible angles while trying to make small steps forward, only prevented from falling by the rope joining their vulvas, which were visibly bulging as they strove to contain the balls stuffed within them.

205

The audience began cheering the girls on, shouting out their names.

Back and forth they tugged, until suddenly a shiny ball popped out of Cassie's cleft. The jerk as the rope momentarily slackened caught both of them by surprise and a ball also slipped from between Sian's pouting labia. Cassie strained to capitalise on this loss and with a heave pulled another one out of Sian's tight slit with an audible pop. But Sian tugged back and managed to extract a second ball from Cassie's by now dripping pubes to even the score. Each girl had one ball left inside her, and they were gasping and groaning in an effort not to let it go.

Finally it was Sian who could not prevail against Cassie's slightly greater weight. The last ball popped free from her and both girls went sprawling. Sian crawled off as Daniela helped Cassie up, the rope still dangling from her vagina, and raised her hand aloft, proclaiming her the winner to much applause.

Sian appeared though the curtain in the top hat and jacket to introduce the next act. Her cheeks were still flushed and she walked with her thighs clenched and hand clasped to her pussy. The audience chuckled.

'And now, ladies and gentlemen, we have a special musical item for your pleasure. I'm sure you've all heard of the "Doh, Re, Me" song from "The Sound of Music". Well, now the Elite Mammary Campanological Choir present a version like you've never heard, or seen, before. Move over, Julie, we're busting to get started!'

The curtain parted to reveal Tara, Gail, Hazel and Daniela kneeling over the backs of a row of chairs facing the audience. Their arms were folded neatly behind them so that their breasts dangled freely. Bells of different sizes, scavenged from the sets Narinda had used, were clipped to their nipples.

Clasped between her teeth Tara had a pair of strikers made from hard rubber balls mounted on sticks. Sian took these from her and waved them about like a conductor's baton before starting to pummel the row of eight breasts before her, making the dangling bells ring. As she struck each breast the girls sang out the note and part of the song associated with it. When she reached the end Sian went back down the line hitting the bobbing mammaries harder, this time just getting a tuneful oww! and a jingle each time.

The recital was received with great appreciation. The girls gave a mass jingle of their nipple-bells as the curtain closed.

After a moment Gail came out dressed as the compère, having quickly removed her nipple-bells.

'Pets can be so embarrassing at times, and girl pets are the worst,' she said. 'They'll put their noses just about anywhere, even where they don't belong. But it's no good telling them off. It's their nature to sniff out exciting scents and of course they're completely uninhibited. Which can be quite a problem for owners, especially when they're trying to maintain their dignity at all costs. We present Hazel, Daniela, Sian and Cassie in: Walking in the Park.'

The parting curtains revealed cut-out trees and a lamppost had been added to the stage. Sian and Cassie entered from opposite wings. Their breasts were still bare, but they wore old-fashioned feathered hats and scarves with long loose skirts, and swanked along to suggest they were clothed in the height of fashion. They were holding Hazel and Daniela on leashes, who padded along on all fours like dogs, sniffing at the cut-out trees and pretending to cock their legs on the lamppost.

Sian and Cassie greeted each other, speaking in exaggerated cut-glass accents.

'Why, hallo!'

'Oh, hallo! Such a long time since I saw you last ...'

As the women chatted, Hazel and Daniela sniffed cautiously at each other's faces, then bottoms. Obviously liking what they smelt they cocked their legs for the other to lick their pouting pubes.

Sian and Cassie suddenly realised what their pets were doing and pulled them apart, smacking their bottoms and telling them not to be naughty girls. Hazel and Daniela squatted down mournfully, looking at each other with lolling tongues as their owners continued to talk. Then an idea appeared to strike them.

They put their heads up their owners' skirts and began to lick them out, to the delight of the audience. The women were clearly too embarrassed to admit to what was going on, apart from surreptitiously slapping at the bulges moving under their skirts, or what it was arousing them. So they continued to talk in ever more strained and high-pitched voices about how hot the weather was getting, giving them an excuse to fan themselves with their hats in an attempt to control their emotions.

The pair eventually orgasmed with such force that they fainted theatrically, leaving Hazel and Daniela free to mount each other face to fanny and consummate their affection, noses and tongues buried in their eager clefts.

The applause was still ringing round the room when Tara, dressed as compère once more, pushed her way through the curtain. She was holding one hand modestly over her pubes.

'And so, ladies and gentlemen, Masters and Mistresses, we come to the finale of our little show. We hope you have enjoyed it as much as we have. And we hope you've given us lots of points for effort, because we all know what that means: not prizes but fewer pricks in our tits! And now we take you back for a second visit to the Follies . . . but this time for some hot anal action!'

She took her hand away from her pubes to reveal a very large upstanding carrot. The base of it was lodged in her vagina and it was held erect by a sling and supporting belt of garden wire. The tapering end had been trimmed slightly with a potato peeler to resemble the head of a penis.

The sight set the audience chuckling as Tara took off her hat and jacket and tossed them aside, then went back through the curtains. The cancan music started up and the curtains parted.

All six girls came on and formed a high-kicking line, all showing off phallic carrots mounted like Tara's, As they danced, the vegetables bobbed about in their slots, alternately stretching their labia as though in a yawn, then rubbing up against their clitorises.

A renewed flush was colouring their cheeks as they sang:

'Now we are about to go,
we hope you enjoyed our sexy show!
You've seen our bums,
seen us kiss and seen us come!
Then there was the spanking,
and the peeing and the wanking!
Now as a send-off,
we're going to screw our ends off,
Just to please you!
What a farce,
to have a carrot up the arse!
Up our bums!
Up our bums!

Here we come,
here we come!'

As they sang they formed a circle, clasping the hips of the girl in front as they went round high-kicking with their outside legs to show off their stuffed pussies and puckered bumholes. The line got tighter and closer as each girl found the anus of the one in front with the tip of her vegetable dildo and then shoved her carrot-cock into it. They gasped and shuddered as their rectums were plugged, then their hips began to pump urgently.

It was not faked. They were all caught up in the wild rhythm of the music, the perverse exhilaration of doing something so abandoned before so many eyes, but above all the need for release from the state of arousal that had grown within them through the show. They sank to their knees, clasping and kneading the breasts of the girl in front of them, pinching erect nipples, while all the time driving into her rear even harder. They were shredding the carrots smooth with their frantic sodomy, staining their bottoms orange, sweating and straining until they shrieked and came, collapsing into a sweating, panting, exhausted heap of naked girlflesh.

Dimly they were aware of the music trailing off, but it was drowned out by the wave of wild applause.

Still woozy from their exertions and cushioned by the post-orgasmic glow suffusing their bodies, the girls slowly gathered themselves together. They pulled the battered remains of the dildo carrots from their sopping and now orange-lipped vulvas, then formed a line across the stage, kneeling submissively with their legs wide and hands clasped behind their necks, ready to accept the judgement of their captors. At least we've done our best, Tara thought, feeling oddly proud of the fact.

After the exchange of nods and muttering between the residents, Major Warwick stood up and addressed the girls.

'That was a highly entertaining show. Well done to you all!'

Tara felt a ridiculous glow of pleasure at his sincere praise. Out of the corner of her eye she saw smiles on the faces of the others.

'And since you've performed so well and shown proper contrition,' Warwick continued, 'we have decided you will suffer the minimum punishment we can let you get away with. Just five strokes each!'

Tara shivered, but five was a lot better than twenty-five.

'As it's fine I think we can leave the frames out in the garden,' Warwick said. 'Now, for the last time, on your feet and march out there smartly.'

They did so, followed by the residents.

The evening air was cool. The last flush of sunset was still tinting the sky. Somebody switched on an outside light while others produced torches and, of course, cameras. This would really be their last performance, Tara thought.

Their hands were cuffed behind them. Thoughtfully the residents had towels ready to rub dry their sweat-streaked bodies and water bottles to replenish the fluids they had lost during the performance. Ball-gags were then pushed between their teeth and blindfolds bound across their eyes.

Dumb, blind and helpless, they were guided to the place on the frames that matched their cup-size.

Tara trembled as she was bent over, unseen hands guiding her breasts into the waiting bowls. She gave a muffled squeak as a pinpoint grazed her left breast. Then the rims of the bowls enclosed her dangling mammaries and the top of the supporting rod pressed against her sternum. The strap was buckled across her back, holding her tight. Her ankles were tied together about the base of the sprung upright rod so she could not brace herself. She wobbled and another tack point grazed her.

The bowls enclosed her breasts completely, making a seal where their rims dug into the surrounding flesh, so that she felt a warm humid closeness building about them. Her rising nipples brushed the bowl bottoms.

She heard the residents moving about, felt the frame tremble as the other two girls who shared it with her were strapped into place. Who was beside her and who was mounted on the companion frame opposite? Whoever you are just try to keep still, she pleaded silently.

The first stroke of the cane seared into her buttocks without warning. She yelped in pain and jerked by reflex. Her big breasts bounced within their tack-lined prisons. Tara screeched again through her gag as her soft flesh was impaled upon what felt like a hundred pinpoints. Panting, she tried to steady herself for the next stroke.

There was a swish of displaced air, the cut of flesh, a yelp of pain, the frame rocked, setting her breasts bobbing again and inflicting a few more lesser pricks. Whoever it was bound beside her had received the stroke. A few seconds later the frame vibrated again, but not quite so severely.

They were punishing them in rotation, administering one stroke at a time.

Waiting for her turn was agony. She just wanted to get it over with, almost willing the next stroke to land, welcoming the pain, because it meant she was one step closer to the end. The tanned heat in her buttocks she could cope with, but the bee-sting fire coursing through her breasts was so sharp it was nearly unbearable. Yet in a twisted way it also felt wonderful because it meant it was nearly finished!

Then the last stroke fell and it really was over.

She heard Warwick announce: 'Your punishment is complete. We'll leave you here to think over what you've learned this last week. At midnight you will have fulfilled your part of the bargain and no longer belong to us. Then you will be released.'

Tara heard the diminishing rustle of footsteps, the click of the outside light going off, and all was still in the garden.

She drank in the silence, the tranquillity, the cool air soothing her burning buttocks, wishing only that some of it could flow round her pincushion breasts. But it was over. She heard a hiss and splutter as one of the other girls relieved herself on the grass. It sounded very loud in the stillness.

The minutes slipped by towards midnight and freedom. And then back to the real world to do – what? She was not sure.

Then Tara became aware of a moving presence in the garden.

Even as she strained her ears, a pair of hands took hold of her hips, the head of a cock parted the lips of her pussy and slid up into her. There was nothing she could do as the man shafted her, not even struggle. Her breasts still bobbed against the pins as they coupled, but only lightly because of his steadying hands. She was actually responding when he came inside her. She heard him sigh, then he pulled out of her now hot slot, which let him go reluctantly.

'Well done,' a voice whispered in her ear, and then was gone. She was almost sure it had been Warwick.

And why not? He only said the punishment was over. They still belonged to the residents to do with as they wished until midnight.

213

A few minutes later fingertips brushed across her outthrust bottom. She tensed, but instead felt the frame begin to shake as somebody else received a secret visitor.

Cassie had flinched so hard when the fingers first caressed her pudenda that she inflicted more pricks on her sore breasts. The fingers were replaced by a probing tongue that took full advantage of her pouting and exposed private parts, making her shiver with helpless delight. As it did so another pair of hands caressed her body and then warm lips were pressed to her ear and whispered: 'When you stop acting like a stuck-up bitch you're quite nice.'

It was Hilary Beck.

With fingers and tongues the pair gently but inexorably brought Cassie to a contained but intense orgasm. She felt suddenly very alone when they finally left, and had to console herself by listening to the other nocturnal visitors as, one by one, they paid their last respects to their chosen playthings.

Gail knew who had come to her from the rough strength of his hands, even before his penis tunnelled into the depths of her lovemouth. She relaxed completely as he used her, not minding the few additional jabs her breasts received in the process. It was still her due to pay and she did so happily.

When he had done he whispered: 'I've never had anything prettier than you in my workshop . . .'

Hazel thrilled at Roberta's touch when it came out of the night. She wanted to say so much as the older woman kissed and caressed her, but her gag allowed only muffled sighs of pleasure. As her fingers stirred the slick hot depths of Hazel's honeypot, Roberta said softly: 'Be good, little puppy . . .'

Narinda Khan's touch roused Cassie from her post-orgasmic reverie. She was surprised to get a second caller. It surprised her even more when she felt a man's hands grasp her hips from behind and then a very hard stiff cock slide into her still wet pubes.

'That's Raj,' Narinda said softly, taking Cassie's shoulders in her hands while her husband set about enthusiastically screwing her. 'Playing with you and your friends this last week has been getting him so excited I've had great sex every night. So as a reward I said he could have one of you. And he chose you because he felt sorry for you dancing so badly for Fred.' She sighed. 'Men are so funny. Perhaps you don't agree. But at least he thinks you deserve something. Think how terrible it would be if a pretty girl like you was not even worth screwing . . .'

Sian's slim body trembled as Tom Fanning sodomised her one last time. He did have a thing for girls' arses, she thought dizzily, gasping from the stretching of her anus and the painful jiggling of her small breasts within the pin-studded bowls. But at least it was a familiar cock. And when he whispered: 'You've got a much hotter bum than Cassie,' she actually felt proud.

Louisa Jessop had pulled Daniela's gag out so that she could kiss and lick her bared breasts while Stan had her from behind. Daniela was delighted to be sandwiched between the two of them once again and hardly noticed the extra pricking her captive breasts received as she bobbed and swayed on her sprung mount.

215

When they were done Louisa kissed her and whispered: 'Don't be a stranger . . .'

Tara gasped through her gag, jerked out of her doze as a garden hose was played over her groin, washing away the drying sperm which had trickled down her thighs. The hose moved on, eliciting squeaks and yelps from the others as they received their sluicing down in turn.

Her blindfold was removed and she saw Narinda Khan illuminated by the outside light. She worked her way round methodically removing blindfolds, releasing the straps that held them bent over the frames, then freeing their ankles.

They straightened their aching backs, cautiously lifting their breasts from the pin bowls, a little fearful of what they might find. Narinda had come prepared with a wet sponge smelling of antiseptic and a towel. After the sweat had been wiped away only a blush and a few small pinpricks remained. It had felt so much worse.

Warwick appeared, having stowed away the hose. He checked his watch and then removed their gags, cuffs and finally their collars. 'It's midnight,' he said. 'You're all free.'

For a minute they just stood there, fingering their now bare necks which felt oddly exposed. They smiled foolishly at each other.

Warwick handed Tara a torch and pointed to the bottom of the garden.

'We've put a stepladder over the fence to make it easy. You can walk back to your camp across fields.' He smiled wryly. 'You should know the way well enough.'

'But . . . what about our clothes and things?' Tara asked, just stopping herself inserting the word: 'Master'.

216

'Oh, we took them round to Simon Pye this morning and told him when we'd be releasing you. I'm sure he'll have waited up. How he receives you is up to him. You see, you've paid off your debt to us, but you still have to square things with young Simon. Of course, if your consciences are clear, then you have nothing to worry about.'

Eleven

The notice, boldly written in red felt-pen, was taped to the back door of Simon Pye's cottage. It was clearly visible under the porch light, but otherwise the windows of the cottage were curtained and dark. The girls huddled together under the tiny porch roof while they rang the bell and knocked, but there was no response.

Their tent, shower and portable toilet were now stowed away in the back of the hired MPV, still parked where they had left it. The vehicle was securely locked and there was no sign of the key, or their clothes.

However something had been added to the back garden since they had left it a week before. Tucked in to one side of the cottage was what might have been an animal pen, built out of salvaged timbers, chicken wire and ragged sheets of bituminous roofing felt. The floor of the pen was covered with straw and was just high enough to sit upright within. Resting against the inside of its front wire wall was a low galvanised metal trough. Beside it was a plastic bucket of water with a length of clear plastic tube sticking out of it like a large drinking straw. In the far corner there was an empty metal bucket.

A door had been let into one side of the pen, but it was padlocked shut. The other entrance was through two smaller sliding doors only high enough to pass through on all fours, linked by a narrow tunnel built out of wooden slats. The doors were locked by large vertical sprung bolts that could only be operated from the outside. At the moment both doors were open and their bolts raised.

'I really thought this whole bloody nightmare was over,' Cassie moaned as they knocked again on the cottage door.

'Where is he?' Sian wondered.

'Either in bed deliberately ignoring us, or else in the woods having a good eyeful,' Tara said.

Uneasily they surveyed the looming mass of trees arrayed about the cottage. From somewhere in its depths an owl hooted. The girls unconsciously edged a little closer.

'We can't blame him for wanting to get his own back,' Daniela said. 'If we had got in trouble with the police they'd have found him minding our secret camp. And he made some of our equipment. They'd probably have accused him of being an accessory.'

'I'd have told them he was innocent,' Tara said.

'But what if they hadn't believed you?'

'We haven't been very nice to him,' Hazel said. 'He must feel so insulted. The way we've been using him –'

'Don't go on about it!' Cassie snapped. 'Let's work out what to do next.'

'Isn't it obvious?' Hazel said, tapping the notice. 'That's what he wants us to do to show we're sorry.

220

The cage or pen is meant for us as well. He's had a few days to plan something special. Maybe he got some ideas from the residents.'

'No way am I playing doggy games for him!' Cassie snorted.

'It made a twisted sort of sense with them at the Close,' Sian said. 'We really messed about with their lives for months. We hurt them so they hurt us back and now we're quits. But with Simon we only –'

'Cheated and lied to him,' Gail interjected. 'Called him sick names he didn't deserve. Got him involved in crime –'

'All right, so we treated him pretty shittily,' Sian conceded. 'But letting him screw us – and worse – is way too much!'

To their surprise Daniela said: 'I think it will be good for us. I mean to help clear our consciences. Simon's part of what we've been doing wrong. Treating other people like they don't matter when they do. We have been acting like bitches. I want to draw a line under it. To feel, well, clean. I'd rather pay back more than I owe than less. If Simon wants to have some fun with me, I'm willing to let him.'

'It's all right for you,' Cassie sneered. 'You like that sort of thing.'

'Maybe I do, but I also know I feel happier now than I have for months,' Daniela replied calmly.

'And I feel my cunt's already had enough use to last a year, my tits are like old pincushions and my bum's sore as hell!' Cassie retorted.

'It doesn't look too bad,' Hazel observed innocently.

'There is another reason to go along with this,' Tara said. 'What if someday Simon gets an attack of conscience and decides to tell our parents, or even the police, what we've been doing? Letting him punish us

221

in private not only proves we're genuine, it also pretty well guarantees he'll keep quiet.'

'So being good little bitches for Simon makes us even, buys us insurance and washes our souls clean at the same time!' Cassie exclaimed.

Tara held out her hands to indicate their collective nakedness. 'What else have we got to offer? Maybe we can bargain for a day's slavery and be ready to go up to two. He knows we can't be away from home much longer.'

'At least he's quite good looking,' Hazel reminded Cassie. 'It might be – fun.'

'You call that fun?' Cassie retorted. 'You and Gail and Daniela are all masochistic, slavish, submissive –'

'You came a few times as well,' Hazel pointed out.

'I didn't have any choice!' Cassie insisted.

'I don't think we should try to bargain,' Gail said slowly. 'We're not the Elite any more. I think we should leave it up to Simon. Do whatever he wants. Accept any punishment. Like Daniela said: we need to do this for ourselves as well.'

Hazel and Daniela were nodding gravely.

'She's right,' Tara agreed, knowing in her heart what careless presumption had already cost her. 'We let him decide.'

'All right,' Sian sighed, 'I suppose there's no other way. At least we've had plenty of practice.'

'There's six of us and only one of him,' Hazel said. 'How many times can he have you?'

'It isn't the sex that's worrying me,' Sian replied. She turned and raised her voice, as though addressing the wood and any hidden watcher they might contain: 'OK, we accept! We'll be your bitches! Let's get this over with!'

There was no answer.

Gail said: 'If we're really sorry and genuinely ready

to accept our punishment, we shouldn't need to be told what to do next.'

She walked over to the pen, got down on her hands and knees and shuffled inside. Through the wire they saw her sit up and look around. 'Come on,' she called to them. 'It's not that bad.'

Hazel and Daniela followed her into the pen. Sian shrugged and went in after them, with a reluctant Cassie at her heels. Coming last, Tara backed into the tunnel, sliding the outer door across as she went. Its bolt snapped down, locking it shut.

'Why did you have to do that?' Cassie demanded.

'So we're not tempted to change our minds,' Tara said, pulling the second door closed so that its bolt dropped as well.

They huddled together for mutual warmth. The low roof kept the dew off and the night air was still. As they got as comfortable as a bed of straw allowed, slumber began to steal over their tired bodies. It had been a busy day, Tara reflected.

'At least we get to sleep without being tied up and screwed half the night,' she pointed out.

'Yeah . . . inside an animal pen . . .' Sian yawned.

'Remember, when we get through this, I'm never talking to you again,' Cassie reminded Tara sleepily.

Tara blinked, bleary-eyed, waking slowly.

Her exposed flesh was chilled, though the straw under her had kept the rest of her body moderately warm. But as she stiffly raised herself onto one elbow the stalks stuck to her skin, which she found was indented with its latticework pattern. Still, she had slept, and surprisingly deeply.

Now it was another dew-fresh morning. She could see out through the mesh of the cage into the garden . . . and saw things that had not been there the previous night. A sack and a bamboo cane lay by the outer door of the cage, while only a few paces further was a garden cart with low planking sides, riding on four small bulbous rubber tyres. A pair of heavy ropes had been fastened to the base of its towing handle. The ropes had hooks on their ends and a pair also spliced into their lengths.

Then Simon Pye appeared from round the corner of the cottage and walked towards the pen. He was carrying a large saucepan.

Tara scrambled across the pen, setting the others stirring and yawning. She grasped the wire mesh, staring up at Simon as he looked down at her. His lips were tight and there was a look of determination and self-assurance on his normally placid face she had never seen before.

'Simon . . . I just want you to know how sorry I am for the way I've treated you in the past,' she said, trying to keep her voice level. 'That was wrong and you didn't deserve it. If it had come to it I would never have let you take the blame for making those things for me. And I promise I'll do everything I can to stop my father selling off Manor Woods. I'm not trying to get out of this and you can do what you like with me now, but I just wanted you to know how I feel.'

Hazel had joined Tara. She said: 'I'm so sorry for the way we treated you. It was stupid and wrong. I'll do whatever you want to make it up to you.'

Gail was also pressing herself against the wire. 'I hope you can keep on living here, Simon. These woods are lovely. I'm sorry for mixing you up in our stupid games . . . and you must do what you want to me.'

By now the rest had crowded about them. Daniela spoke up: 'I hope you stay here as well. We deserve to be punished. Have fun with us until you feel we've properly paid you back.'

Sian sounded genuinely contrite. 'I should never have called you "stupid" like that. I was being a stupid cow myself. That's on top of the way we've used you and were never even properly grateful. So you just ... do what you have to to make it right.'

Cassie's words did not come easily, but she forced them out. 'Calling you "Simple Simon" was nasty and I'm very sorry for it. I won't blame you if you treat me worse than the others for saying it. I'd want to get back at somebody for talking about me like that. Do what you want now, as long as when it's over I know that it's for good and we'd be even. Please say you'll ...'

Simon was frowning at them. He put down the saucepan, picked up the bamboo cane and tapped the inner pen door meaningfully. Only now did they see it had a copy of the notice on the back door of the cottage pinned to the inside. The line BITCHES DO NOT SPEAK seemed to jump out at them.

They fell silent. Gail sat back on her heels, spread her legs and clasped her hands behind her neck in the position Warwick had taught them. The others quickly copied her. Tara felt her nipples rising automatically, standing to attention in a way that would have pleased the Major.

When he was satisfied they understood, Simon tipped the contents of the saucepan through a slot in the wire into the metal trough.

'Eat,' he said simply.

They crowded shoulder to shoulder as they bent their heads over the trough, not even attempting to use their fingers. It was salted porridge, which they ate greedily.

When they had licked the trough clean and drunk from the water bucket, they re-formed their line, kneeling on display once more. Simon, who had watched them in silence, nodded slightly, as though approving of their posture.

He emptied the sack out onto the grass where they could see. There were bundles of plastic-coated nylon clothesline, half a dozen large metal rings, what seemed to be small mesh baskets with pairs of straps trailing from them, plus several smaller lengths of rope and cord.

'You've been bad, you've hurt people, you've been real mean bitches,' he said simply. 'So that's the way I'm going to treat you. I don't want to hear another word out of any of you 'til I say, because bitches can't talk, right?'

They nodded meekly.

He slid open the inner door of the pen and pointed his cane at Gail. 'You: get out here,' he said.

Nervously, she went down on all fours and shuffled into the tunnel.

The cart rattled along the twisting path through the woods. Simon was standing on the platform holding its raised towing bar like a tiller, occasionally calling out directions to his team of sweating bitches. Tara gasped at every bump and turn, but she dared not fall out of step. She was part of the team, harnessed to the cart and to the other girls like animals. It was painful, degrading, exhausting and cruelly exciting.

Tara, like the rest, was bound in an improvised harness of plastic-coated nylon clothesline. Its many coils circled her waist, crossed between her breasts and over her shoulders, looped about her upper arms, pulling them in to her sides, and bound her wrists behind her back. The cord was perfectly smooth but it was tight and cut into her flesh. A large metal ring had been tied to the coils where they crossed her navel, so that it dangled against her lower belly. Clipped to it was one of the snap-hooks spliced to the left-hand towing rope. This ran forward from the cart between Tara's legs and then Daniela's and finally Cassie's, linking all their belly rings. The right-hand rope ran from the cart through Gail's legs, then Hazel's and then Sian's.

As they strained to draw the cart the ropes were dragged up between the slippery lips of their now sodden pubes, their twisted cords grinding and rubbing and teasing their swollen clits. Tara drooled round her muzzle at the sensations this generated. She was not gagged but muzzled like a real bitch. A plastic-coated wire cup, designed for some short-snouted breed of dog, was strapped in place over her nose and mouth. An extra thick wire crosspiece had been added inside the muzzle so that it acted like a bit.

As if that was not enough, Simon had ensured each of his pairs stayed shoulder to shoulder and in step by tethering them together with short lengths of rope clipped between their navel rings and also lighter cords fitted with spring clamps linking their breasts. Tara's right nipple was thus linked to Gail's left, tugging painfully as their big sweating breasts bobbed and bounced in and out of synchronism.

And so through the woods they went, following a meandering path that led eventually to the spot where a birch tree had fallen, opening a gap in the canopy overhead. Simon called a halt and jumped off the cart, while the girls sank down gratefully onto their knees.

The birch was in the process of being cut up. Some of the main trunk had already been reduced to firewood-sized blocks, while the thinner straighter branches had been roughly trimmed into manageable

227

lengths and were stacked in piles. It was these that Simon began loading onto the cart, while the girls trembled at the prospect of hauling such a weight.

The cart took about half the pile. Simon tied a cord in series to the middle of each of their nipple tethers, then began to lead them back along the path. They had no choice but to follow, straining to draw the cart along, whimpering as the heavy tow ropes cut into their vulvas even as they stained it with their secretions. They walked hunched over to reduce the angle through which the ropes grated across their tender flesh.

The return journey to the garden seemed twice as far as the outward one, and they were gasping and panting by the time they arrived. But Simon gave them little time to rest. He unloaded the branches, jumped on the cart and turned them round for a second load. When they had delivered the remainder of the branches to the garden, he took them back once more to collect a load of firewood. The last trip almost finished them. It was the heaviest of them all. Pulling the roller over Gerald Spooner's lawn had been light work by comparison. But they were just mute beasts of burden, and what they felt did not matter. With tottering steps they finally dragged the cart back to the garden and sank to their knees; breasts heaving and splattered with drool, hair lank with sweat, eyes smarting, thighs wet with lubrication and pubes raw.

Once the wood was unloaded, Simon freed them from the cart but left them harnessed and nipple-tethered. He briefly removed their muzzles so they could drink, then allowed them to sprawl on their backs to recover, their legs spread wide to allow cool air to soothe their sore groins. Meanwhile, he began laying out the branches on a little secluded patch of lawn next to their pen and trimming them with a saw and axe. Through her multitude of aches and pains, Tara wondered what he was building and whether it had anything to do with them.

Simon extended the arrangement of nipple tethers for lunchtime and also put one of the thinner birch branches to use. He cut it into two waist-high posts and hammered them into the ground in the shade of a tree. The stakes were far enough apart so that the six of them could kneel in a row, shoulder to shoulder, between them, with the short lengths of spring-clipped cord linking their nipples to those of the girl on either side. The two on the ends had their nipples fastened to the posts.

Simon took off their muzzles and sat in front of them eating his own meal, while tossing them chunks of bread, cubes of cheese or slices of apple. They soon learned to catch the titbits in their mouths like dogs being fed treats, though if they moved too energetically they risked giving both their nipples and those either side of them a nasty yank. Anything they missed they had to hunker down awkwardly and pick up off the grass with their teeth.

Nevertheless, their nipples were painfully erect and pussies shamefully moist as they watched Simon eat and snapped at the morsels he tossed them. They were helplessly expectant, waiting for the moment when he would start screwing them, as he must be planning to do, secretly wondering who would be first.

But he kept them in suspense while he put them through another degradation. He had dug a small latrine pit in a patch of rough grass near their cage. Replacing their muzzles he led them, still nipple-tethered together, over to it. One by one they had to squat over the pit with their thighs spread wide and pee and void their bowels while he watched.

Cassie and Sian stared fixedly at the ground while they falteringly relieved themselves. Tara did not try to avoid Simon's grinning face, but met his gaze calmly, trying to show she accepted this further indignity without looking as though she was actually attempting to defy him. Daniela and Hazel both gave Simon shy smiles through their muzzles, suggesting mingled embarrassment and excitement at him witnessing their private functions. Gail gazed at him with curious intensity, as though readily offering her shame in payment for past misdemeanours.

When they were done he unselfconsciously wiped them clean with handfuls of grass, adding one more intimate defilement of their persons. Was this calculated? Did he know he was sowing the seeds of shame that would haunt them for months if not years? How could they ever see him tending their gardens back in Fernleigh Rise after he had wiped their bottoms clean? Yet what possible reason could they give their parents not to employ him again?

Simon tethered them round a tree while he used a post driver to hammer a ring of six trimmed branches into the ground until they stood at about head height. He then nailed lighter branches across the post tops to form lintels, bridging the gaps between them. Tara chewed on her bit as she watched the structure take shape, knowing it was meant for them, fearful of how it would work yet perversely desperate to find out.

Simon brought out a high stool from his cottage and set it down under the crossbars. One by one he laid the girls on their backs across the stool and raised and spread their legs so he could tie their ankles to the lintel posts. He lifted them easily onto the stool as

230

though they were children. Tara had not realised how strong he was. It made her sense of helplessness seem even more profound.

Once each girl's ankles were bound, Simon ran more rope through the coils of her harness where it crossed between her breasts and tied its ends to the crossbar by her ankles. The tension bent her like a fishhook until her head was level with her knees. Then he pulled away the stool from under her bottom, leaving her dangling in the air.

Soon he had all six of them suspended and facing inward while he stood at the centre of the ring, a cane in his hands, grinning at the spectacle they made as they displayed their intimacies. Six exclamation marks sculpted in flesh: six red-lipped pussy clefts gaping and glistening, dotted underneath by dark anal puckers. In turn they looked helplessly back at him through the V's of their widespread legs.

Slowly Simon unzipped his flies, releasing an erect penis of impressive dimensions. The girls squirmed in their bonds. He walked round the circle stroking and pinching their pouting lovemouths, sliding his fingers into their honeypots and drawing them out wet and scented, bringing forth muffled groans from his captives. Tara could smell the sensual aroma of apprehension and need filling the air, knowing she was contributing her share to the intimate perfume. Just get it over with, she shrieked silently to herself.

Simon began to cane them. Not hard strokes, but enough to paint blushing stripes across their thighs and taut backsides and cause their anuses to pinch tight as the tendons on the backs of their knees contracted, making them jerk and sway in their bonds. Because of their doubled-over postures their pubic mounds protruded beyond the stretched flesh of their haunches and so received a proportion of the cane's stinging kisses. But such modest pain had by now become hard for their bodies to distinguish from foreplay, and their labia gaped even wider as they blossomed in anticipation while their clitorises rose brazenly from their hoods.

Then Simon dropped his cane, grasped Gail's hips and drove his hard cock into her sex. At last, Tara thought, wishing it could be her.

But Simon only thrust half a dozen times into Gail's passage before he withdrew, transferring his now glistening manhood to Sian's waiting hole that was hanging beside her. Another half dozen pokes, and then he moved on to Hazel. Tara understood. This was for his pleasure, not theirs. Which cunt he came in did not matter to him, nor the frustration it created. There was a cruel downside with six to one when you were one of the six.

Tara tried desperately to come when it was her turn, but six thrusts were not enough to bring her off. He pulled out of the hot clutches and moved on to Daniela. He came halfway through pumping out Cassie's vagina. He sagged against her for a minute as he recovered, then withdrew his softening prick from her sticky cleft. Tara saw anguish written large on Cassie's muzzled features.

Now their master was satisfied, while they were left agonizingly wanting. How could they ever have been brought to this state, Tara thought? Having to contend with not getting what they wanted when they wanted it was torture! Was that a reflection on their privileged lives up until now? Had they been spoilt? But it got even worse.

Simon used some short springy twigs to wedge their vulvas wide open, pushing apart the thick outer lips of flesh and their finer inner petals, so that the smallest details of their private anatomy were open to the air, and they could look across the circle into the dark crinkle-mouthed passages of the girls opposite. Then he simply left them, exposed and unrequited.

Time passed with agonising slowness as the pain of stretched tendons behind their knees and across their lower backs grew. Flies buzzed curiously around their fragrant exposed pudenda, a few settling for a closer examination despite their desperate wriggles. It only made their miserable state seem even more acute.

At teatime Simon emerged with a large plate of sandwiches, cake and bottles of water. They were silent as he briefly removed their muzzles to feed them, pleading with their eyes not their mouths. It did no good. He took the twigs from their labia and made the rounds a second time with his cock, satisfying his pleasure even as he brought them once more to heights of frustrated lust. When he was done he replaced the twigs in their aching lovemouths and left them again.

Not long afterwards the need came upon them, one by one, to pee. With their labia pulled back their exposed urethras squirted like fountains. The intimate sensation of passing water in such circumstances roused them once more, but still not enough to bring release.

It must have been gone eight that evening when Simon finally let them down. He took off their muzzles, removed the twigs holding them open then freed their ankles and set them on the ground. They lay still doubled over, groaning softly, too stiff to move, their tendons on fire and their stretched pubic lips slowly contracting.

He carried them to their cage like sacks of potatoes, opened the larger padlocked door and laid them on the straw on their backs side by side and head to toe. He spread their legs again and re-tied their ankles to the salvaged poles, then tied the poles to the sides of the cage. Then he shut and locked the door and left them.

There was a long silence as they luxuriated in being allowed to lie flat and straight, not even caring they were still in harness or how cold they might get that night. Finally Cassie said in a small, miserable voice:

'He's broken me. I admit it. I'll do anything to be allowed to come. You'd think after a week of all that sex I could go a day without more . . . but I can't. I'm ready to beg him to screw me properly, if that's what it takes.'

Tara agreed but was too exhausted to say so.

'He'll do it . . . if we ask him in the right way,' Gail said. 'We've got to show we've learned our lesson . . .'

The next morning, as Simon approached the pen with their breakfast pot of porridge, he was greeted by a series of mournful whines and howls such as miserable dogs might make.

He looked in on them, bound as he had left them, their nipples crinkled with cold but eyes bright. 'So, my bitches are unhappy, are they?' he asked.

The girls nodded and whimpered even louder.

Simon opened the cage, freed their ankles and allowed them to crawl outside on their knees. Despite their stiffness they crowded round his feet, kissing and licking his boots, looking up at him and panting hopefully, then turning round and presenting their backsides for his inspection.

'I get it. Maybe later, if you're good girls . . .'

He poured the porridge into the trough and they ate it all up, licking the metal clean. When they were finished he did not put on the muzzles but simply pointed to the latrine pit. They scampered over in stooping postures, not needing to be reminded that bitches kept low. When they squatted to pee they looked proud and excited that he should find it pleasing to watch them.

Simon took them for a long walk in the woods, and they fussed around him like eager puppies, sniffing at tree trunks and rubbing against his legs. He threw sticks and they fetched them. The woods were a delight to roam about in naked. When the need came again to pee they did so as dogs might; cocking their legs against trees. They forgot the time and were surprised to find Simon leading them back to the cottage for lunch. They ate on the lawn. When they were done they looked at him again pleadingly, whimpering to be allowed relief.

'I suppose, as you've been good bitches, you've earned it. Get in a line all facing the same way . . . closer, noses up bums . . . Now Hazel, Daniela and Tara you roll over on your backs, legs wide. That's right. The rest get your heads down between the legs of the one in front and your muffs down on the face of the one behind . . . Right. But none of you is allowed to come until I've had you, got it?' They nodded and whimpered their assent, trembling with anticipation. 'Now start licking!'

They tongued each other uninhibitedly, past caring about pride or shame, willing to do anything to gain the relief their bodies demanded. Cassie was first in the line. Though she had her face buried in Hazel's crotch she had nobody to lick her upturned and hungry pussy. Simon knelt down behind her, unzipped his flies and slid his shaft into her wet cleft.

Such was her state of pent-up arousal that a dozen thrusts were all it took to send her into orgasm. Simon rolled her aside while she was still shuddering, opening the way to Hazel as she lay on her back, her upturned face covered by Sian's grinding pubes.

Simon shuffled forward, lifted Hazel's splayed legs until her hips left the ground and he could slid his cock into her already wet cleft. A short bout of determined thrusting was all it took to push her over the brink. He dragged her twitching body out from under Sian and rolled her aside to join Cassie. Sian's haunches rose eagerly to meet him and he drove hard into her slim body, rocking her on her knees. She came inside half a minute and was easily pushed aside onto the grass.

Daniela's hot vagina welcomed Simon's cock and she soon came joyfully. The hot split peach of Gail's sex responded with equally uninhibited passion, and she was in turn rolled aside onto the grass with a look of perfect delight on her face.

And then there was just Tara left, sprawled on her back, her legs splayed in utter abandon, lifting her hips desperately to meet him, offering herself, her eyes hollow with need. As they coupled she knew his hard cock was carrying the juices of all the other girls with it and mingling them with her own and thought it was filthily, disgustingly wonderful. She cried out aloud as his sperm was pumped inside her and she was free to come, letting herself be carried away on a wave of raw pleasure that sucked her down into warm pink-tinted depths of total satisfaction and blissful release from all cares.

An unknown time passed. As the rosy haze that had enveloped her melted away, Tara realised she was still lying on the lawn beside Simon's cottage but something had changed. Her clothesline harness had been removed.

It hurt to lift her arms, the flesh of which was scored with red and purple grooves from her bonds. Her fingers seemed to belong to somebody else, but she was free.

In a daze she looked around her. The others had also been unbound and were sprawled awkwardly on the grass trying to pump life back into their numbed limbs. Simon was standing over them, a bundle of clothesline in his hand and a couple of black bin bags by his side.

'We're even,' he said simply. 'If you need time to get over it you can put up the tent again and stay the night. Your clothes are in the bags.' For a moment his eyes met Tara's. 'I hope you meant what you said.'

She nodded. 'I did.'

Simon took one last look at them, then turned away and went back into his cottage.

It took them almost half an hour to regain enough feeling in their arms and hands to dress themselves. The fabrics felt oddly rough and heavy to wear. Putting up their tent took longer but they managed it. They hardly spoke a word, whether because there was too much or too little to say Tara was not sure. Even Hazel, Gail and Daniela seemed subdued, though perhaps for different reasons to the others. They made a sketchy snack meal and retreated to their sleeping bags early to wrestle with their thoughts.

They were free. It really was over. But what now?

The next morning, Monday, as they were packing away the last of their gear into the car, Simon appeared with a parcel that had just been delivered. It was from Katy Mitchel in Cornwall and it contained their phones, cards and receipts, plus a note hoping everything had gone well and saying she was eager to hear all the details.

Tara didn't know whether to laugh or cry. Could she ever dare tell Katy the truth? Well, irrelevant as it was now, at least that was one part of her deception which had worked perfectly.

Simon had been watching her, perversely making her feel more embarrassed being clothed than she had naked. Now he said bluntly: 'It wouldn't have worked.' (No 'Miss Tara' now).

The echoed word disconcerted Tara. 'What?'

'Pretending you were all in Cornwall. If anybody'd checked. Car hire firms keep records of the odometer readings. That would've shown you'd never been there.'

I know nothing, Tara thought savagely as she drove them out through the cottage gate. I'll have to start all over again . . .

Twelve

It was a Friday evening seven weeks later.

Tara was preparing to go out. Though it was well into autumn the weather was still mild, so she was lightly dressed in a matching black hooded sweat top and jogging pants. She carried with her a single travel bag.

Her parents thought she was going to Brierston, a village about fifteen miles away, to stay over the weekend with Milly Raymond. In fact Tara was doing no such thing, though Milly was ready to cover for her should the need arise. Until recently Milly had been merely a casual acquaintance, but Tara had contrived to strengthen the friendship during the last month or so. Milly, who was overly romantic, thought Tara was secretly visiting a boyfriend of whom her parents disapproved. Tara tried not to think too badly of this shortcoming, reminding herself that Milly was providing her with an essential alibi.

Tara breezed out of the house, calling out goodbye to her parents, who said to give their regards to Milly. They were pleased Tara was making new contacts. After her 'return' from Cornwall it had become obvious the relationship between her and the rest of her old friends was now strained. They assumed there had been some sort of group falling-out while on holiday, but Tara had refused to go into details. From what she heard later the others had done much the same with their respective families. Shortly afterwards, Daniela's father had come round to see her father saying that he hoped whatever had happened between their daughters would not spoil their business relationship. All Tara's parents had done, after accepting her silence on the subject, was to observe that at least she had come back from her holiday looking very fit and with a nice even tan.

Tara had seen little of the others since then. In chance encounters Daniela had smiled and nodded, but had not initiated any conversation. Hazel and Gail had chatted briefly about nothing of importance, but seemed distracted. Sian and Cassie had simply ignored her. A couple of times she had seen Gail on the path across the fields that led to Manor Woods and Simon Pye's house. Tara wondered if she had been tempted back by the beauties of the woods or the size of Simon's cock or both. If so then it was none of her business. They did not want or need her any more.

As for herself, she tried to avoid Simon when he came round to tend their garden. For his part he made no sign that anything had changed. She would never forget what happened, of course. In many ways she did not want to, because it had been part of a major event in her life. It was just that he was not what she was looking for. But she had kept her promise and talked to her father about conservation and the importance of preserving woodland for wildlife. He was now looking into whether he could get more money from the Government or European Union for keeping Manor Woods in its natural state than developing it.

Tara got into her new red Mini, a birthday present, and set off, ostensibly, for Brierston. But after turning out of Fernleigh Rise she quickly took another turn off the Styenfold road into Nooks Lane. Shortly she turned on to a track which led to an old wooden garage, half-smothered in brambles and set beside an equally venerable cottage. Tara unofficially rented the rambling structure from Mrs Merril, whom she had met while doing 'good works' as a cover for her war on the Close. The old lady was also a romantic at heart and Tara almost felt guilty about deceiving her.

Padlocking the rickety garage doors on her car, Tara checked her watch then pulled her sweat-top hood up and headed back the way she had come though the gathering gloom. Crossing the Styenfold road at the turning, she scrambled up the grassy bank opposite. She was about to push her way through the scrubby hedge onto verge of the field when she heard voices.

Crouching low she saw two figures approaching along the edge of the field, chatting in low but excited tones as they went. She recognised them at once. It was Hazel and Daniela.

They passed by Tara heading in the same direction she planned to go: the route they had all taken from Fernleigh Rise when they made their clandestine raids on the Close. But what were they doing here?

Tara shadowed the unsuspecting pair as they made their way along the edge of the field and then round the perimeter fences of Cheyner Close. Where were they going?

They stopped two thirds of the way round outside the back fence of Number 7, the house shared by Hilary Beck and Rachel Villiers. The small gate set in the fence, which had been heavily locked and bolted during the war, now opened silently on oiled hinges.

The two girls went through and closed it behind them.

Tara crouched in the shadows, debating whether she should follow them. She didn't want to upset her own plans, yet she had to know what was going on.

Giving them another minute to get clear, she slipped through the gate.

Light was streaming out of the uncurtained kitchen windows. Tara cat-footed up the garden and round to the smaller side window of the kitchen, which looked out over the narrow passage where the bins were kept, and cautiously peered inside.

Hazel and Daniela were kneeling side by side on all fours on the kitchen table. Both were completely naked and beaming happily. Hilary and Rachel were fussing round them, petting and stroking the girls as though they were prize pets on display at a dog show. Full pendant breasts, already tipped by swollen erect nipples, were cupped and squeezed. Smooth buttocks were patted and pinched. Pouting pubic clefts were tickled and vaginal passages probed.

And in response to this intimate inspection the pair were acting just like excited puppies. If they had tails they would have been wagging them. They were loving it.

At a word of command they sat back on their heels and extended their arms. Disposable cotton gloves were slipped onto the hands and then these were bound round with tape, turning them into 'paws'. Another order and they knelt forward again so that collars could be buckled round their necks and bright red ball-gags were stuffed into their mouths. Going down onto their stomachs they lay flat and crossed their wrists behind their backs so that the two older women could cuff them together.

Hazel and Daniela's responses were quick and sure.

Tara suspected they'd gone through this little routine more than once before.

The latch of the front gate rattled. Tara shrank away from the window, crouching down into the shadows between the wheelie bins.

Roberta Pemberton walked past and around the side of house to the back door. Tara heard the murmur of voices from the kitchen for a minute or two, then Roberta reappeared leading Hazel on a leash. The light from the window illuminated the younger girl's face as she passed. She was looking up at her mistress with joyous excitement.

The pair went out of the gate and round out of sight to Roberta's house. Tara stood up and went back to the window.

Daniela was now standing between Rachel and Hilary as they caressed and fondled her; telling her everything they were going to do with her, while she squirmed in delight. Then each woman took hold of one of Daniela's nipples and led her out of the kitchen. The light went out, leaving Tara alone in the dark alleyway.

Well, she thought, they all had somehow to fill the void left in their lives by those nine incredible days they had spent as captives and slaves. She knew ordinary life was, by comparison, rather dull. Hazel and Daniela had chosen outright submission and simply handed themselves over to those they most wished to serve. She did not begrudge the girls whatever happiness they could find with their respective mistresses, but that way was not to Tara's tastes. She had a different objective, though it was not far away.

Tara made her way back down the garden, through the gate and turned right, taking the few paces that led to the back of Number 8. Aware of the excited thudding of her heart, she felt along the fence until she came to the pair of loose boards. She pried them open and slipped through into the narrow space between the fence and garden shed.

All was still and quiet. She stepped out onto the lawn, heading towards the house . . .

A strong hand closed over her mouth while another caught her wrist and twisted her arm behind her back.

'You're late,' Major Warwick grunted in her ear. 'That's going to cost you . . .'

Tara struggled but he was too strong for her. She would not have had it any other way. Tara Ashwell did not give herself to just anybody. She had to be conquered by somebody who proved himself worthy of her. A mature man, not a boy . . .

Warwick dragged her through his back door, kicking it shut behind him, and into his kitchen. Bending her across the kitchen table he said: 'Girls who sneak round other people's gardens at night must expect to get punished.'

'You can't do this to me!' Tara shrieked, her stomach knotting with exquisite anticipation.

'I can do anything I like to you, girl.'

There was a rope coiled waiting on the table, one end already tied about its right front leg, slip-knot loops halfway along its length. Dragging Tara's wrists together, Warwick pulled the loops tight around them, then tied the rope's free end about the table's back left leg. Now she was held face down over the table, her hardened nipples sunk into the flattened pancakes of her breasts.

'Let me go,' she demanded, kicking desperately.

But Warwick caught hold of her flailing legs and one by one wrenched off her trainers. Hooking his fingers round the waistband of her jogging pants, he stripped both them and her knickers down her legs and pulled them free. Suddenly naked from the waist down she clamped her thighs defensively together, knowing it was a last futile gesture. Warwick dragged her ankles wide and tied them to the foot of the table legs with more rope ready for just that purpose.

Her perfect backside was now open and trembling at his mercy. He could do anything he liked to her, she thought with near delirious pleasure, her loins churning, pumping oily warmth into her vagina.

'Don't you dare!' she cried aloud, tugging against her bonds.

Extracting her knickers from the bundle of her discarded jogging pants, Warwick balled them up and stuffed them into Tara's mouth. She was gagged with her own underwear. She could taste a smear of her own excited juices on them. Now she could protest to her heart's content in complete abandon and wonderful futility.

The first crisp slap of his hand across her bottom lifted her pale fleshy hemispheres, drove her hips against the edge of the table and brought hot tears pricking to the back of her eyes. She gurgled and shrieked into her gag, but of course he took no notice.

By the sixth spank she had stopped struggling. Her bottom was burning so hotly she thought it must be glowing and her eyes were wet with tears. Convention and 'honour' had been satisfied. Now she could allow herself to slip down the slope of sweet surrender. She had no choice. She wanted no choice. He was too strong for her ... she was helpless ... he could do anything her liked with her ... she was just a silly little girl ... she deserved everything that was coming to her ...

His hands were on her hips. The plum of his erect cock was finding the ready-greased mouth of her anus. She felt the ring of muscle being stretched wide as he forced his way through. Then his shaft was sliding up inside her, making the contours of her rectum conform to its dimensions. He began to pump her, grinding her against the side of the table, careless of her feelings. She was being sodomised, bruised, degraded . . . which at that moment was exactly what she wanted.

Joyously she let go of her last vestiges of shame and surrendered to her master's pleasure like the slavish slut she was.

Sometime later they were in Warwick's sitting room.

Warwick, now dressed in robe and slippers, was sipping a glass of wine while he rested his feet on Tara's sore and blushing bottom. She was hogtied face down on the rug.

An elastic cord was hooked to the back of her new collar of broad black studded leather. It ran down her back to twist round the chain of her handcuffs, where they secured her wrists to the small of her back, and then on to loop about her crossed ankles, its tension excitingly bending her legs over and bowing her body. Her hands were gloved and taped, binding her fingers. She would not have the use of them again until six o'clock on Sunday evening, and the knowledge added deliciously to her sense of helplessness. Besides, the binding would protect her hands when her master took her out for a walk on her leash or during meals, which like a good bitch she would eat straight out of her bowl on the floor.

Tara relaxed in her bonds, feeling perfectly content . . . except for one small detail. Best to get it out the way now so she could enjoy the rest of the weekend.

She made the little throaty whimper that signalled she was begging for permission to speak.

'Is it important?' Warwick asked.

Tara nodded.

'Then you may speak.'

'Thank you, Master. I want to tell you I saw Hazel and Daniela coming here this evening. I know where they went . . . and what they're doing.'

Warwick smiled. 'You've only just found out? This arrangement began less than a week after we had had you all as our unexpected guests.'

'They came back so soon, Master? It took me nearly three weeks to get up the nerve.'

'You're very different in some ways. Submission comes more easily to them.' He rubbed his toes over her scarlet bottom cheeks. 'You had to find a different accommodation with your nature.'

'They're like Gail, Master. I think she's seeing Simon Pye.'

'She is. But she hasn't forgotten us either . . .'

Warwick got up and left the room for a minute. He came back with a folder which he opened on the floor where she could see its contents.

'Entertaining you as we did made Jim Curry realise there was a specialised market for certain novel restraining devices,' Warwick explained. 'He's been very busy ever since, and has already made several sales. Gail was delighted to try out his new inventions, and even model for the catalogue . . .'

There was an A4 sheet headed: 'Dual Function Head and Breast Stocks', complete with price, specifications and dimensions, together with photos taken from different angles of the device in use. The naked girl shown bent forward in the stocks was wearing a ball-gag held in place by straps running under her chin, across the bridge of her nose and over the top of her head which partly concealed her features, but there was no mistaking who it was. Her neck and wrists were secured between the two halves of a board tilted on its side, while her large pendant breasts ballooned out from under holes in a horizontally mounted board that pinched tightly about their roots. Another horizontal board set at ankle height held her legs spread wide.

Tara thought Gail looked unbelievably arousing and vulnerable, yet at the same time perfectly at ease. She was where she belonged.

'This reminds me of something else I was thinking of showing you,' Warwick said. 'We had a visit from Sian and Cassie last week . . .'

He went to a rack of DVDs beside his television, selected one and put it into the player. Clasping Tara's upper arms he hauled her onto her knees and twisted her round so she could sit back on her heels and watch the recording.

Sian and Cassie's faces appeared side by side on the screen. The pair looked nervous but determined, staring straight at the camera.

'This is to prove not all of us lose control as easily as Sian and the others who peed themselves on Mr Fanning's electric machine,' Cassie declared.

'I bet her she couldn't help doing exactly the same,' Sian interjected.

'But I said I'd only have a go if she did too,' Cassie added.

'So to make sure nobody chickens out after the other one's gone, we've agreed to let Mr Fanning tie us up and told him we're both to get exactly the same treatment whatever happens,' Sian said.

'Which is why we're recording this bit to say we're doing this voluntarily,' Cassie continued. 'And we're having the session videoed as well as proof for whoever wins the bet . . . which'll be me.'

'You wait!' Sian retorted.

'We'll see, Miss Wet Knickers!' Cassie jibed.

The scene dissolved into a view of Sian naked and strapped securely to the electrical stimulator she had described to them. Cassie, also naked, stood in the background looking on, her arms tied behind her back.

The camera moved round to show the electrodes clamped tò Sian's nipples and her clipped and widespread labia, and the rod up her rectum. She gazed back into the lens grinning foolishly. Tara wondered at her willingness to revisit an experience that only a short while ago had been seen as painful, shaming and deeply embarrassing; all for the purpose, supposedly, of settling a bet. Whatever the truth of it, she was hardly in a position to criticise.

Tom Fanning, who must have been operating the camera, said from off screen: 'Cassie won the coin toss and decided Sian should go first. To make it less messy I've arranged a bucket to catch the evidence ...' The camera dipped to show that beyond the motor-driven foam rubber dildo there was now a bucket tilted at an angle and mounted on a bracket between Sian's legs, so half of its rim showed above the top of the blockboard platform, which was covered in a plastic sheet.

'The test is to see if Cassie can come without wetting herself like she says,' Fanning continued. 'Both of them went to the loo half an hour ago, then drank the same amount of water, so their bladders should be equally full. I've set up a programme to run the stimulator automatically, ensuring each subject will get exactly the same pattern, duration and intensity of shocks. Sian's session will start – now!'

The motor hummed into life and started to crank the dildo in and out of Sian's vagina, while at the same time she began to twitch and gasp as electric shocks coursed through her crocodile-clipped nipples and labia. It was fascinating, and deeply exciting, to watch. Tara felt her own lovemouth growing oily at the sight.

Sweating and straining at her bonds, Sian appeared to be in the throes of mounting pleasure despite the jolts of electricity passing through her most sensitive flesh. As the camera revealed in lingering close-up, her vagina was clamping round the dildo as it mechanically pistoned into her. The shaft was dripping so wetly with her juices it seemed as though it was pumping out a well. Even her anus was pinching about the electrode rod as though it did not want to let it go.

She was being screwed by a machine and was loving every minute of it.

Sian came with a plaintive cry of delight and a shuddering of her captive body. Her vulva clenched visibly and then sent a pulsing stream of pee arcing through the air into the bucket.

'We have involuntary urination!' Fanning announced.

The image flickered and shifted, returning to show Cassie now strapped to the machine and clamped by electrodes, while Sian, her cheeks flushed by her recent exertions, looked on. Cassie appeared less confident than she had earlier, and the smooth taut domes of her breasts, adorned with their shining crocodile clips, rose and fell rapidly.

The machine started its programme once again. Cassie grunted as the dildo penetrated her and simpered and yelped as the shocks coursed through her nipples and flesh-lips. As the voltage increased she lost all vestiges of her normally aloof manner. Her eyes bulged as the rod up her backside came alive, she writhed in her bonds, her pussy clamped onto the thrusting dildo. If anything her cleft looked wetter than Sian's had been. Tara had never seen her looking so abandoned.

She came with raw passion and a yell of amazement, pee squirting from her like a fountain.

'Cassie loses her bet,' Tom Fanning declared triumphantly.

Warwick turned off the player and looked at Tara with a smile. 'I suspect they'll find other excuses to visit again. Perhaps I should borrow that machine of Tom's and see if it has the same result on you.'

Tara gulped, her loins knotting in anticipation. 'As you wish, Master. You can try it out on all of us if you want. We all seem to belong to you now.'

'Not belong. This time you came to us. We've only taken what's been freely offered.' He looked at her narrowly. 'Does that make you sorry you started all this?'

'Of course not, Master. I mean, I'm only sorry I underestimated all of you. But then, if I hadn't, I wouldn't be here now, would I?'

Warwick laughed. 'Unrepentant as ever. I think you need another lesson in humility.'

Tara lowered her eyes meekly. 'As you wish, Master . . .'

Warwick looked down on Tara with satisfaction.

She was chained spreadeagled on his bed. Her mouth was stopped with a red ball-gag, so she could respond freely to the punishment he was about to give her without troubling the neighbours. Cords ran down from the top of the bedposts to spring clips that bit into her nipples, lifting and stretching her heavy breasts up and outwards, exposing the soft swell of their pale undersides to his gaze. A holly cane lay at the ready across her palpitating stomach. Her engorged lovemouth gaped invitingly wide: salivating with hunger, eager to be filled. She looked mutely back up at him through eyes bright with need and excitement.

She was very beautiful, he thought. But though he might briefly possess her body and she might play the part of his slave, she was not and never would be truly his.

They had broken up her gang and had their revenge, but they hadn't really beaten Tara herself. More truly they had won her grudging respect by demonstrating they were not the grey cheerless non-entities she had imagined. They had provided her with a new form of amusement which gave an outlet for her scheming energy and desire for dangerous sensations.

She had become a weekend slave on her terms. Warwick knew the arrangement wouldn't last for ever, but then what did? Be grateful for such pleasures life gives and enjoy them to the full, he told himself philosophically.

He took up the cane, laid it against the naked undercurves of her breasts, drew back his arm and swung. Tara's muffled yelp of pain and pleasure filled the bedroom . . .